ACADEMY FOR
ROBLOX PROS

AN UNOFFICIAL ROBLOX GRAPHIC NOVEL

ATTACK OF
THE ZOMBIES

By Louis Shea

First published by Scholastic Australia Pty Limited in 2024.

ISBN 978-1-5461-0331-8

10 9 8 7 6 5 4 3 2 1 24 25 26 27 28

Printed in China 62

This edition first printing, June 2024

Written and illustrated by Louis Shea
Cover design by Chad Mitchell and Ashley Vargas
Internal design by Chad Mitchell
Typeset in Extra Crunchy, Owners, Zemke Hand, and Low res 9 Plus

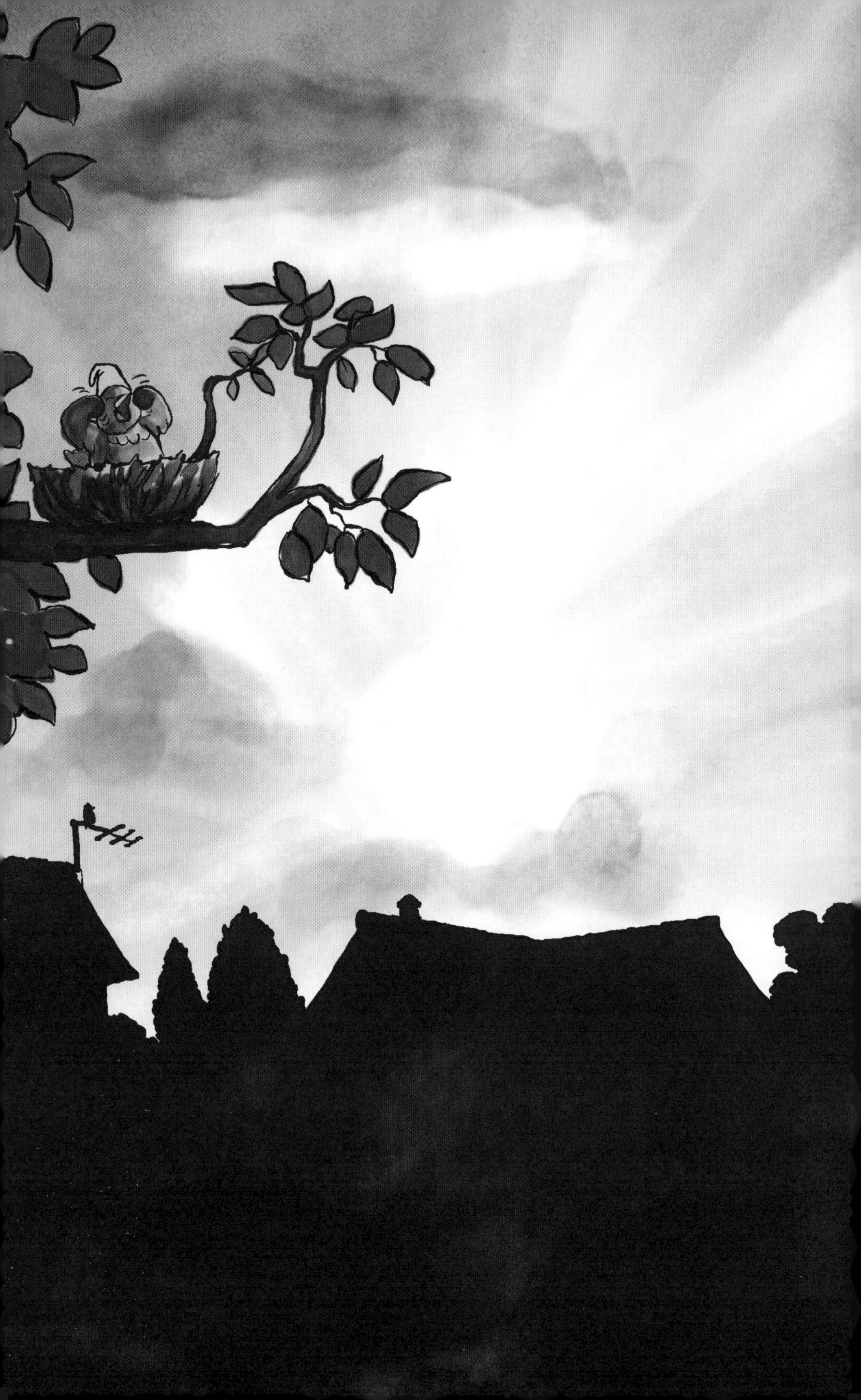

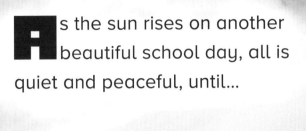

As the sun rises on another beautiful school day, all is quiet and peaceful, until...

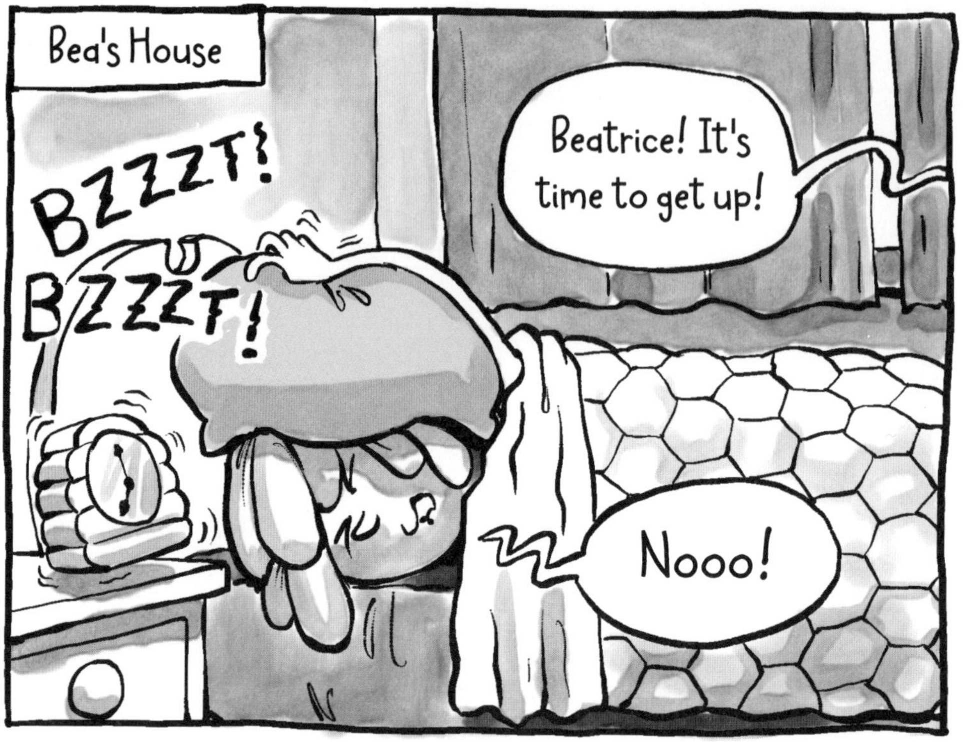
Bea's House
BZZZT!
BZZZT!
Beatrice! It's time to get up!
Nooo!

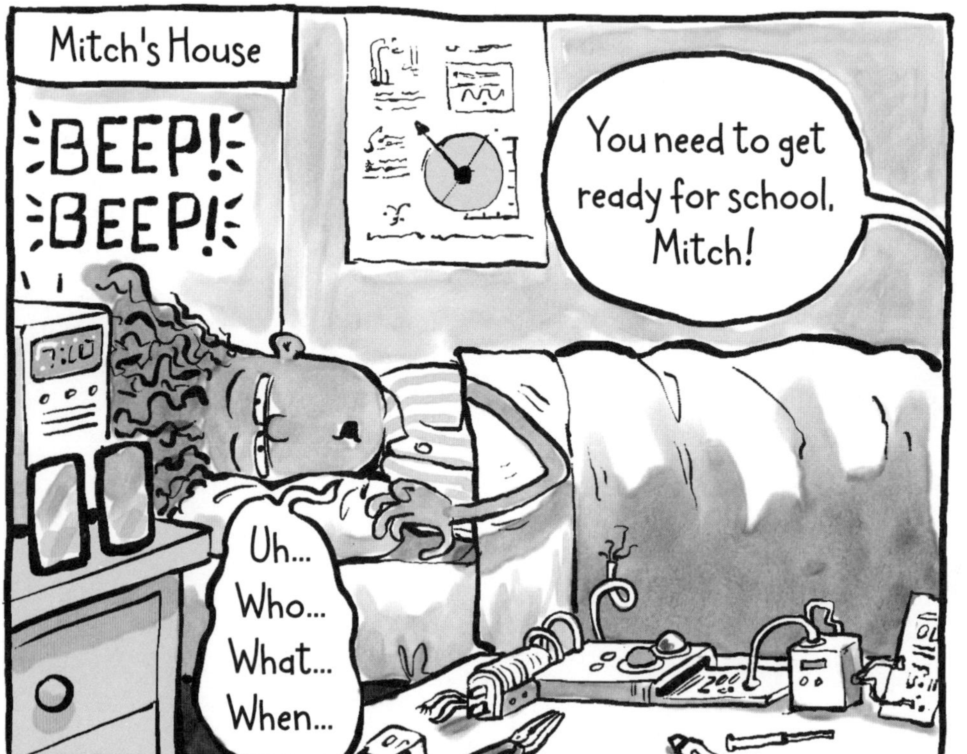
Mitch's House
BEEP!
BEEP!
You need to get ready for school, Mitch!
7:00
Uh... Who... What... When...

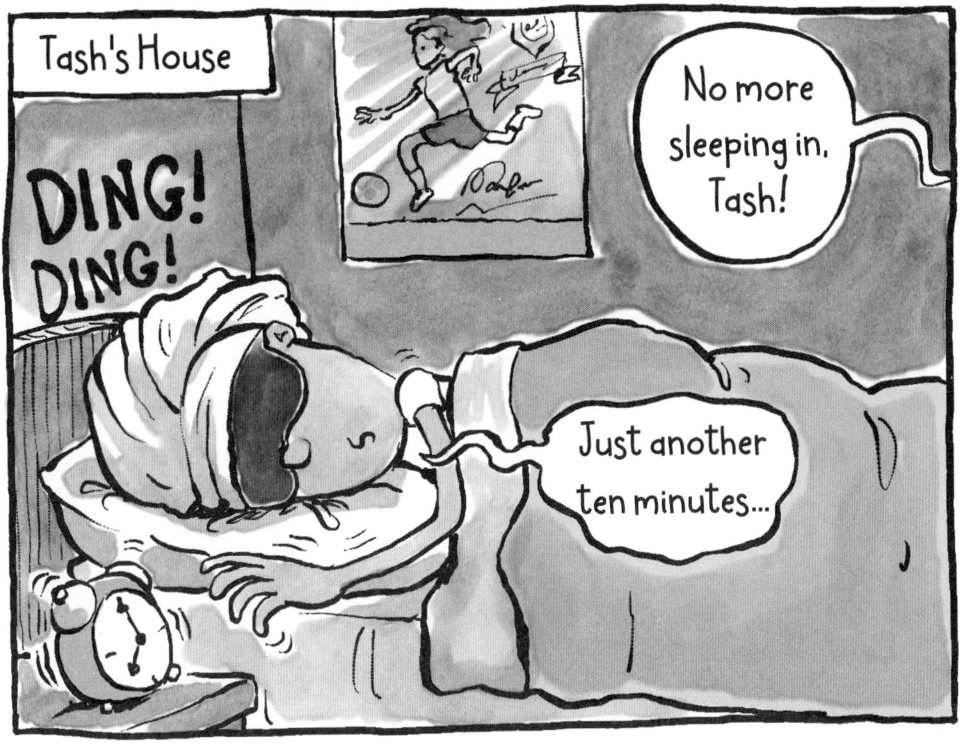
Tash's House
DING!
DING!
No more sleeping in, Tash!
Just another ten minutes...

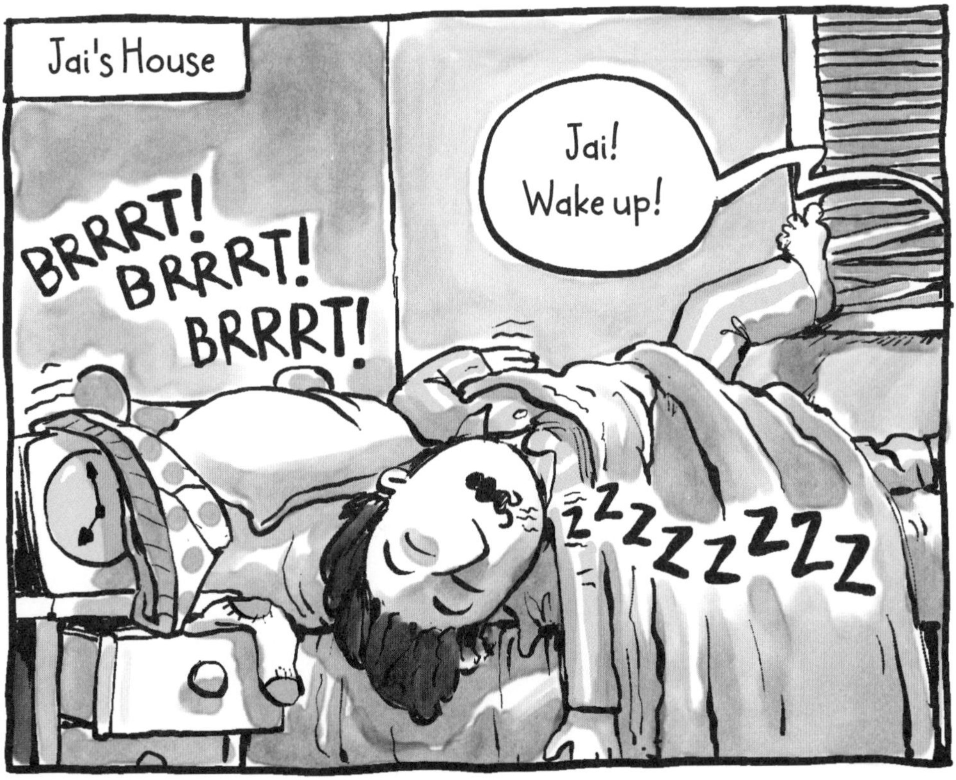
Jai's House
Jai! Wake up!
BRRRT!
BRRRT!
BRRRT!
ZZZZZZZZZ

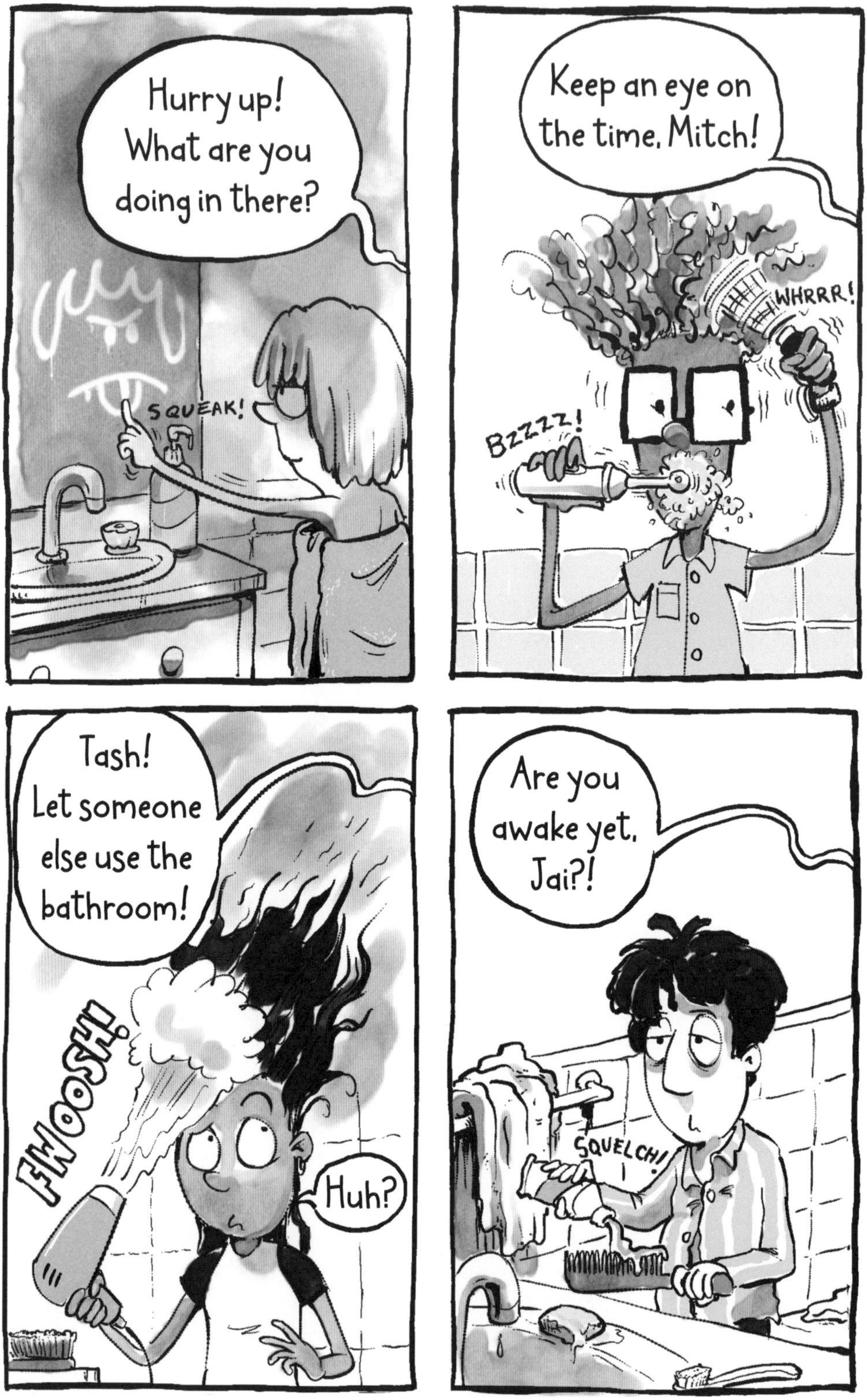
Hurry up! What are you doing in there?
SQUEAK!
Keep an eye on the time, Mitch!
WHRRR!
BZZZZ!
Tash! Let someone else use the bathroom!
FWOOSH!
Huh?
Are you awake yet, Jai?!
SQUELCH!

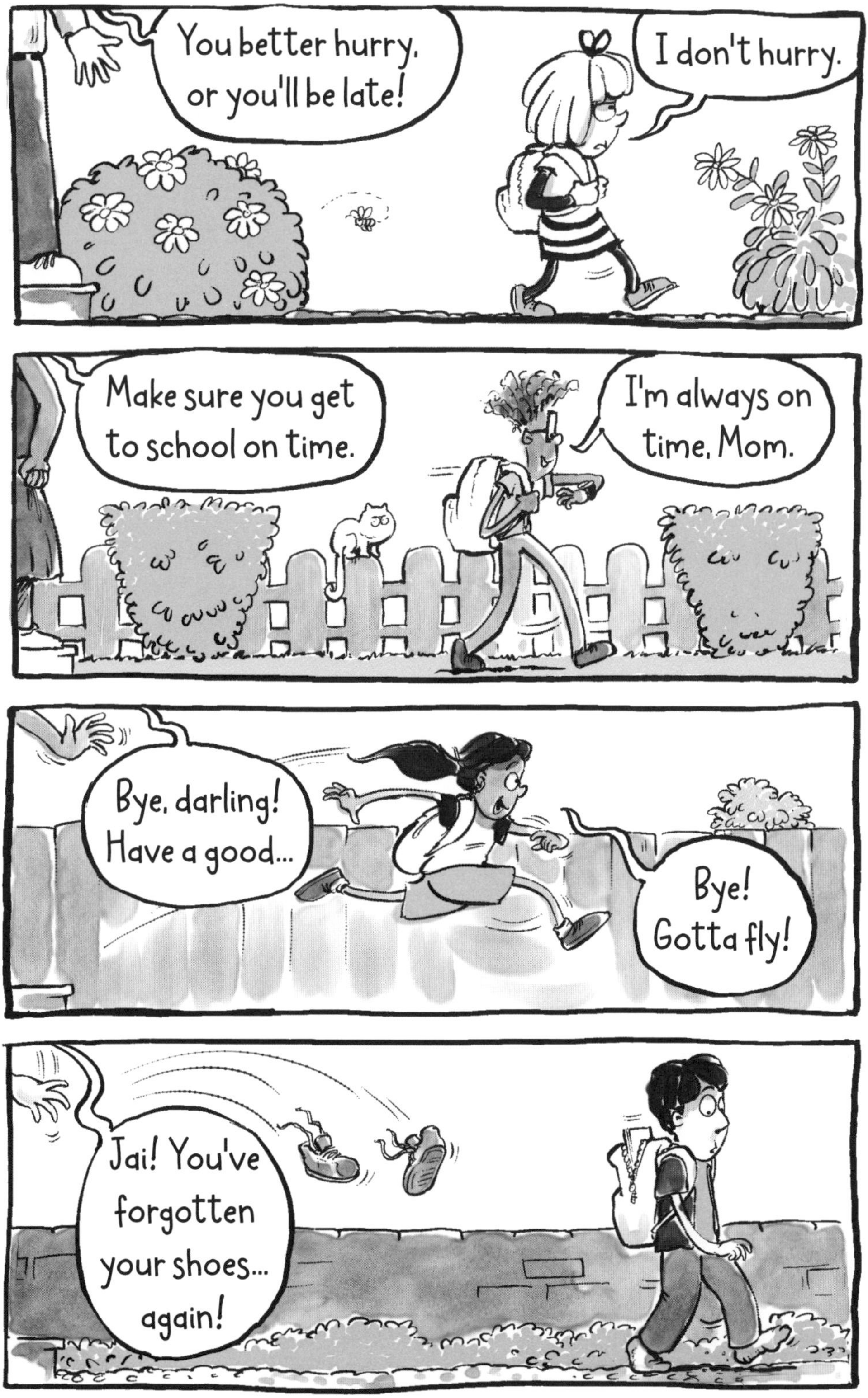
You better hurry, or you'll be late!
I don't hurry.
Make sure you get to school on time.
I'm always on time, Mom.
Bye, darling! Have a good...
Bye! Gotta fly!
Jai! You've forgotten your shoes... again!

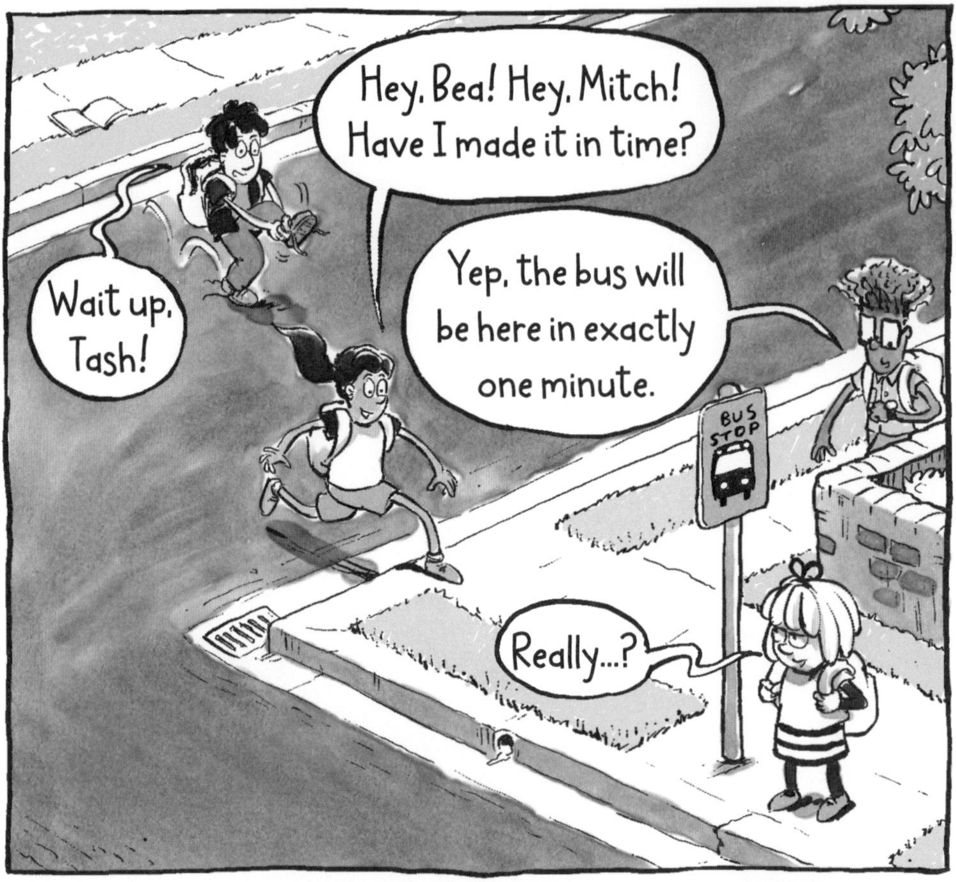
Hey, Bea! Hey, Mitch! Have I made it in time?
Wait up, Tash!
Yep, the bus will be here in exactly one minute.
BUS STOP
Really...?

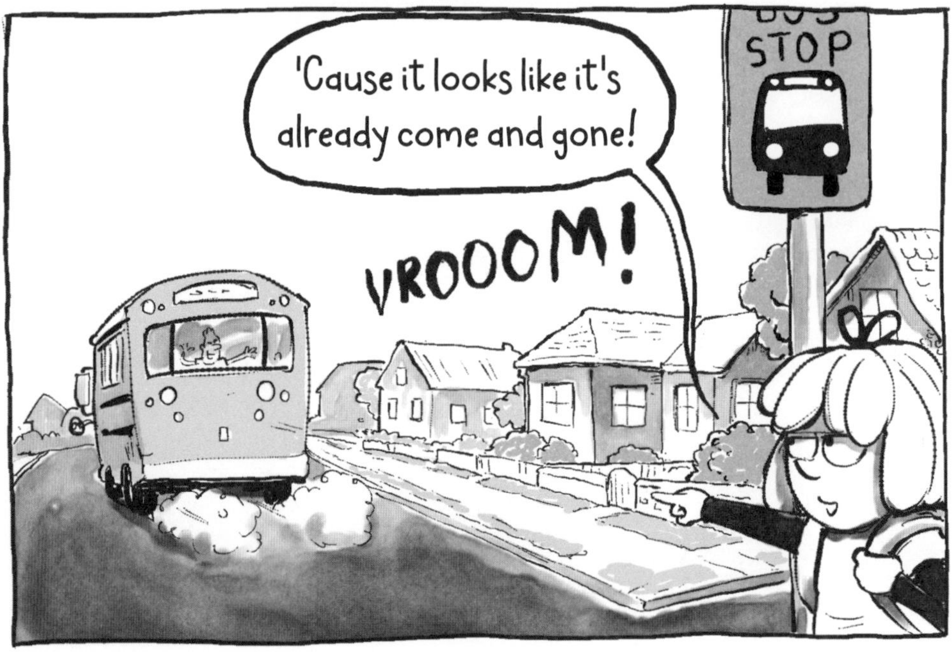
STOP
'Cause it looks like it's already come and gone!
VROOOM!

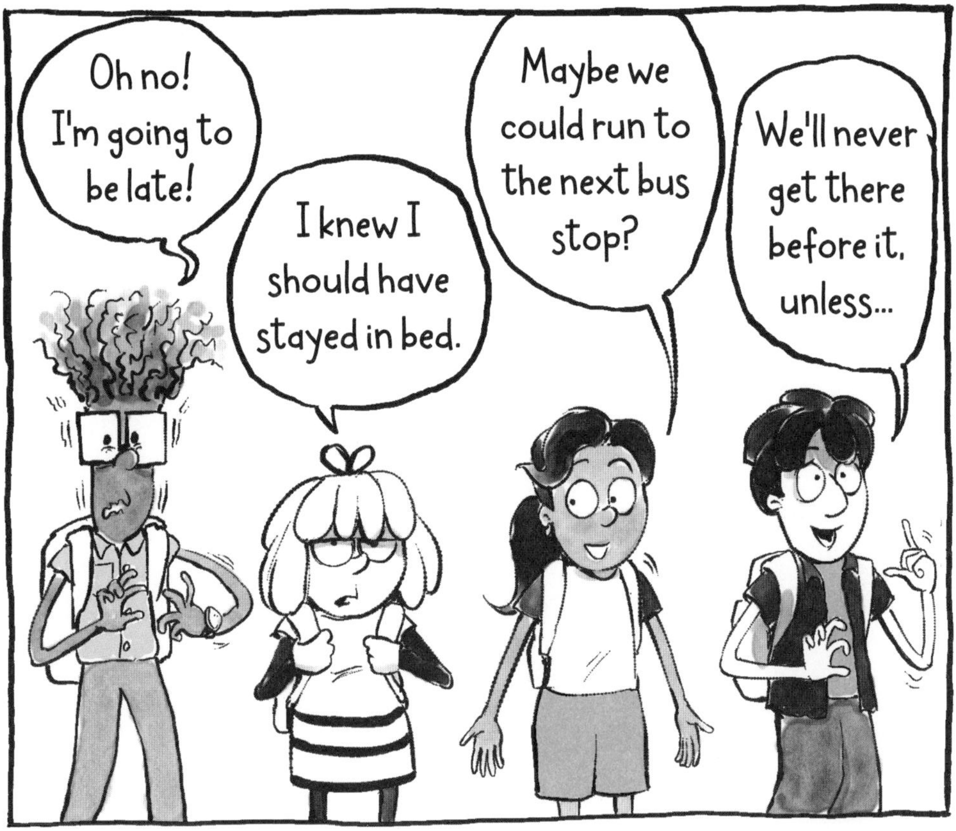
Oh no! I'm going to be late!
I knew I should have stayed in bed.
Maybe we could run to the next bus stop?
We'll never get there before it, unless...

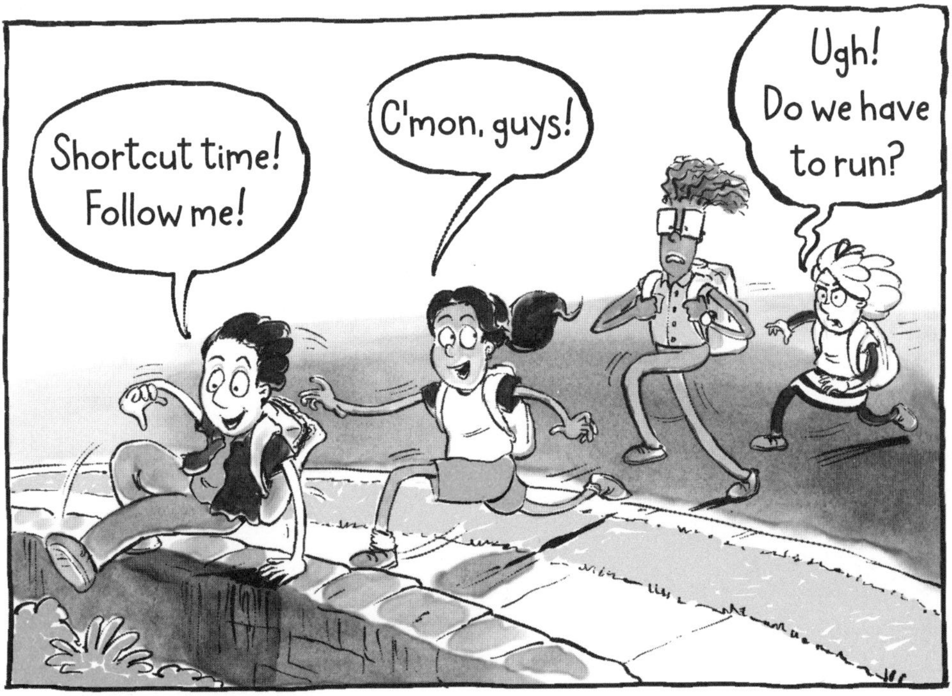
Shortcut time! Follow me!
C'mon, guys!
Ugh! Do we have to run?

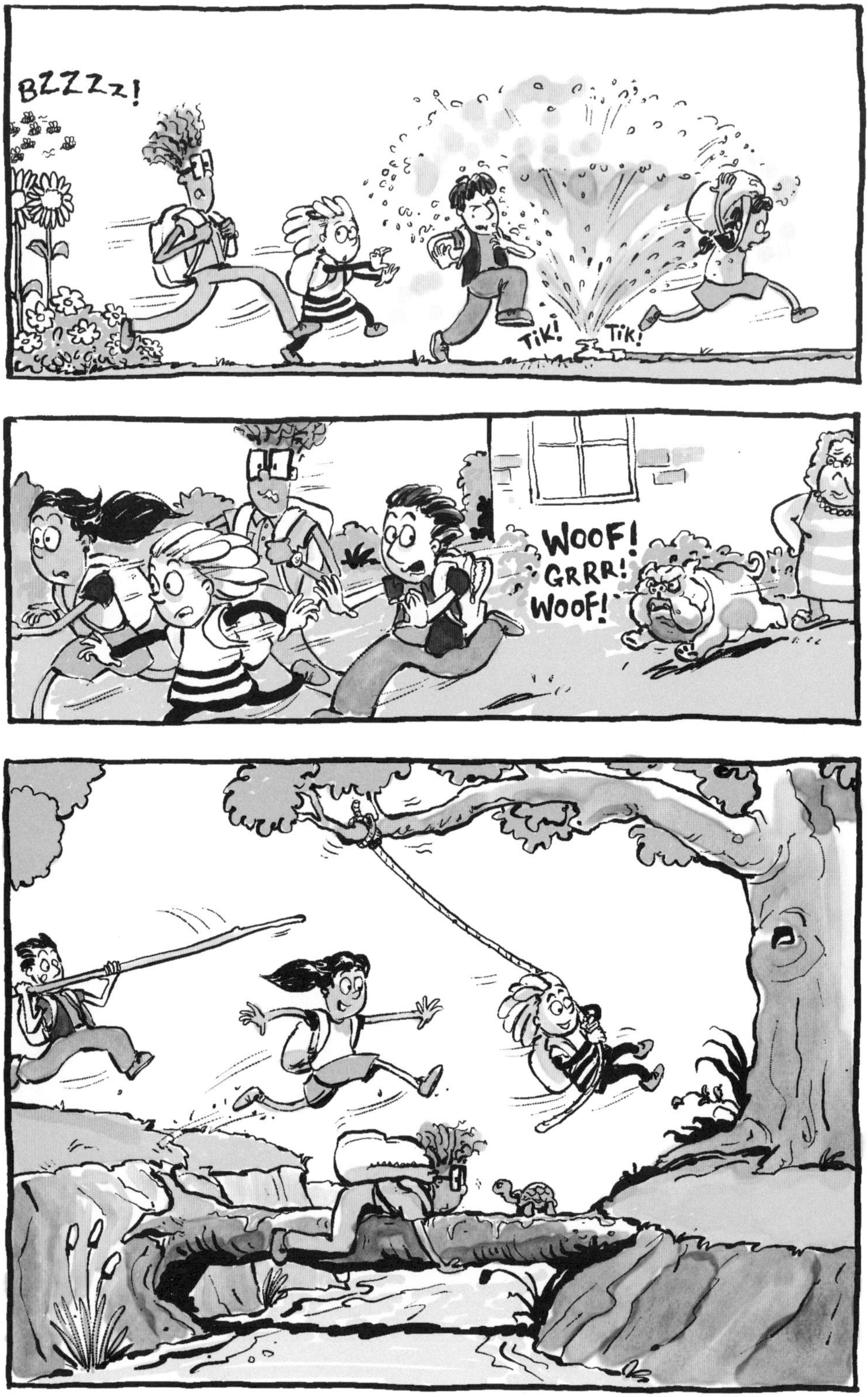
BZZZZz!
TIK!
TIK!
WOOF!
GRRR!
WOOF!

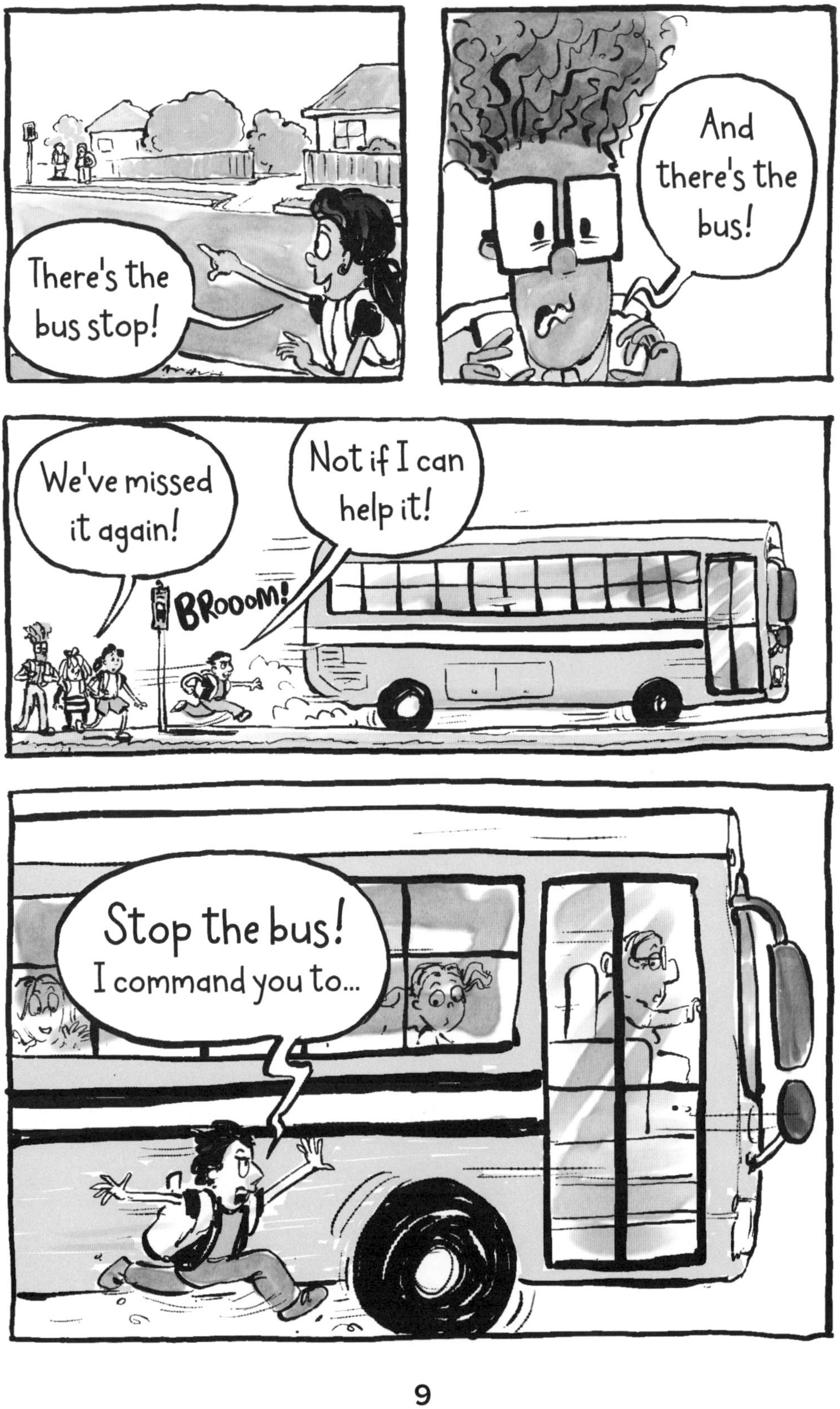
There's the bus stop!
And there's the bus!
We've missed it again!
Not if I can help it!
BROOOM!
Stop the bus! I command you to...

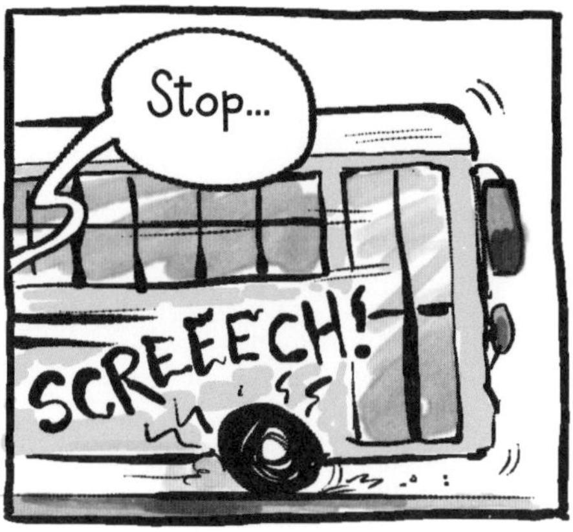
Stop...
SCREEECH!

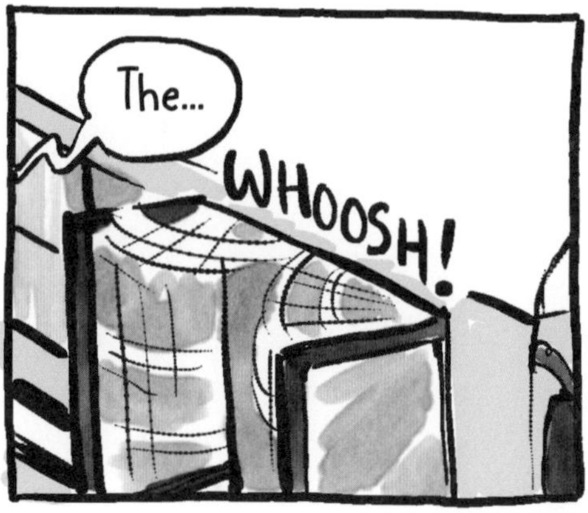
The...
WHOOSH!

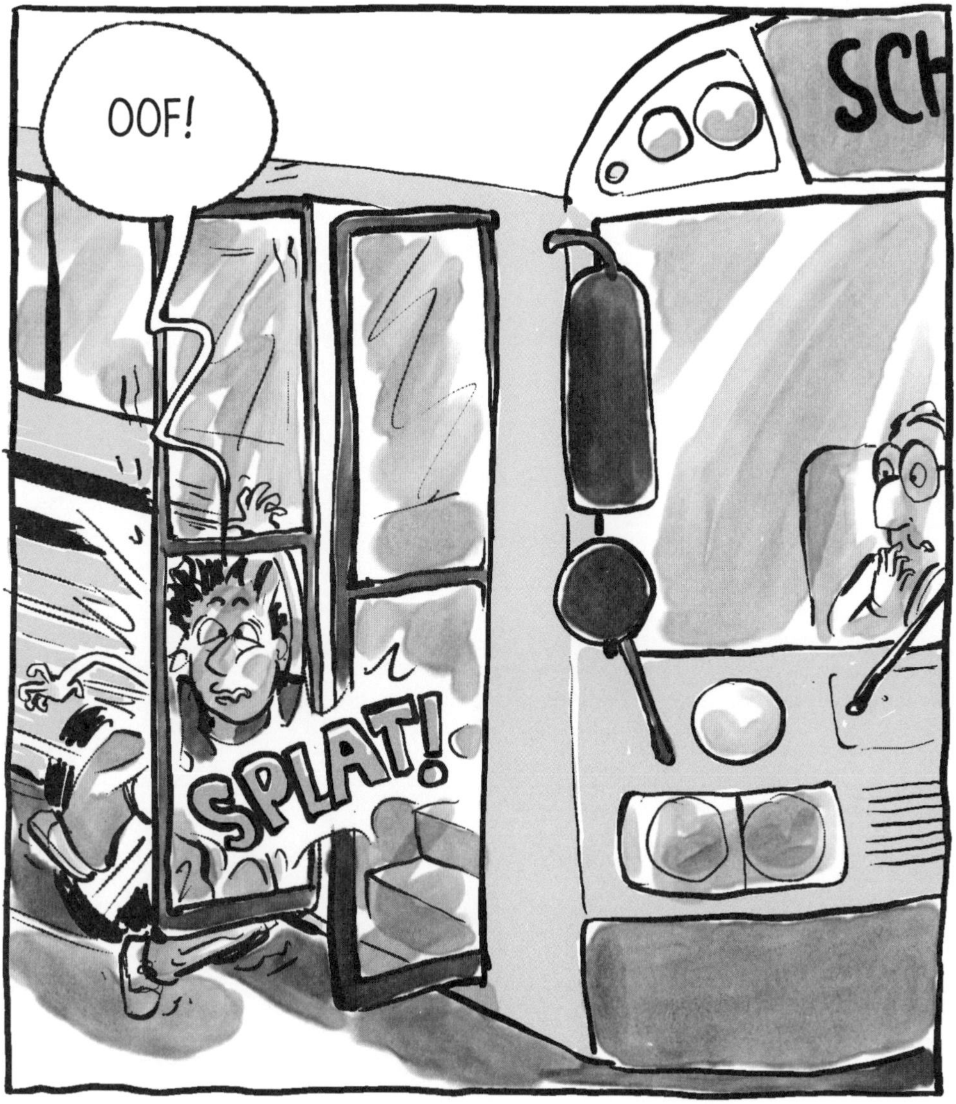
OOF!
SPLAT!
SCH

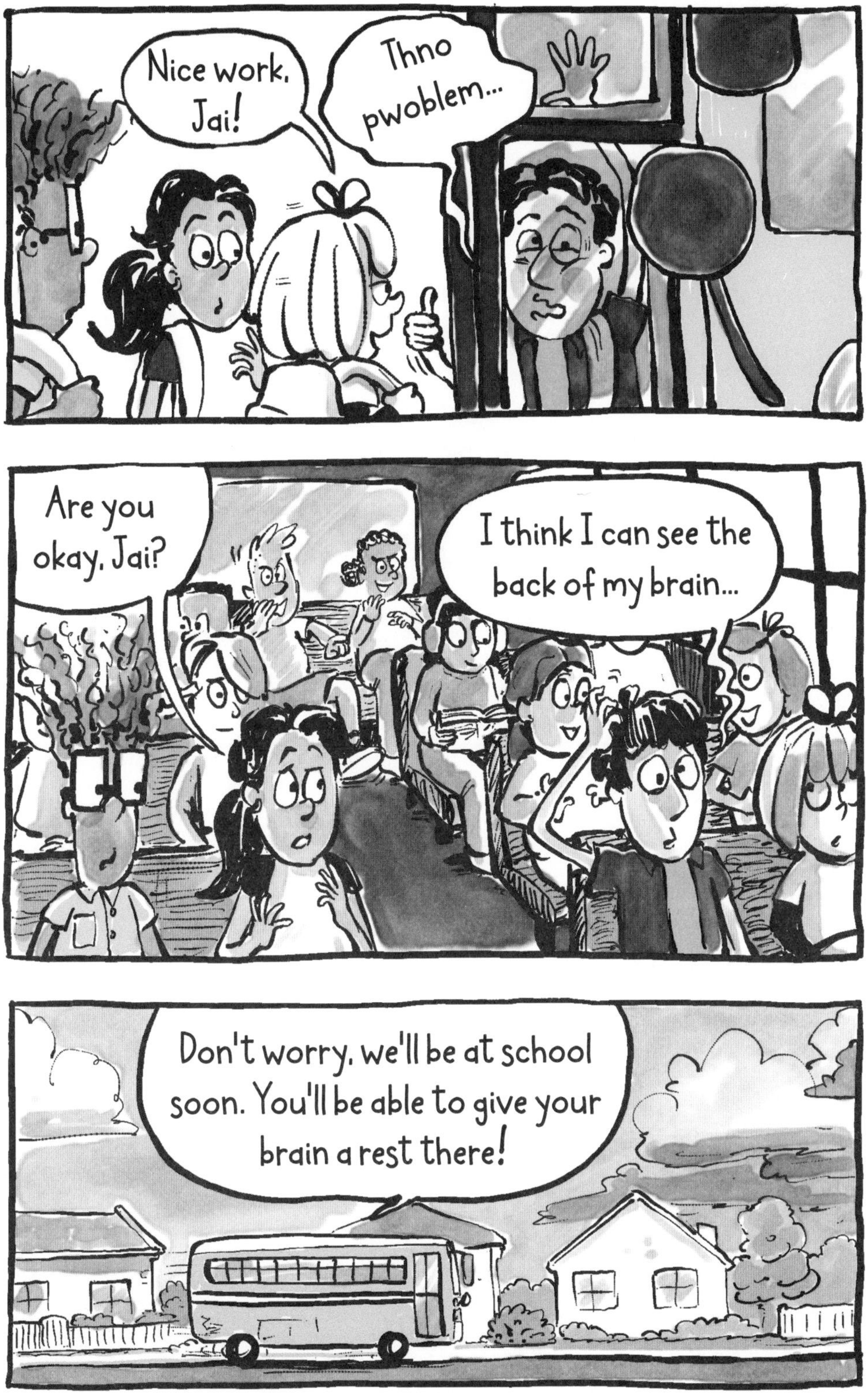
Nice work, Jai!
Thno pwoblem...
Are you okay, Jai?
I think I can see the back of my brain...
Don't worry, we'll be at school soon. You'll be able to give your brain a rest there!

ROBLOX PRO PROFILES

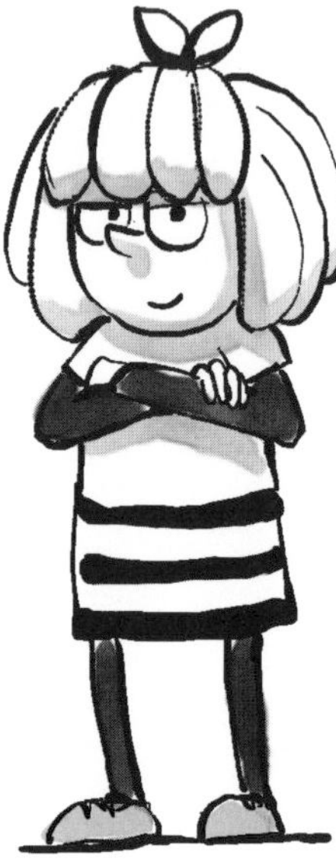

Name: Beatrice
Favorite subject: Art
Most hated subject: PE
Likes: Loud music
Dislikes: Loud people
Special skills: Rolling her eyes

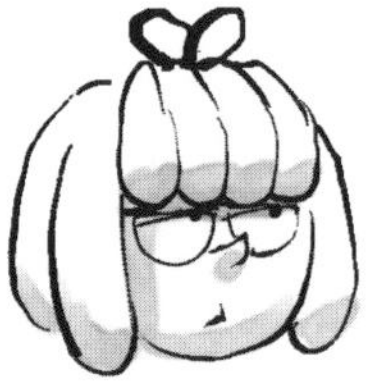

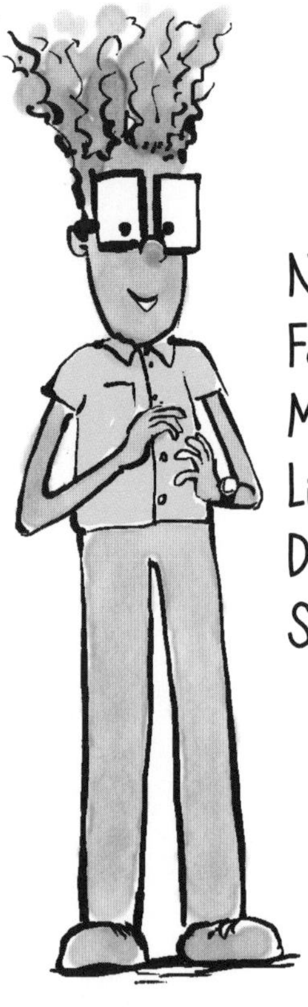

Name: Mitch
Favorite subject: Science
Most hated subject: Music
Likes: Knowing how things work
Dislikes: Decision-making
Special skills: Electronics

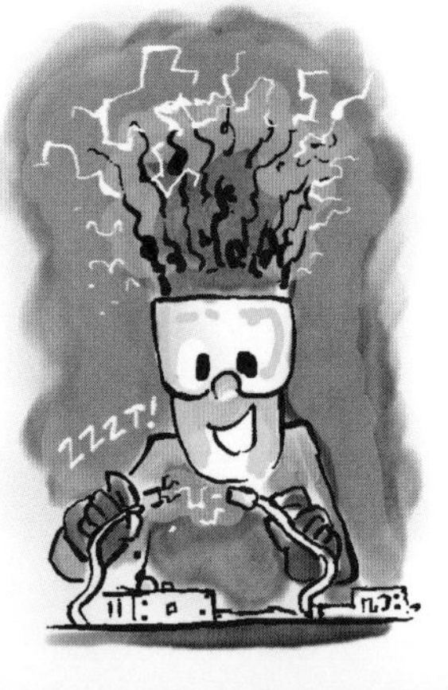
ZZZT!

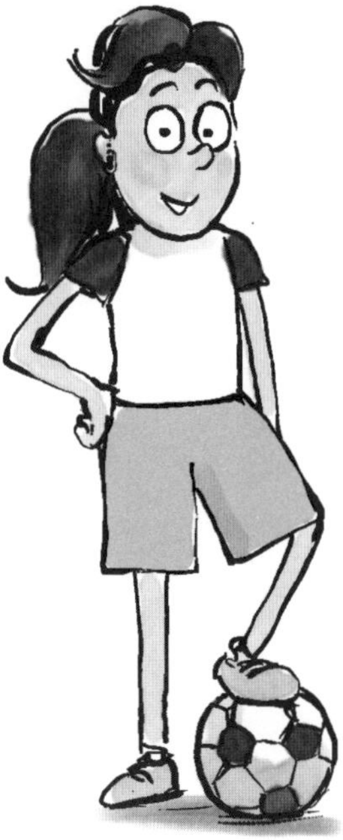

Name: Tash
Favorite subject: PE
Most hated subject: English
Likes: Sports
Dislikes: Messy hair
Special skills: Kicking things hard

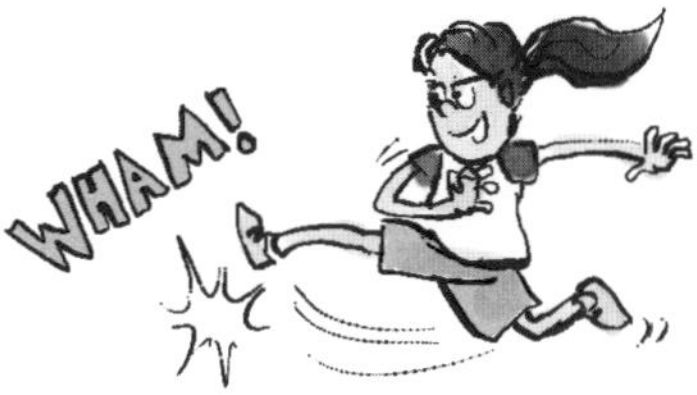
WHAM!

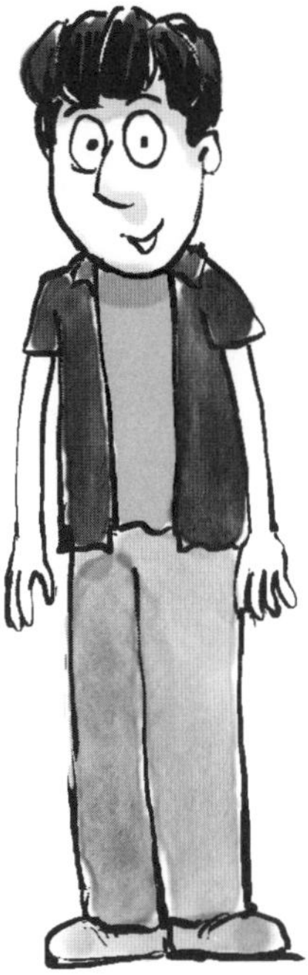

Name: Jai
Favorite subject: Lunch
Most hated subject: History, math, geography...
Likes: Food
Dislikes: Celery
Special skills: Making Hamdozas (a combination of hamburger, hot dogs, and pizza)

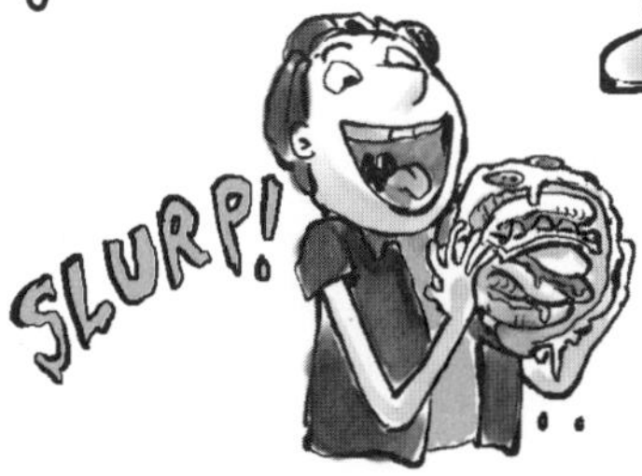
SLURP!

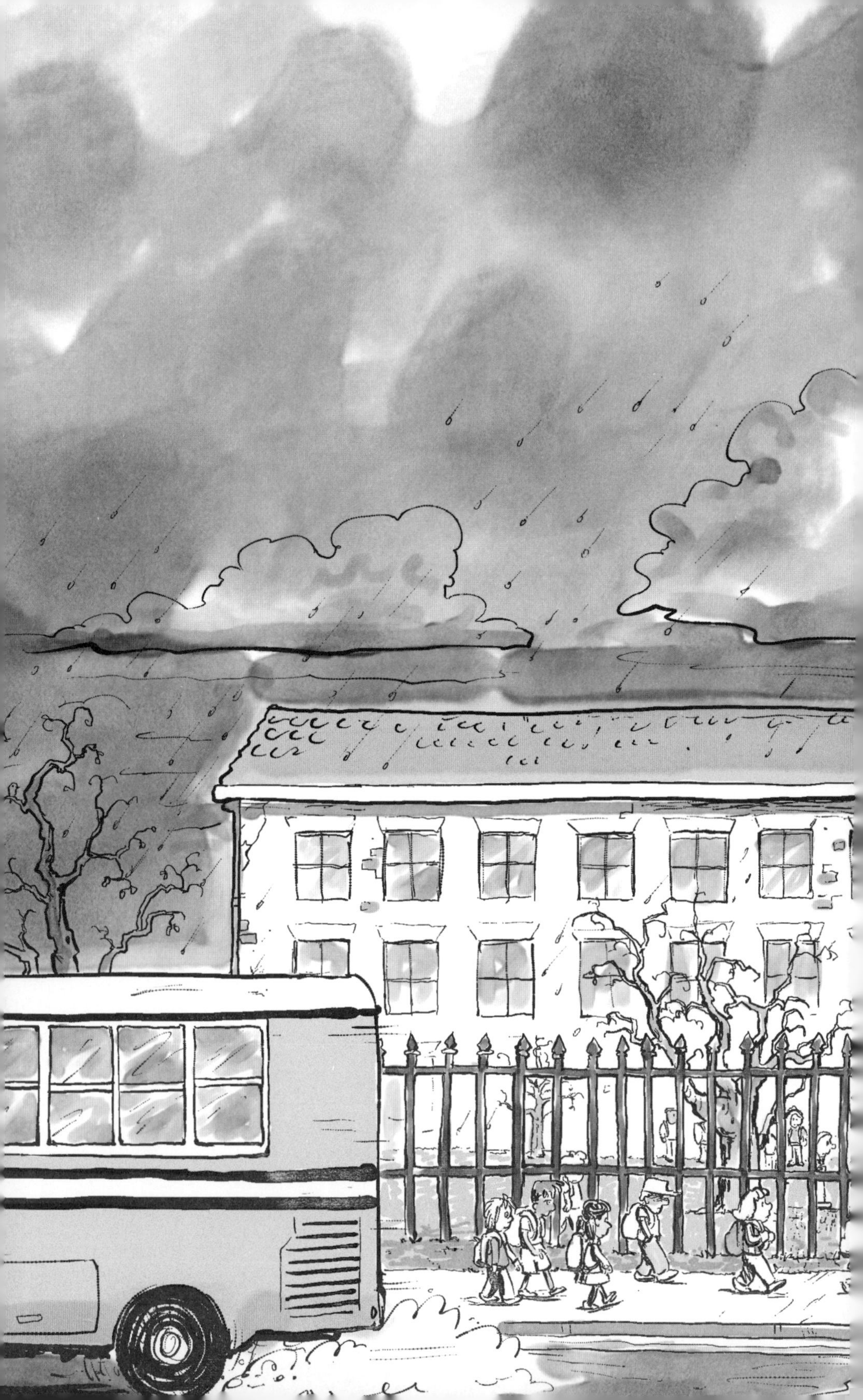

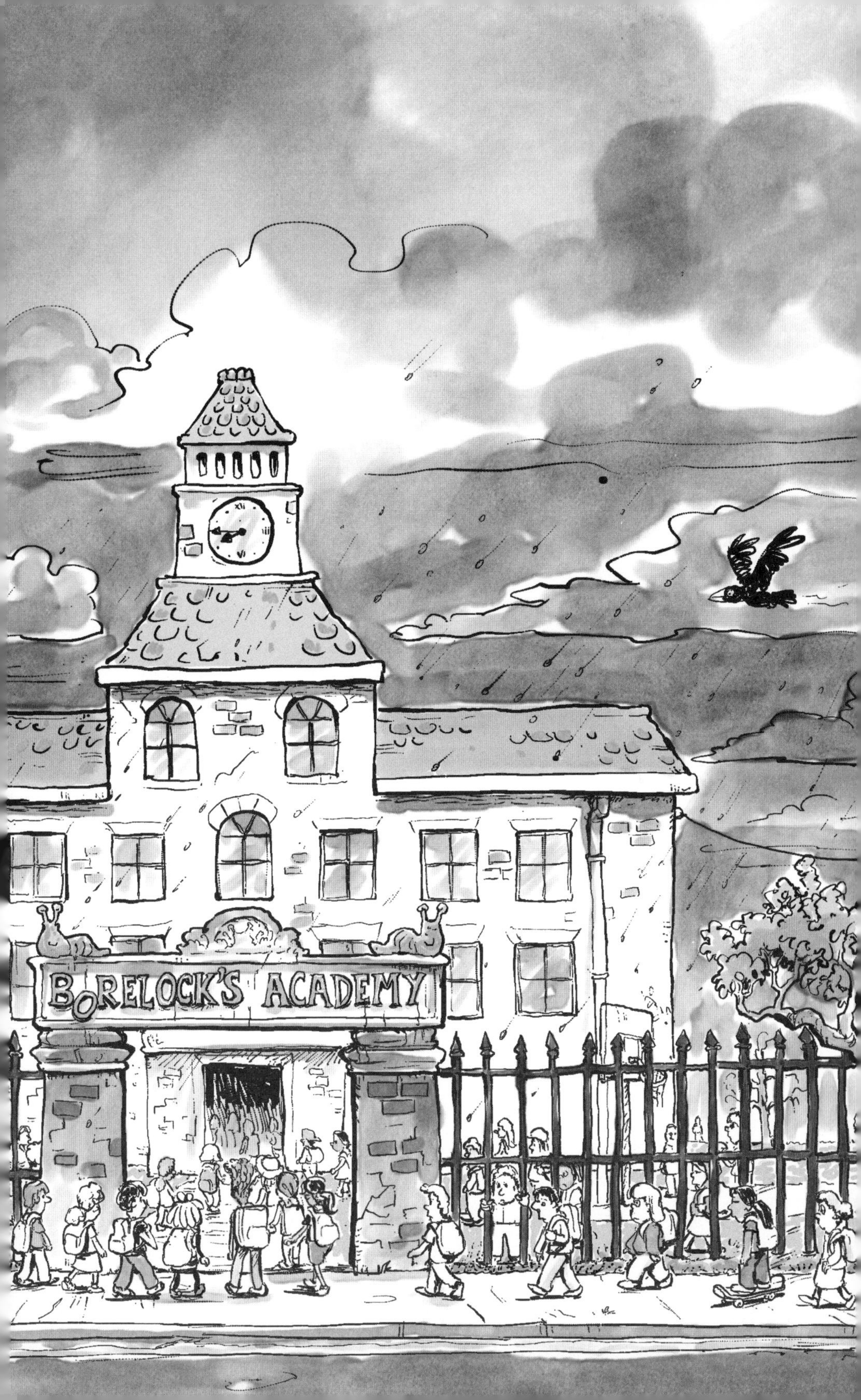
BORELOCK'S ACADEMY

Borelock's Academy is a ~~proud~~...~~noble~~... ~~prestigious~~ old institution that was founded by the Borelock family long ago.

Originally starting out as slug farmers, the Borelock family soon realized that no one really wanted to eat slugs...or keep them as pets, so they decided instead to build a school.

Since then, Borelock's Academy has educated many generations of children on the joys of slugs and other less interesting stuff.

BRUNHILDA BORELOCK

URIAH BORELOCK

WOLFGANG BORELOCK

The current principal, Warren Borelock, proudly continues his ancestors' love of slugs and ~~hatred~~...*tolerance* of children.

As he can often be heard muttering, "They might be slimy and horrible, but someone's got to teach them!"

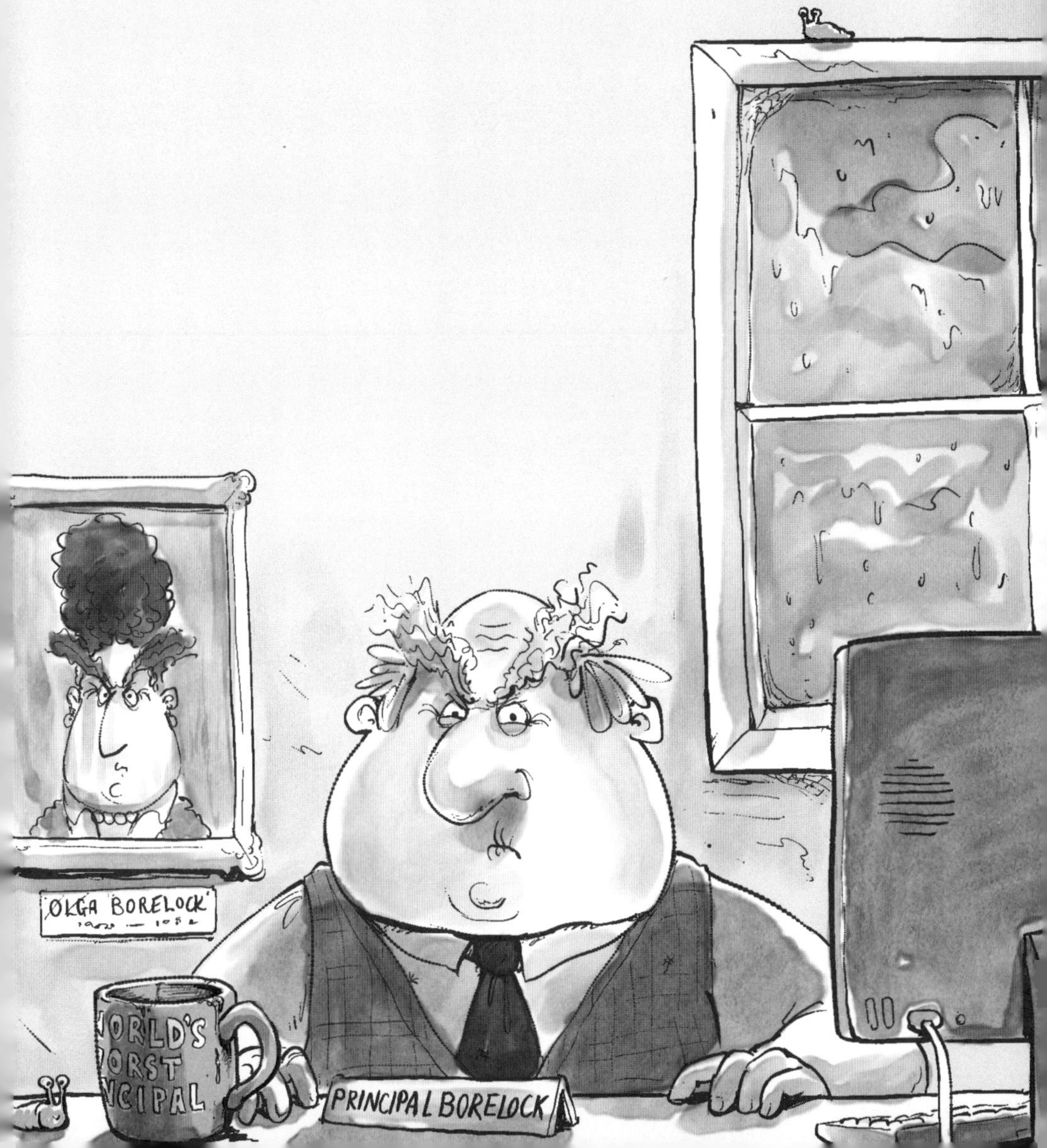
OLGA BORELOCK
PRINCIPAL BORELOCK

But Borelock's Academy is not just about fun and slugs. There are plenty of other exciting classes, too! There's science...

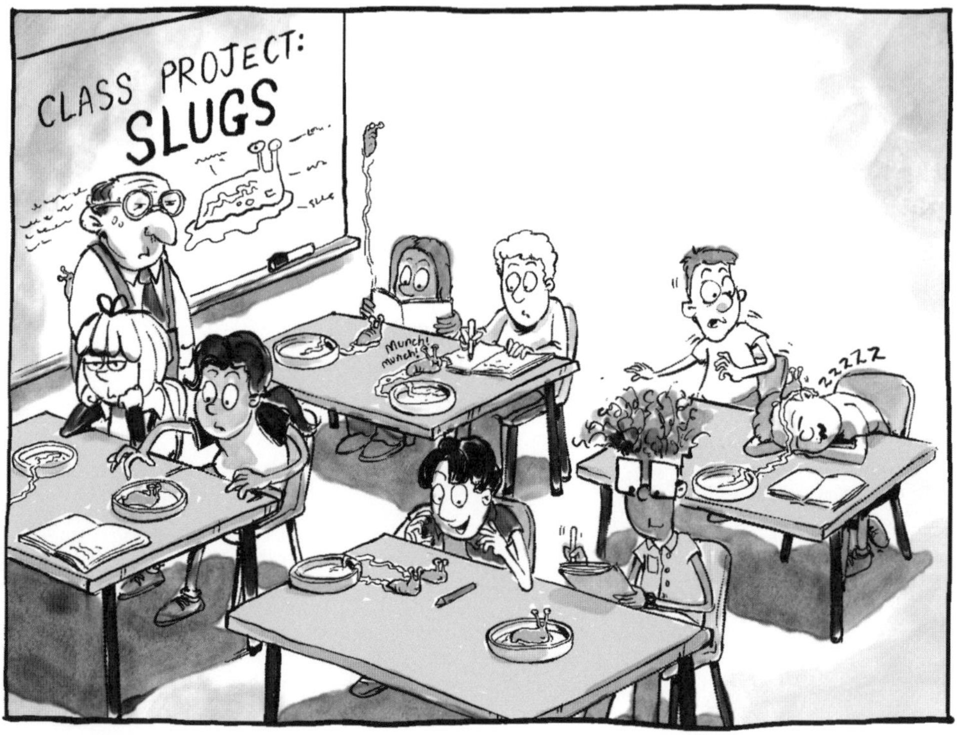
CLASS PROJECT:
SLUGS
Munch! munch!
ZZZZZ

And English...

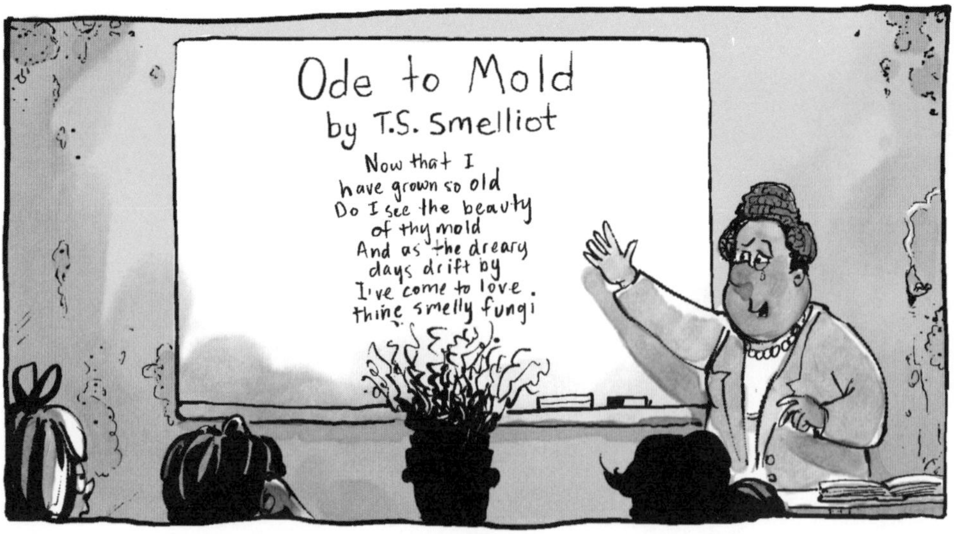
Ode to Mold
by T.S. Smelliot
Now that I
have grown so old
Do I see the beauty
of thy mold
And as the dreary
days drift by
I've come to love
thine smelly fungi

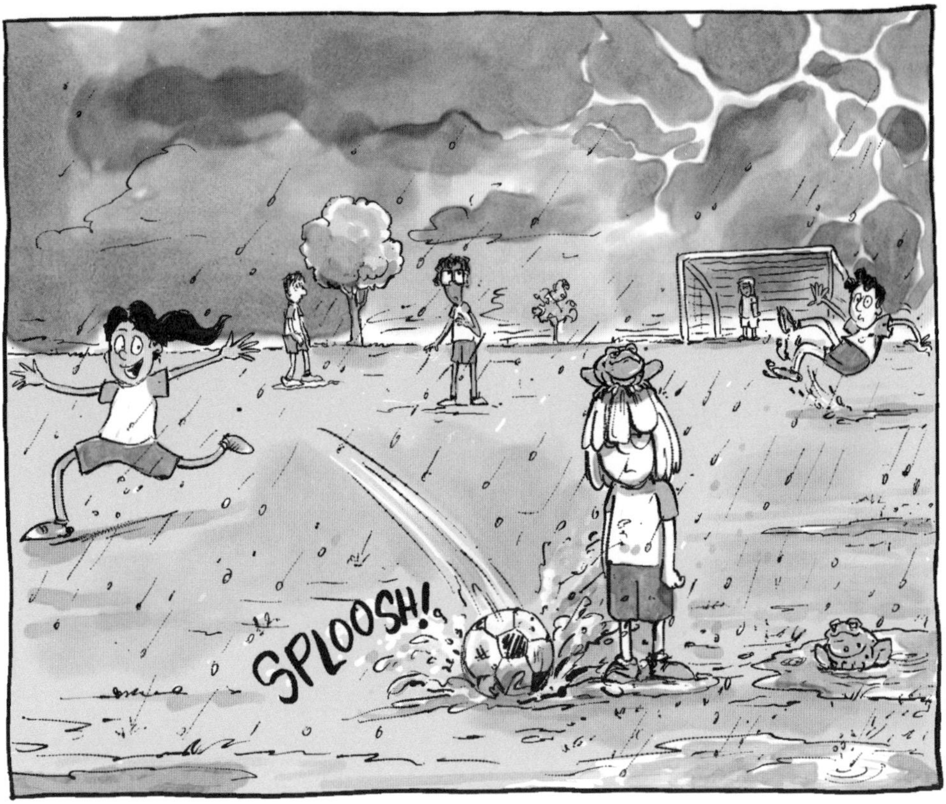
SPLOOSH!

Fun outdoor sports, and ~~music~~ noisemaking!

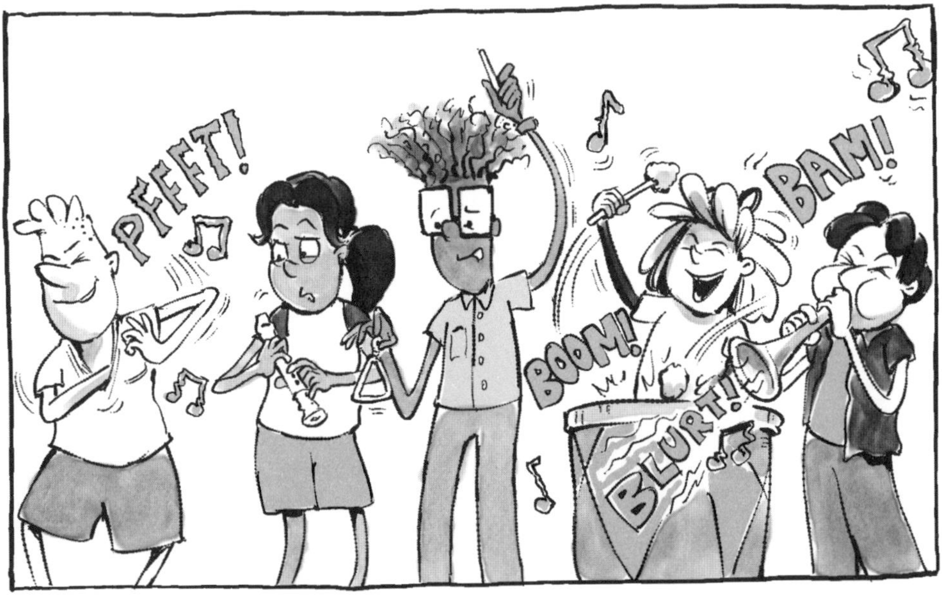
PFFFT!
BOOM!
BAM!
BLURT!

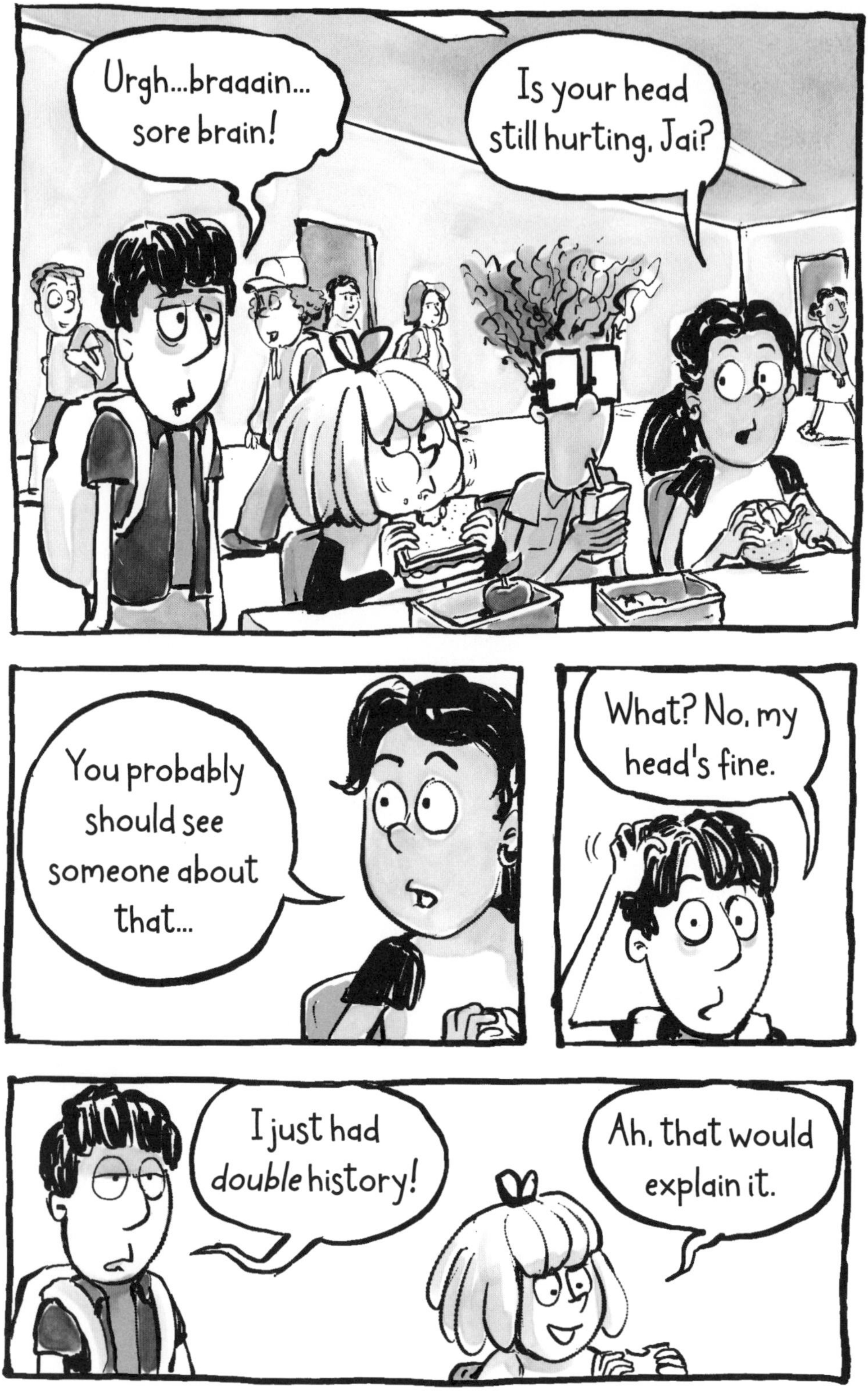
Urgh...braaain...
sore brain!
Is your head
still hurting, Jai?
You probably
should see
someone about
that...
What? No, my
head's fine.
I just had
double history!
Ah, that would
explain it.

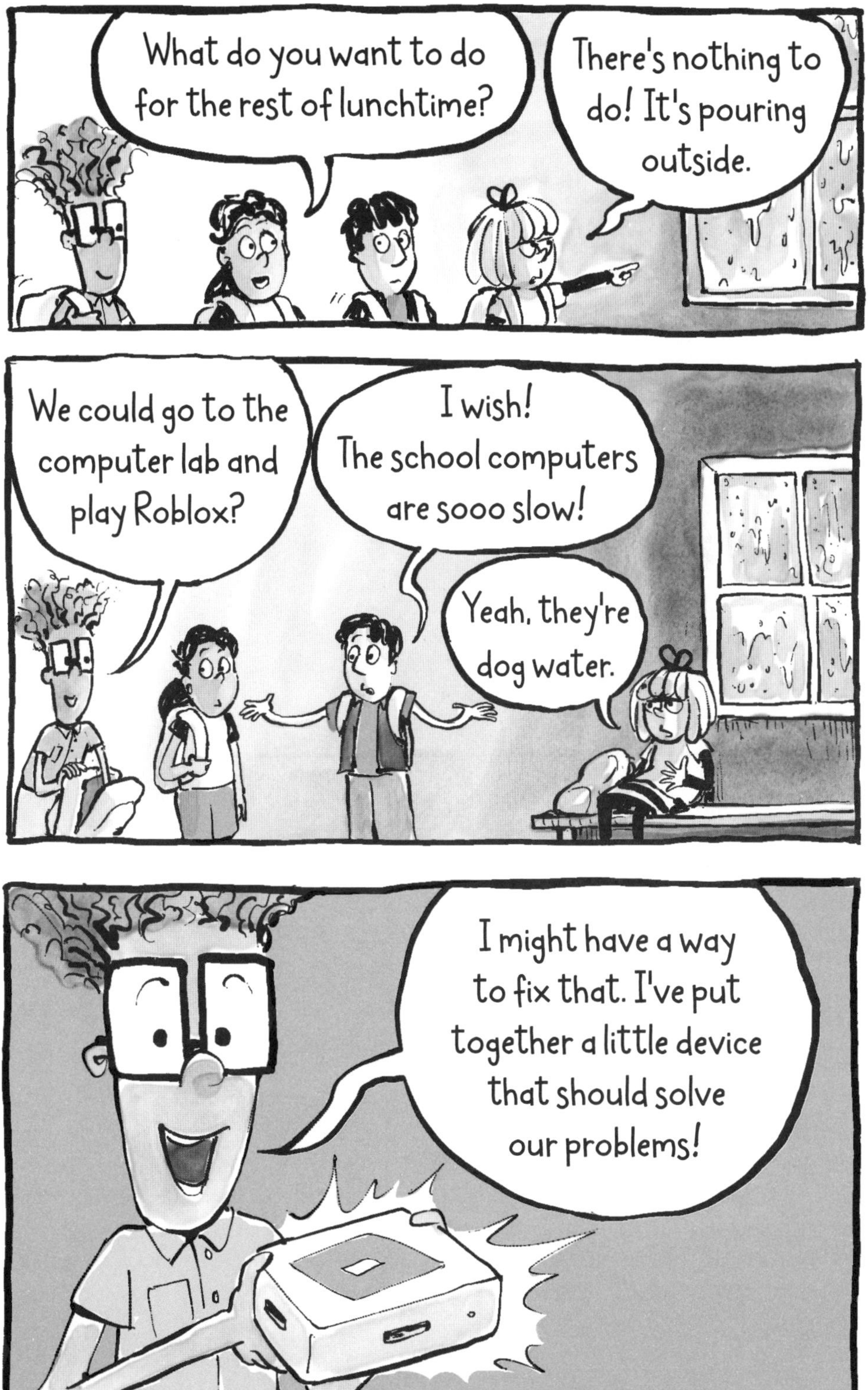
What do you want to do for the rest of lunchtime?
There's nothing to do! It's pouring outside.
We could go to the computer lab and play Roblox?
I wish! The school computers are sooo slow!
Yeah, they're dog water.
I might have a way to fix that. I've put together a little device that should solve our problems!

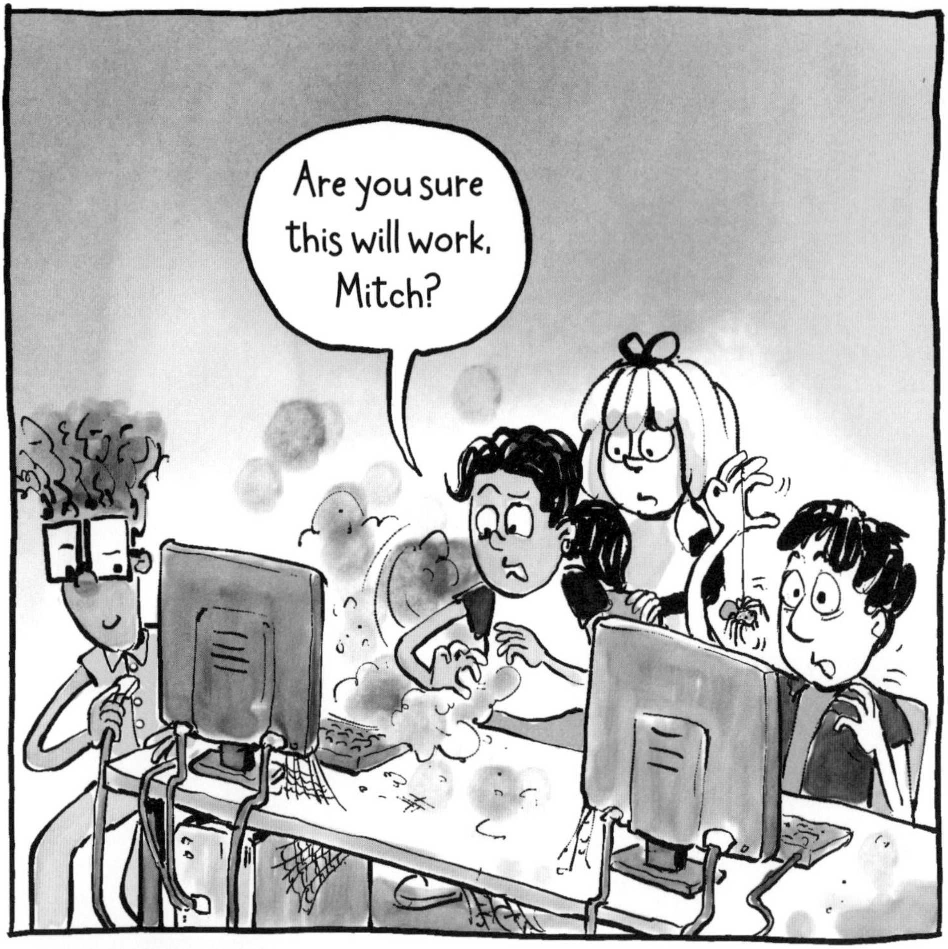
Are you sure this will work, Mitch?

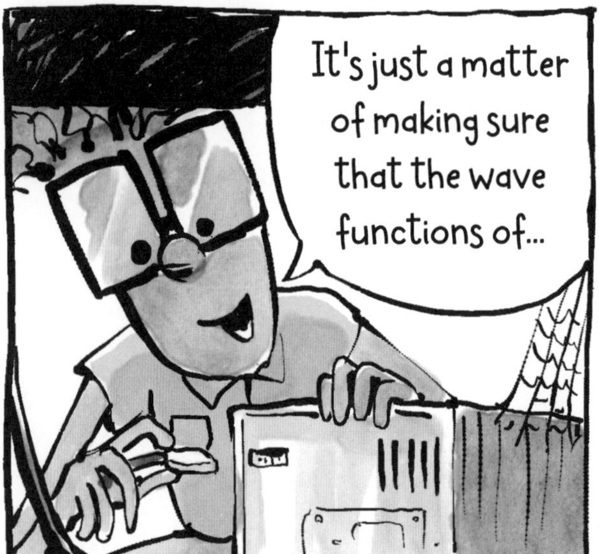
It's just a matter of making sure that the wave functions of...

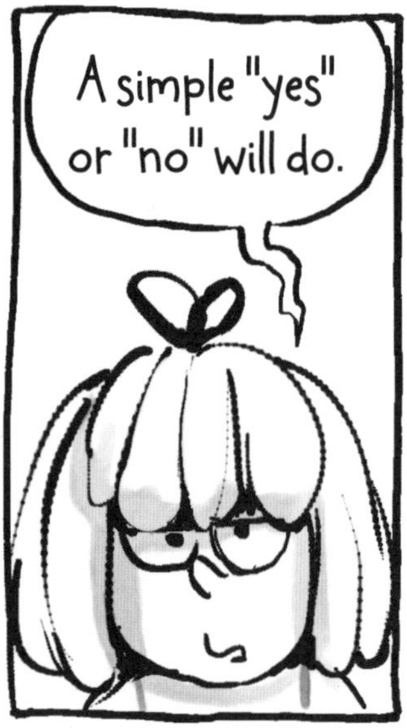
A simple "yes" or "no" will do.

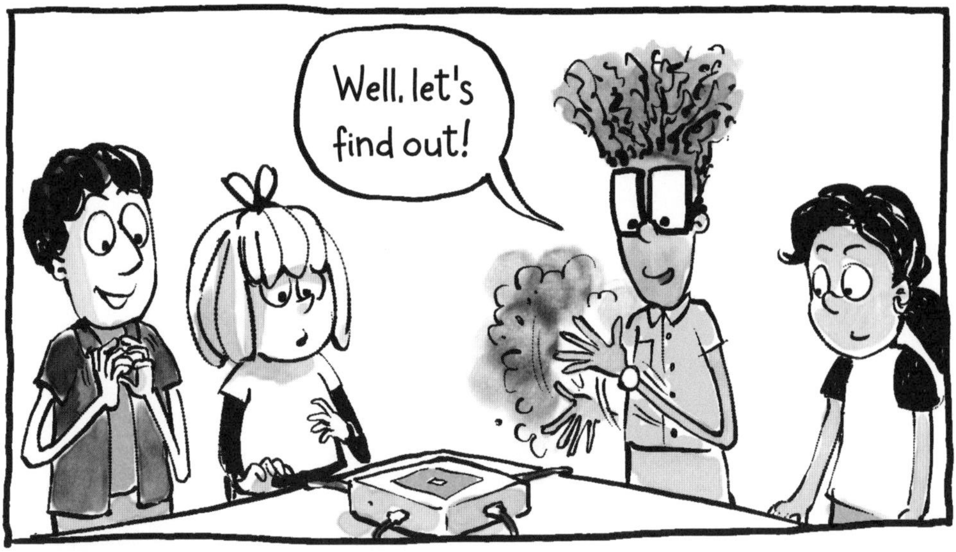
Well, let's find out!

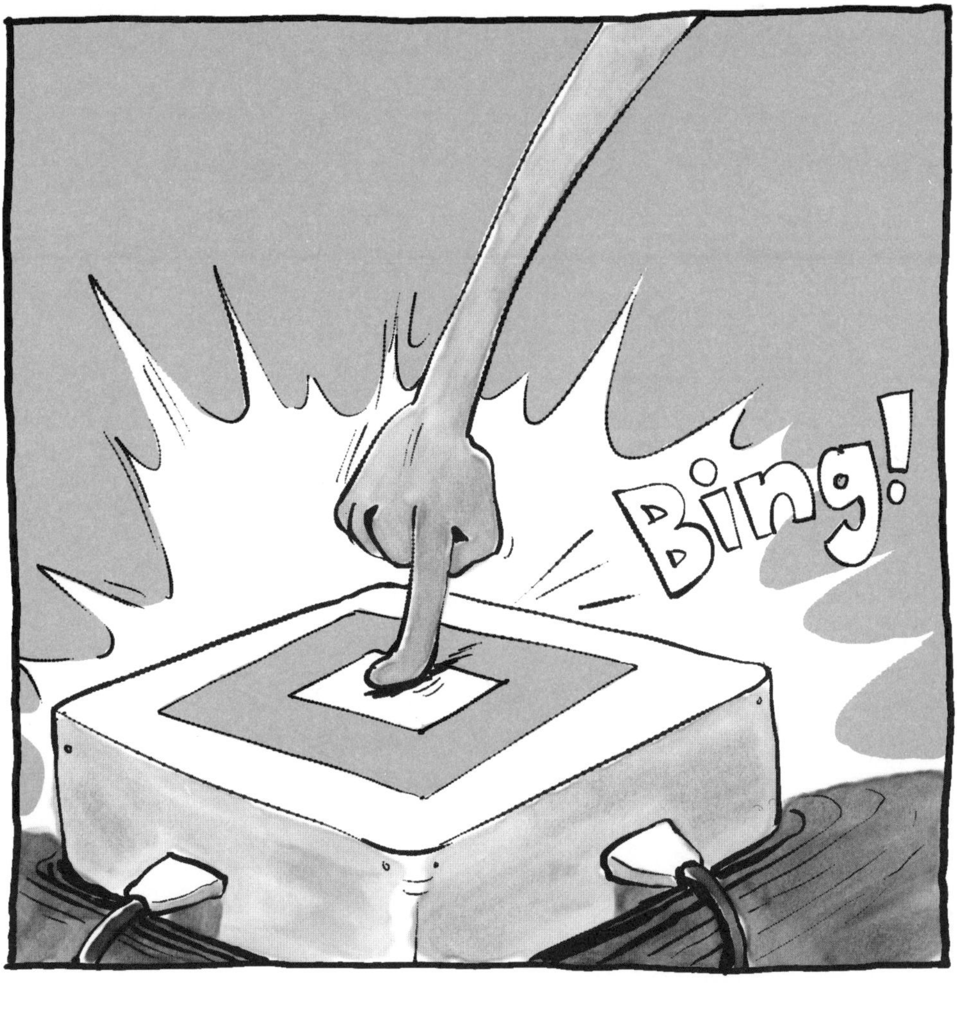
Bing!

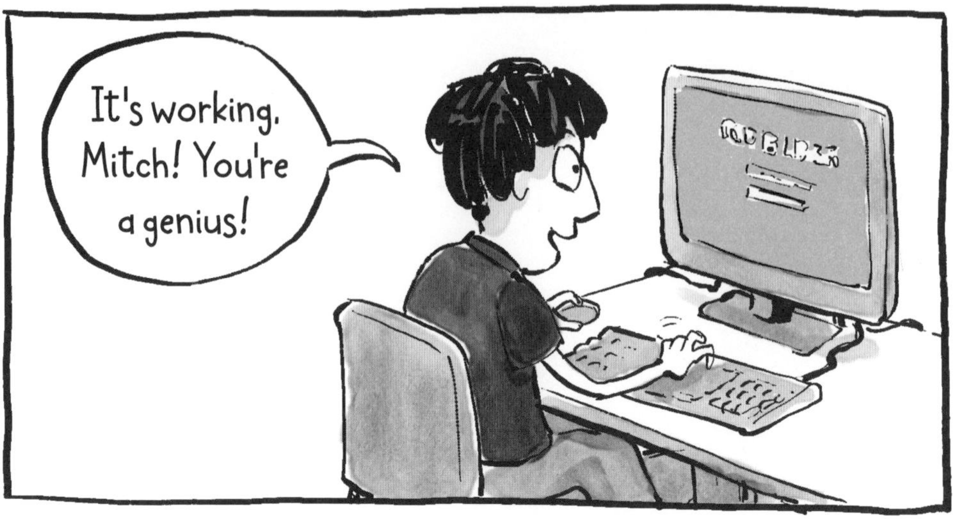
It's working, Mitch! You're a genius!

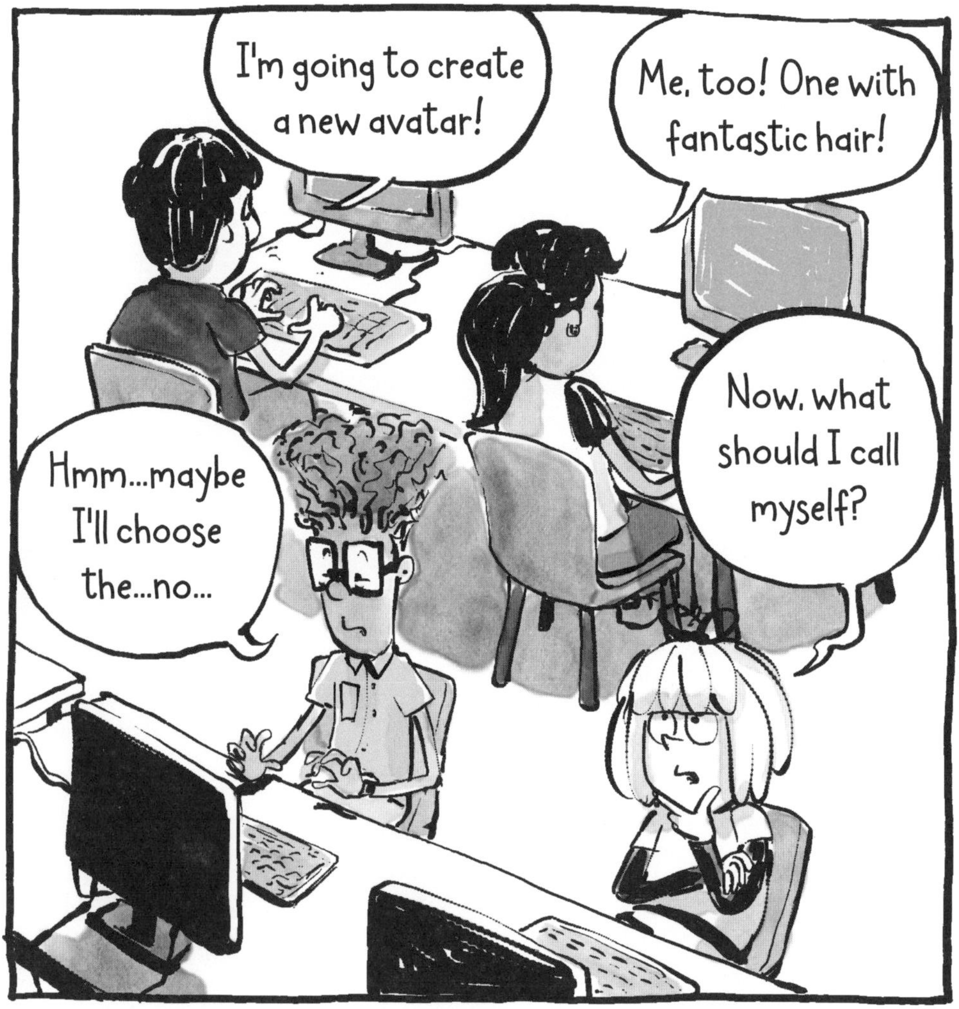
I'm going to create a new avatar!
Me, too! One with fantastic hair!
Hmm...maybe I'll choose the...no...
Now, what should I call myself?

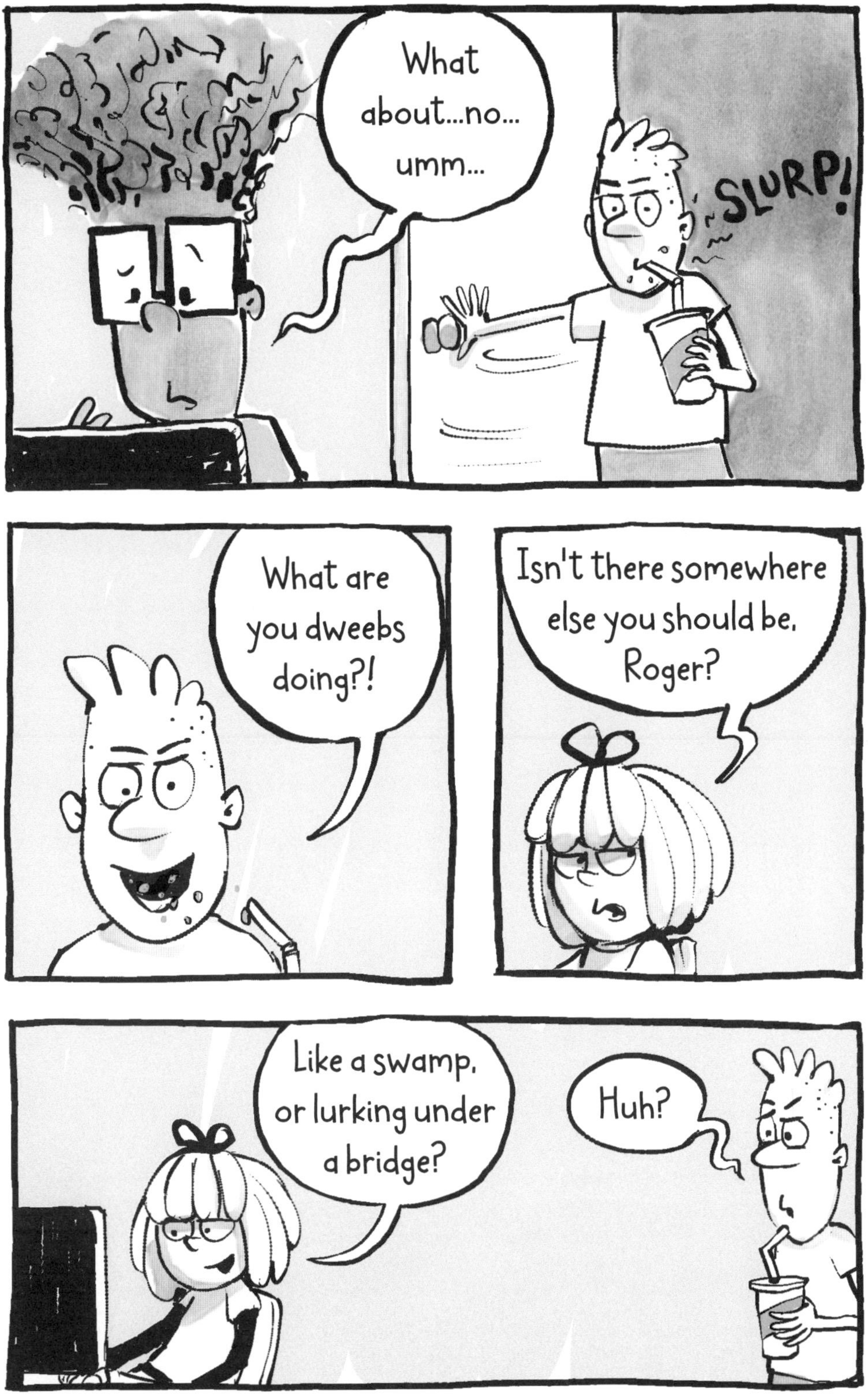
What about...no... umm...
SLURP!
What are you dweebs doing?!
Isn't there somewhere else you should be, Roger?
Like a swamp, or lurking under a bridge?
Huh?

26

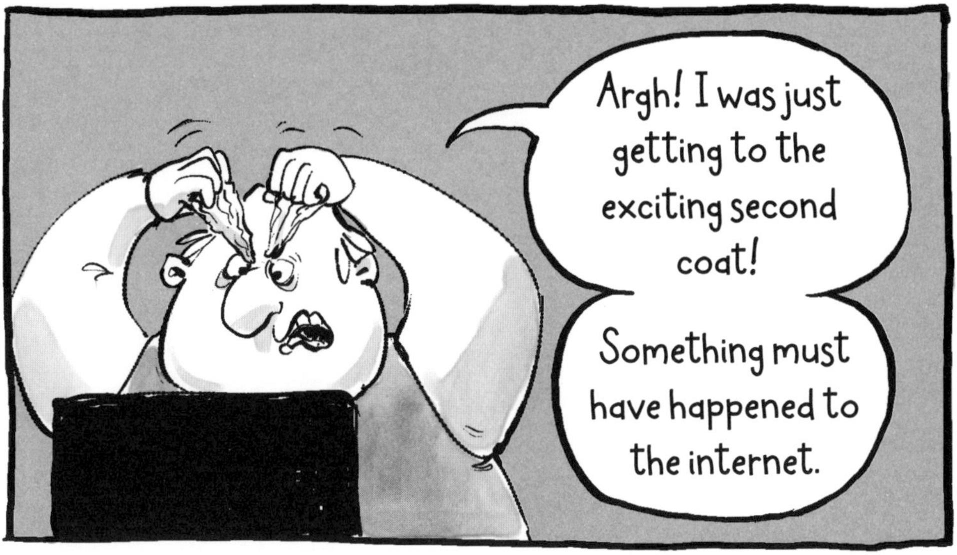
Argh! I was just getting to the exciting second coat!
Something must have happened to the internet.

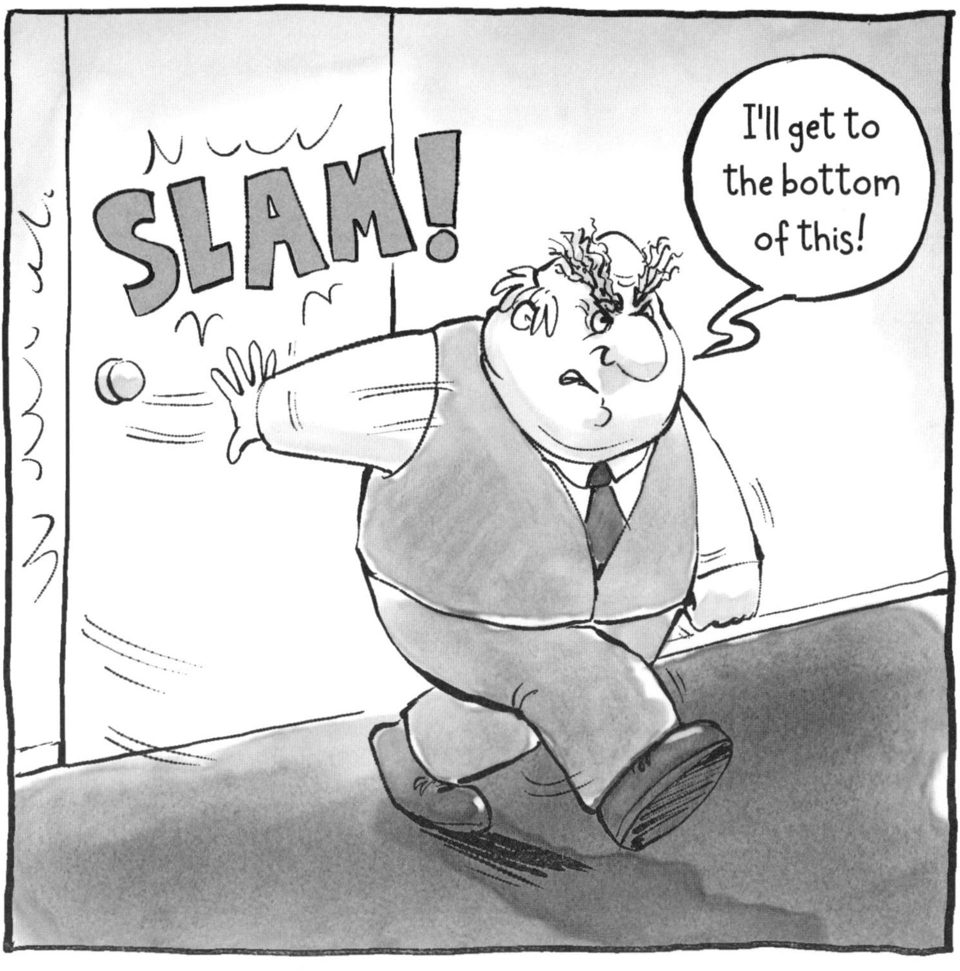
SLAM!
I'll get to the bottom of this!

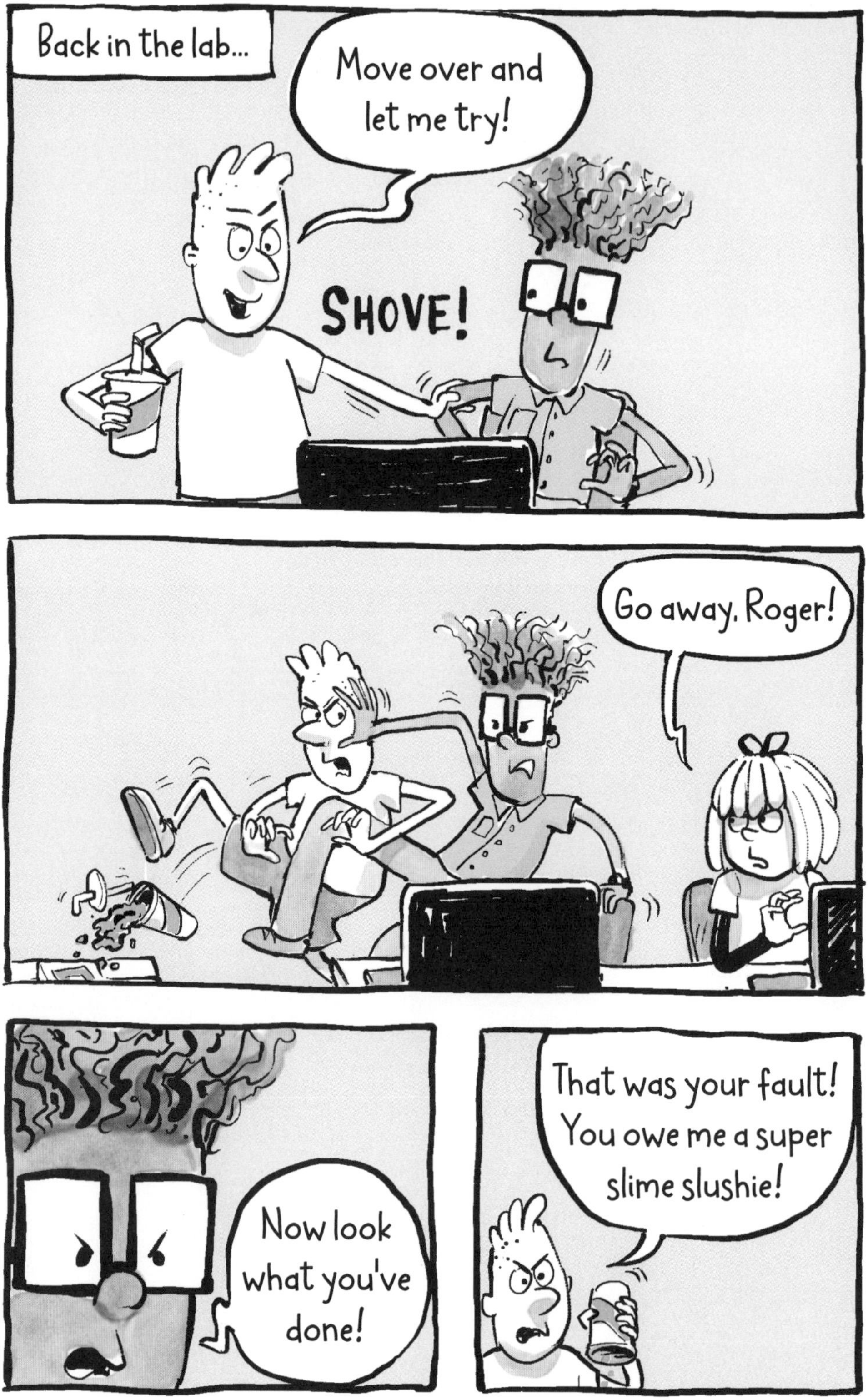
Back in the lab...
Move over and let me try!
SHOVE!
Go away, Roger!
Now look what you've done!
That was your fault! You owe me a super slime slushie!

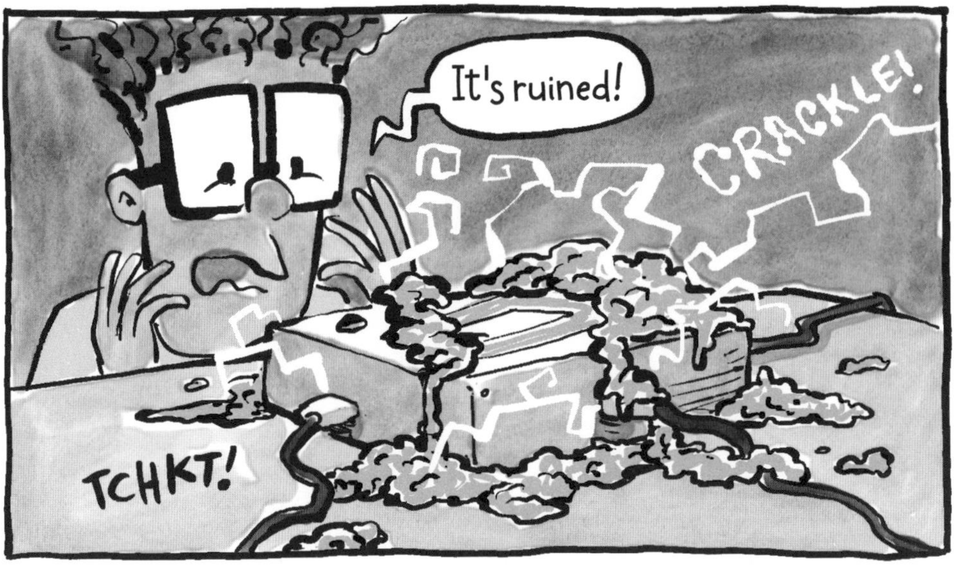
It's ruined!
CRACKLE!
TCHKT!

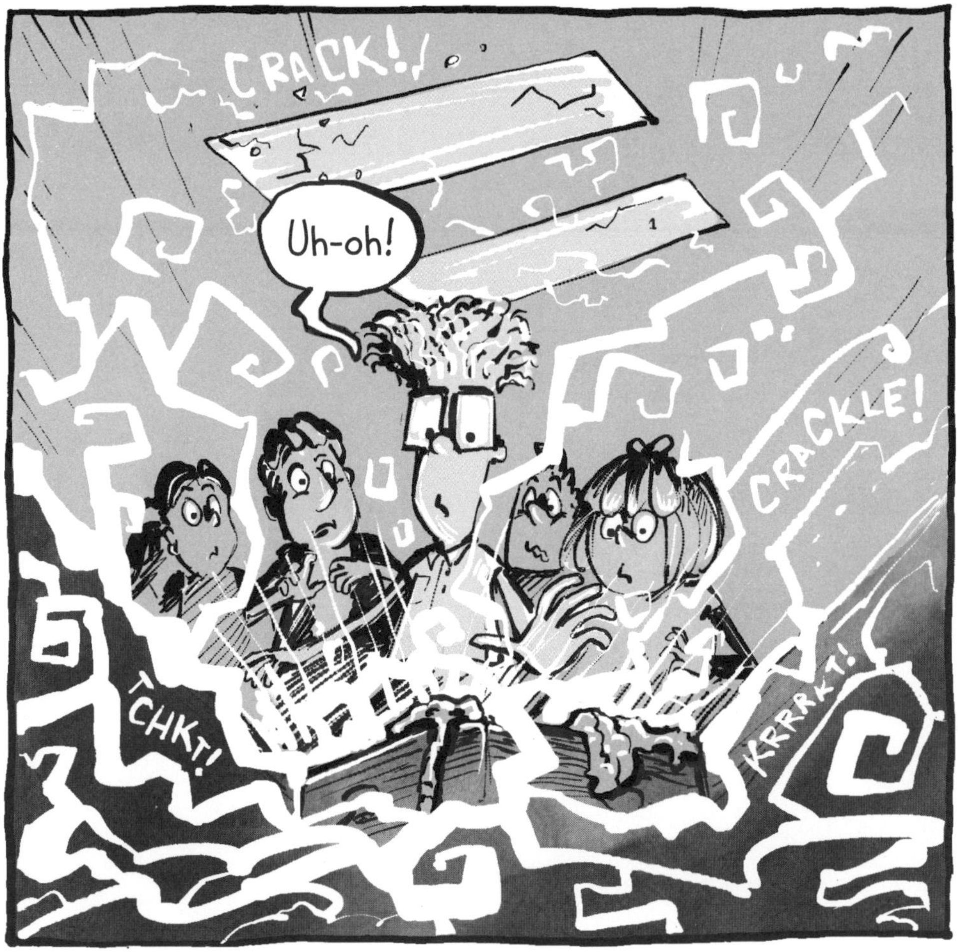
CRACK!
Uh-oh!
CRACKLE!
TCHKT!
KRRRKT!

As Mitch's device malfunctioned, the computer lab was plunged into darkness.

"Nice one, Roger!" snapped Bea.

"I didn't do anything," replied Roger. "Mitch made me..."

"How about we stop fighting and try to find a way out of here instead?" said Tash. "There should be an exit sign somewhere..."

But the kids, stumbling and bumbling in the pitch black, couldn't find the door anywhere.

Panic started to set in as Roger became more and more hysterical.

"We're trapped!" he wailed. "We're all going to die in here! I'm running out of air...need oxygen...Help! Help! Heeeelp!!!"

"I don't think there's any help for him," muttered Bea.

"We've got to get out of here soon," stammered Mitch. "We'll be late for class!"

At that moment, an eerie green light began glowing in the corner of the room. An outline of a doorway, with a sign above it, slowly became visible.

"There you go," said Jai. "No need to panic at all. I knew we'd find the exit..."

But the sign read ENTER, not EXIT, and as they watched, a strange square shape appeared in front of them.

Trembling a little, the kids approached the glowing door and opened it...

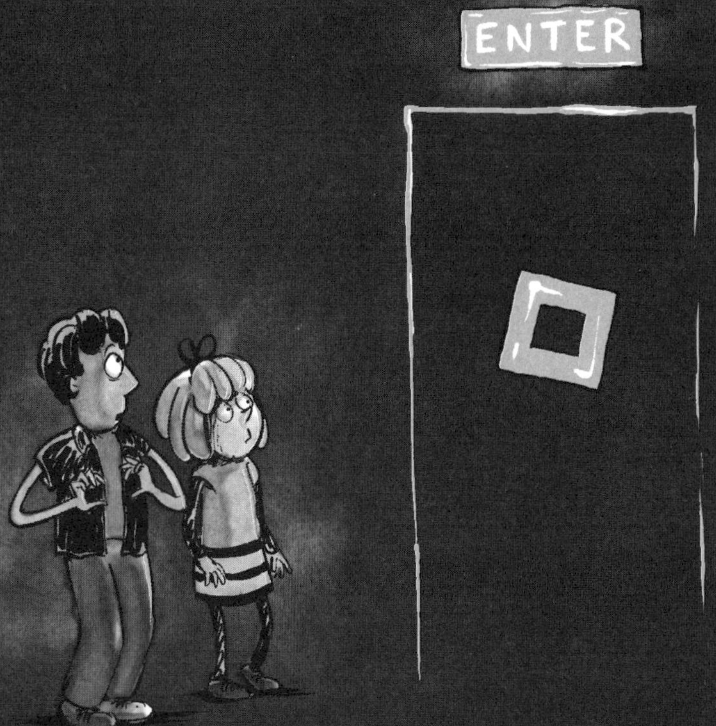
ENTER

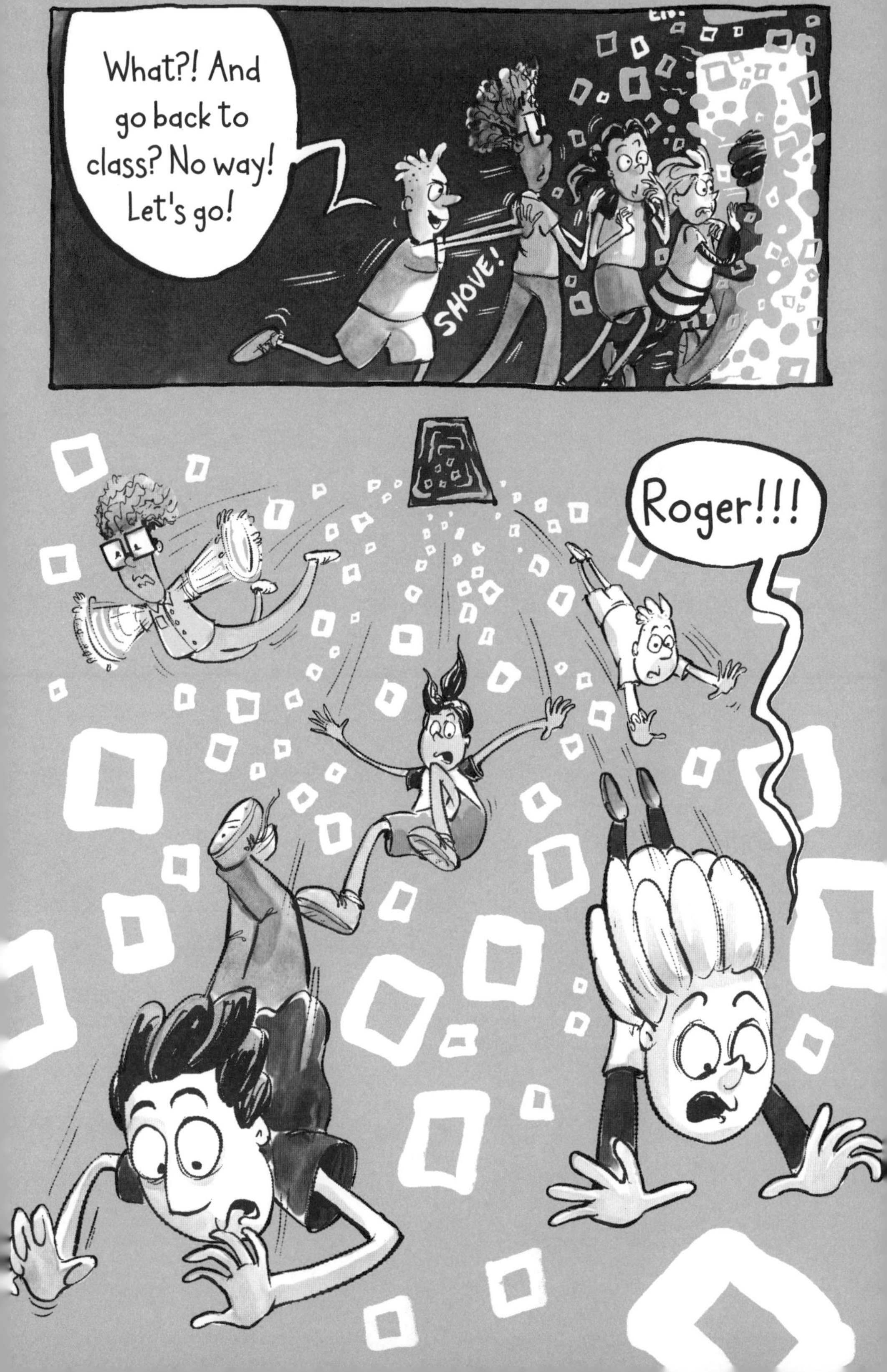
What?! And go back to class? No way! Let's go!
SHOVE!
Roger!!!

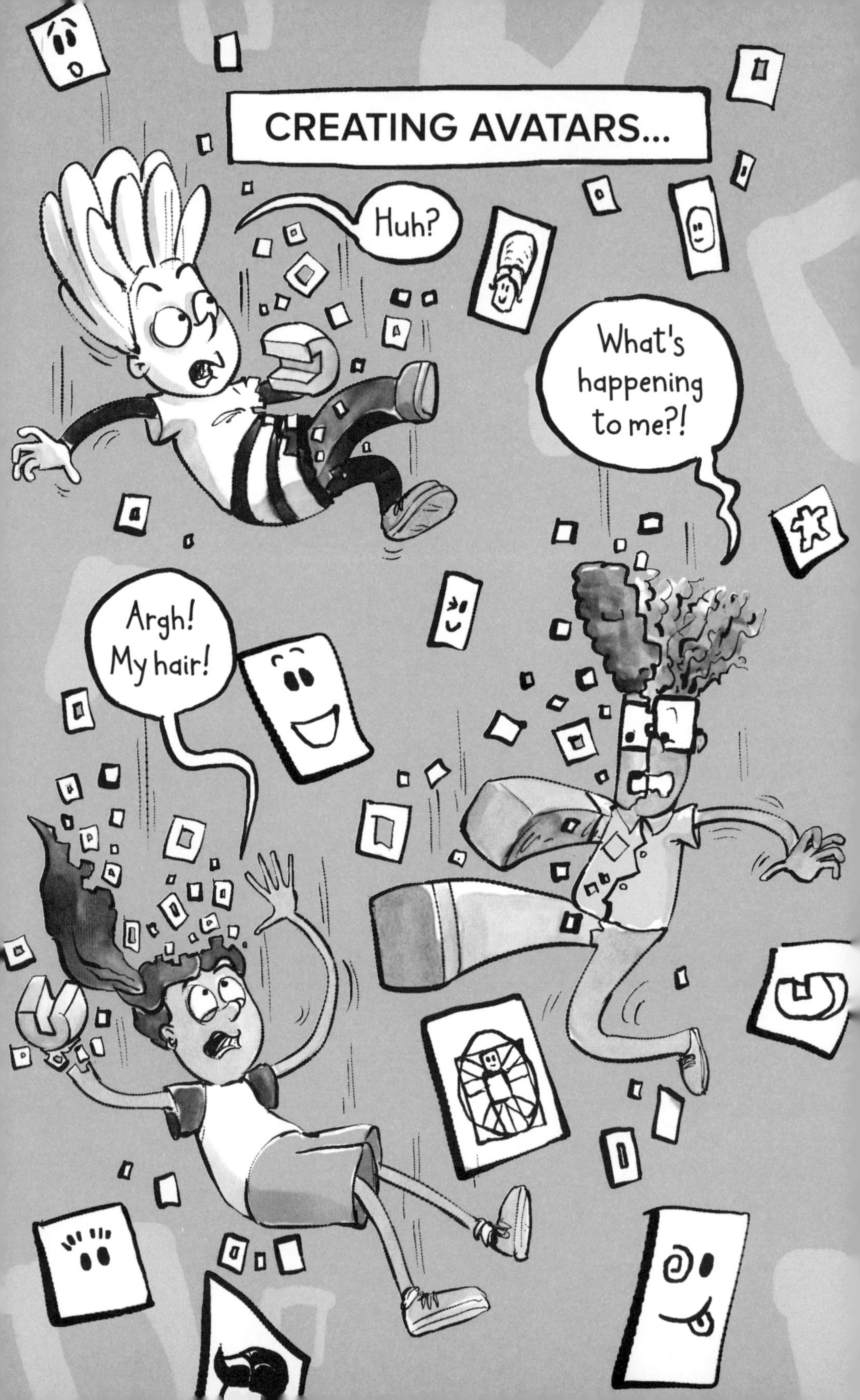
CREATING AVATARS...
Huh?
What's happening to me?!
Argh! My hair!

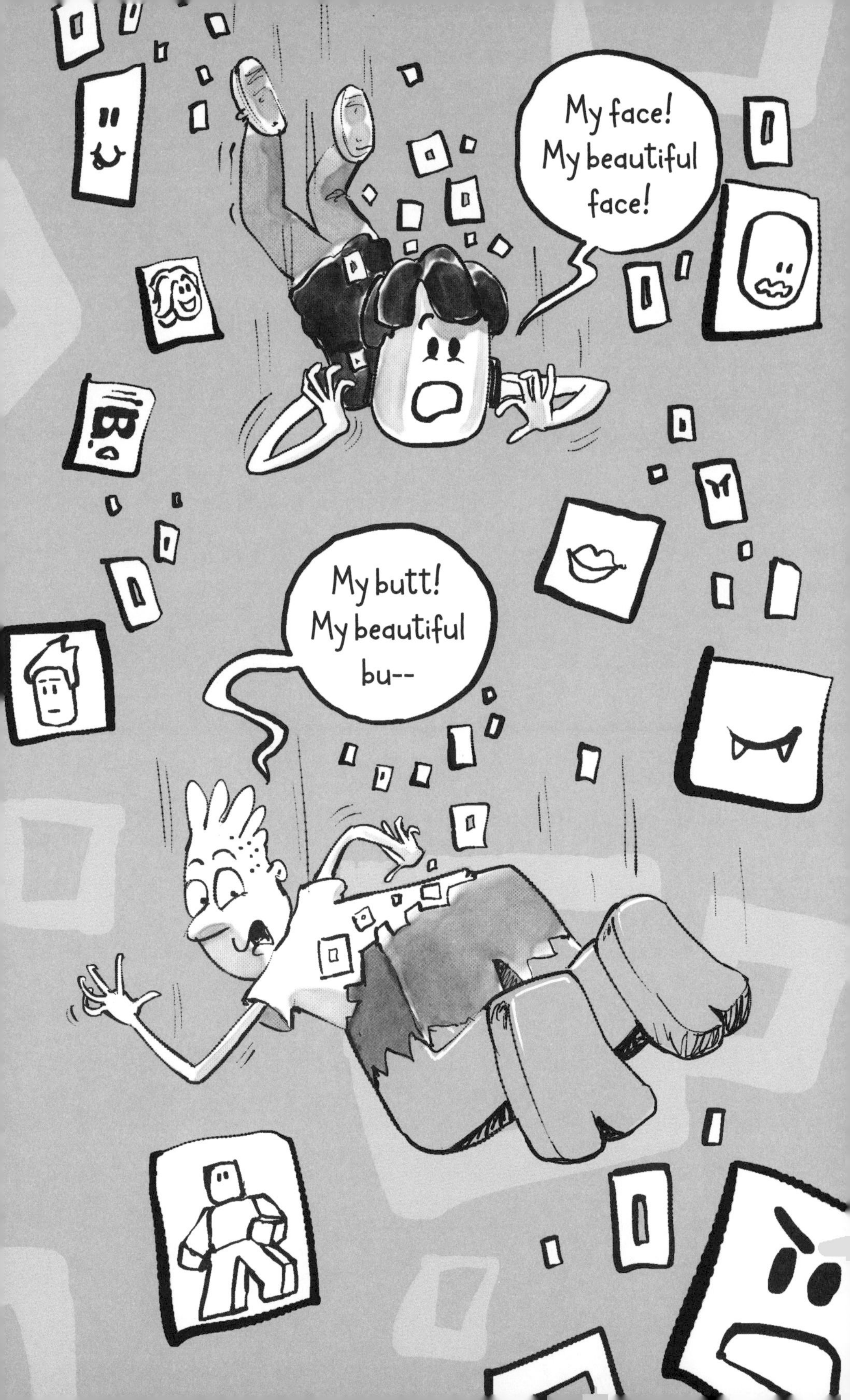
My face! My beautiful face!
My butt! My beautiful bu--

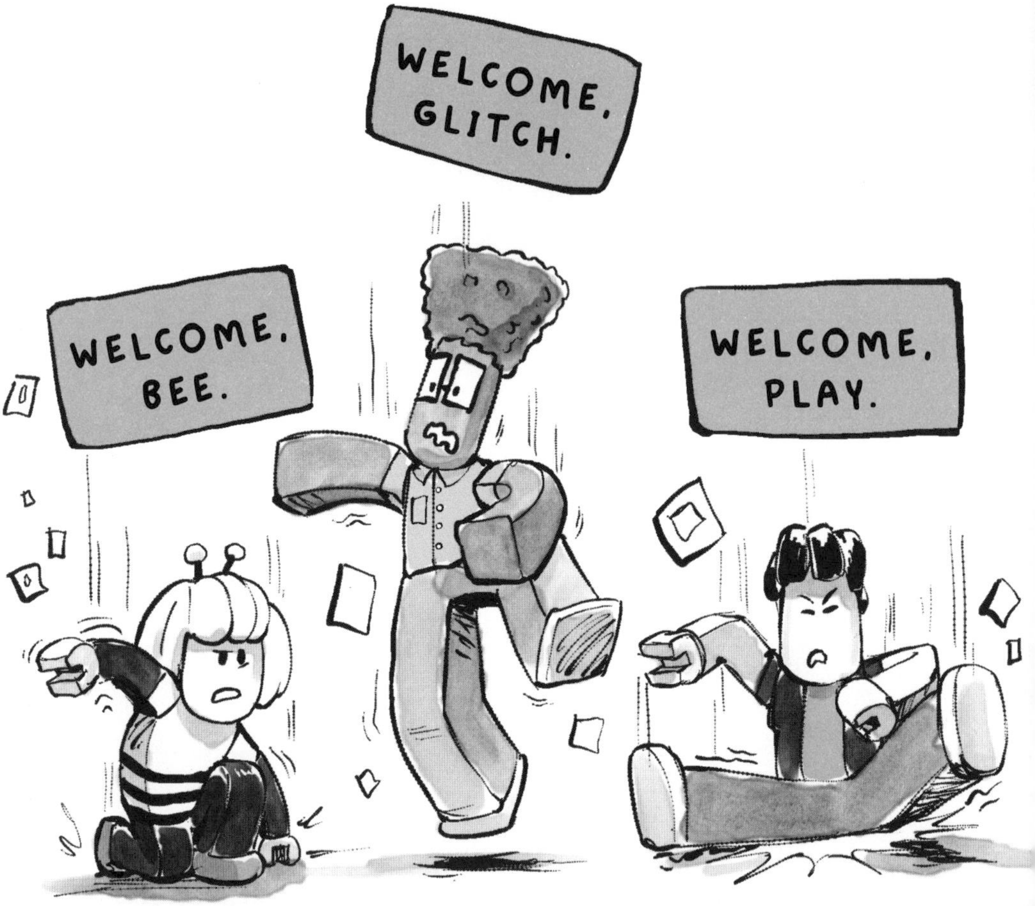
WELCOME, GLITCH.
WELCOME, BEE.
WELCOME, PLAY.

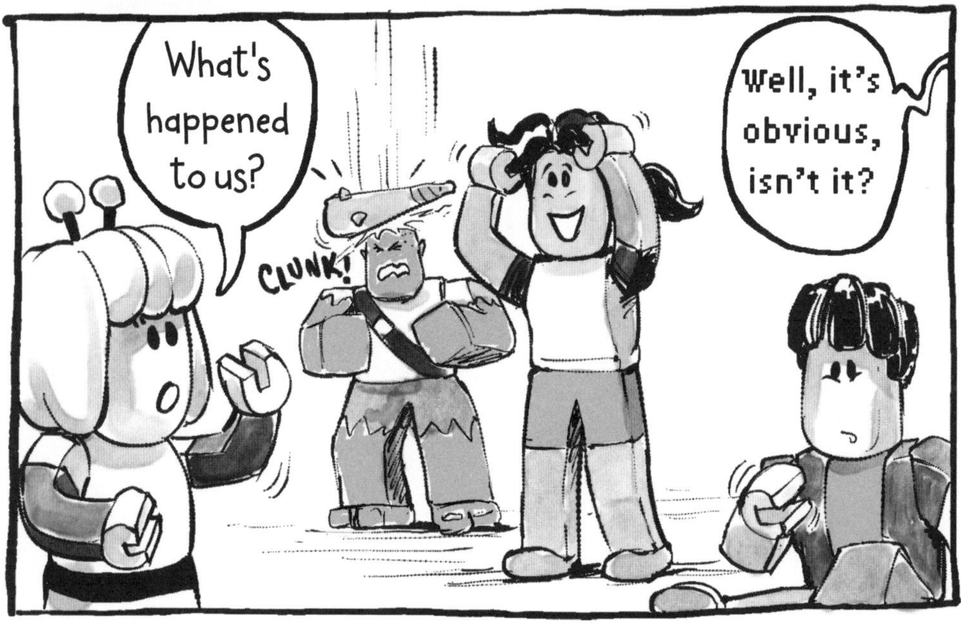
What's happened to us?
CLUNK!
Well, it's obvious, isn't it?

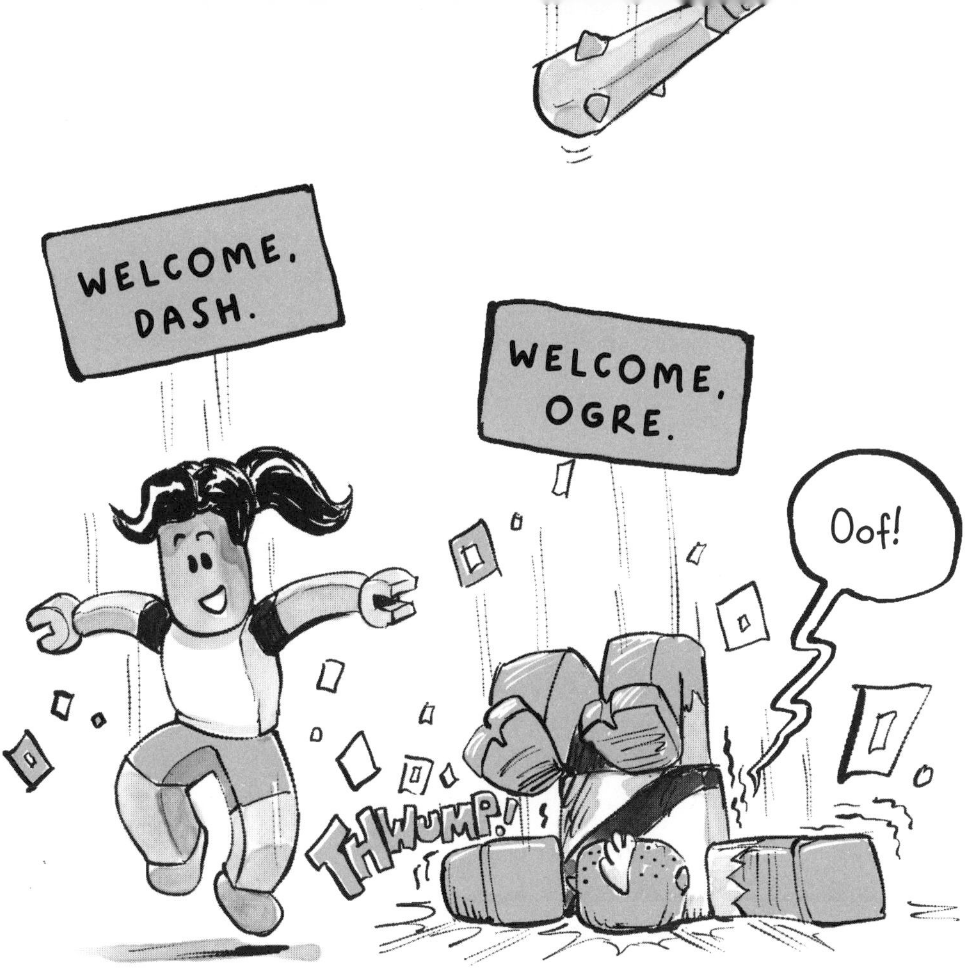
WELCOME, DASH.
WELCOME, OGRE.
Oof!
THWUMP!

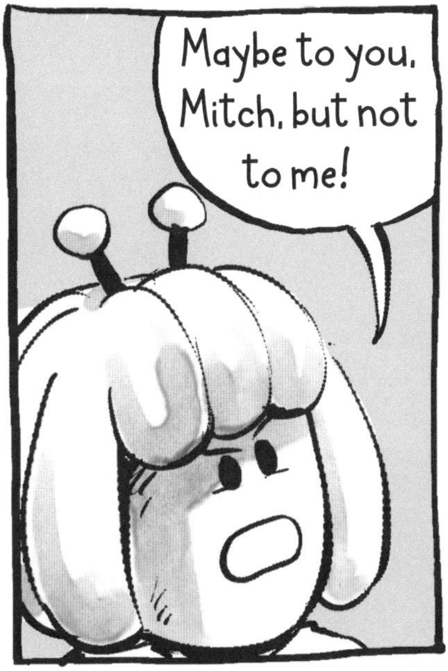
Maybe to you, Mitch, but not to me!

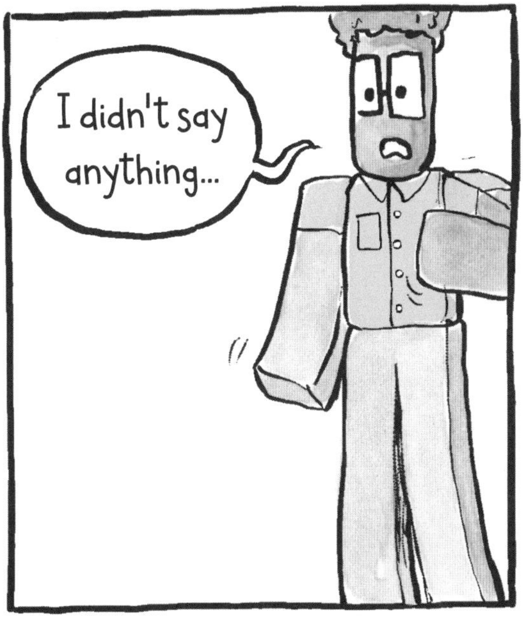
I didn't say anything...

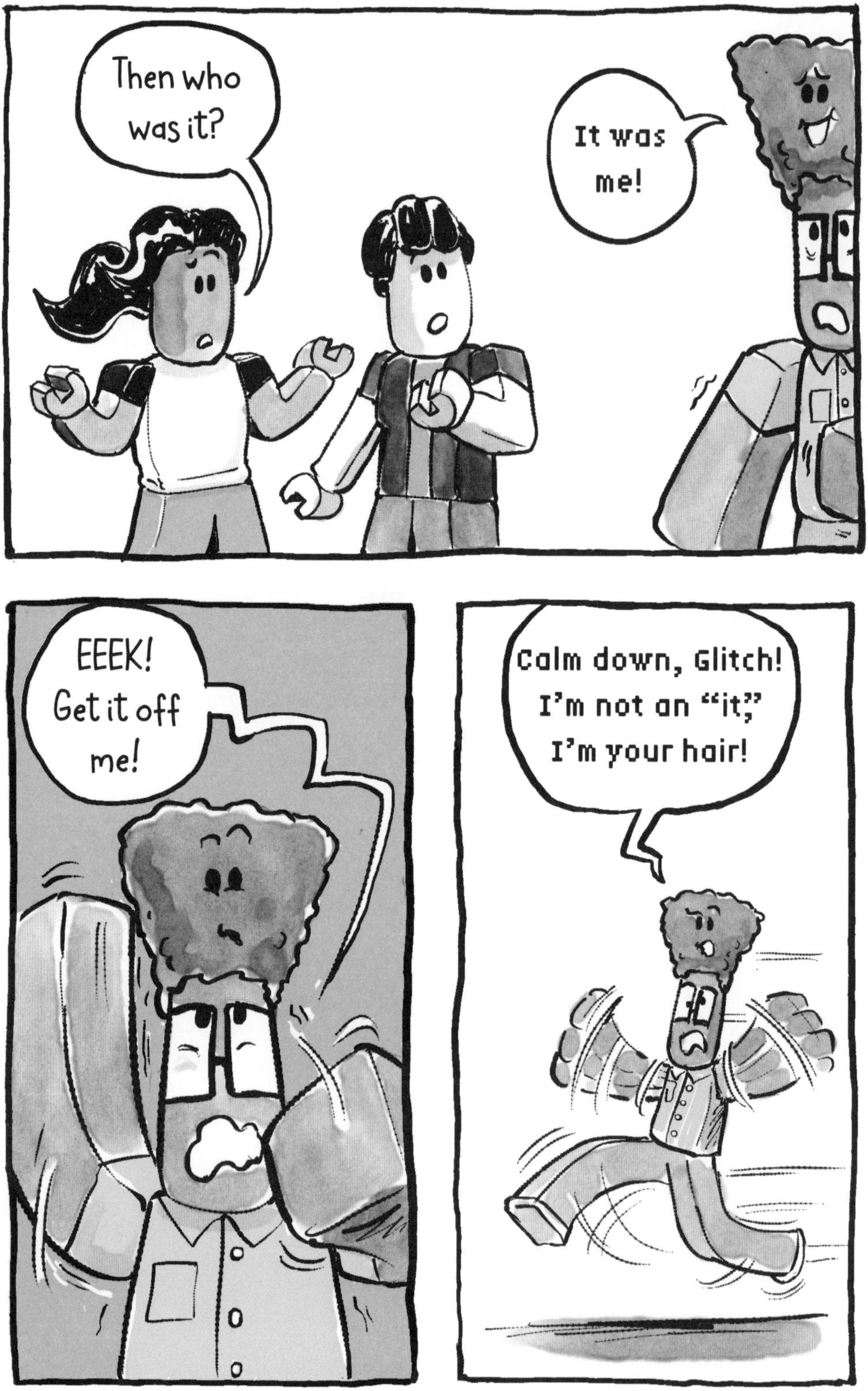
Then who was it?
It was me!
EEEK! Get it off me!
Calm down, Glitch! I'm not an "it," I'm your hair!

ROBLOX AVATAR PROFILES

Beatrice's avatar name: Bee
Though her avatar doesn't have an actual sting, Bee's sharp comebacks more than make up for it!

Mitch's avatar name: Glitch

Mitch's hair's avatar name: Fritz
As his friends pointed out, Glitch's ample brain is always of two minds! Fritz has all the confidence and is ready to guide Glitch and his friends in the Roblox universe!

Tash's avatar name: Dash
Just like in the real world,
Dash loves to move! She's
ready for any obby Roblox
throws at her!

Jai's avatar name: Play
Play by name, Play by
nature! Always ready for
fun, Play will sometimes
learn stuff, too!

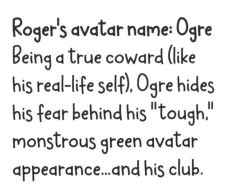

Roger's avatar name: Ogre
Being a true coward (like
his real-life self), Ogre hides
his fear behind his "tough,"
monstrous green avatar
appearance...and his club.

The avatars followed the green arrows until they reached a door with another ENTER sign above it.

"Not another one!" said Glitch. "I think we should turn back. Who knows what's on the other side?!"

"Whatever it is, it'll be better than school!" replied Ogre.

"I hate to agree with Ogre, but I think he's right, Glitch," said Play. "Look, there's a sign on the door. Let's see what it says at least."

Under the heading BUS RUN was a description of a challenge that needed to be completed to go any further in the game.

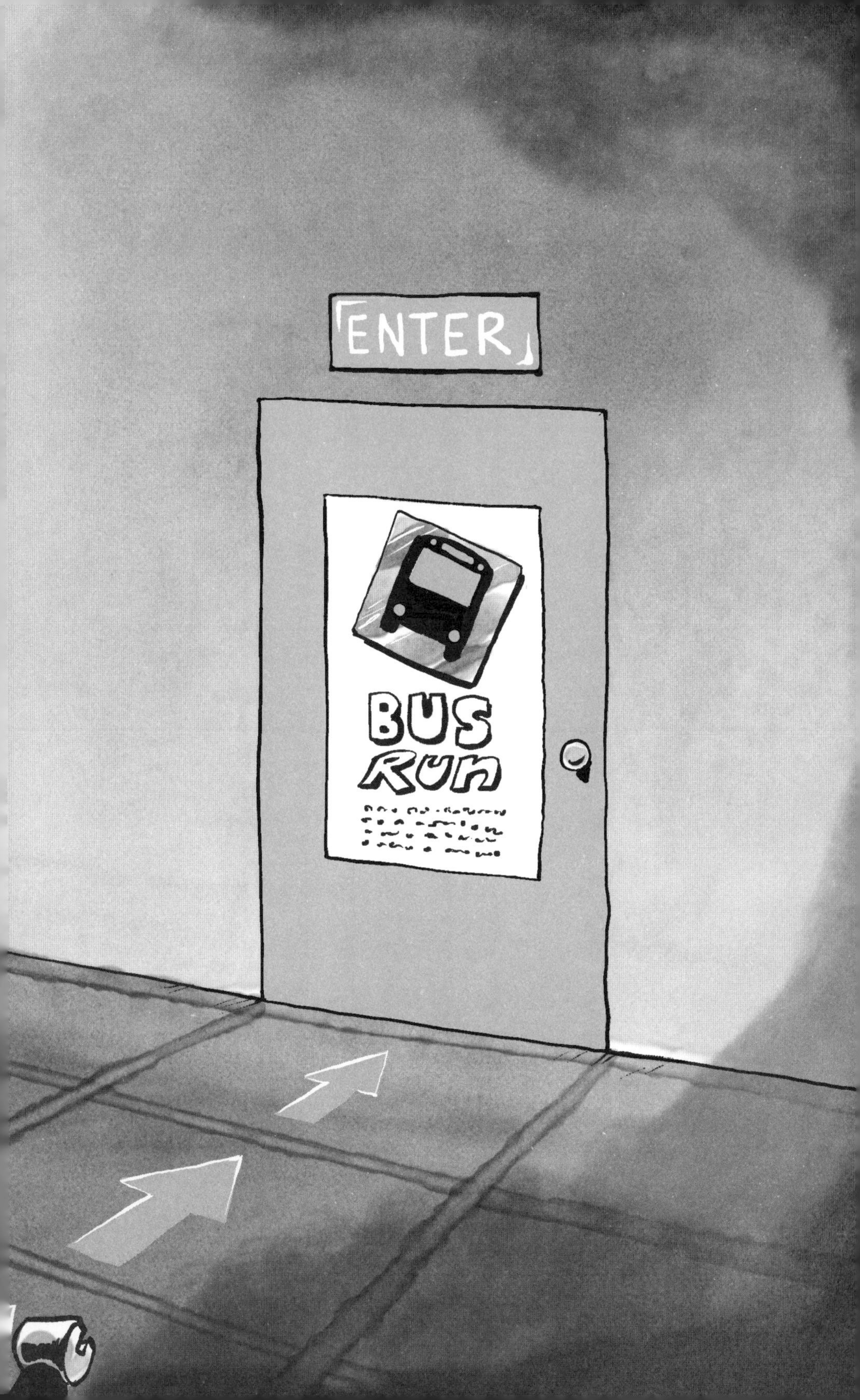
ENTER
BUS
Run

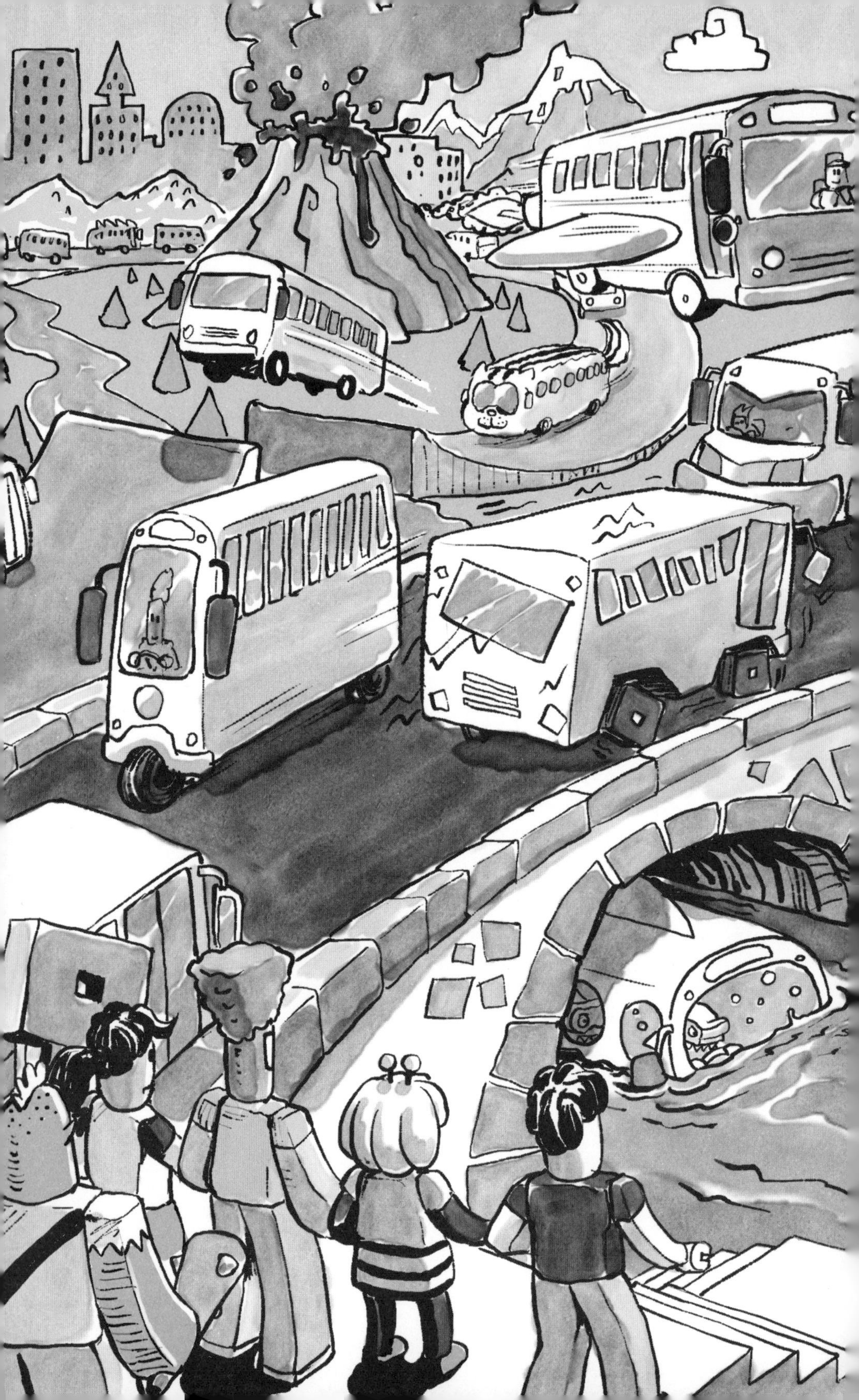

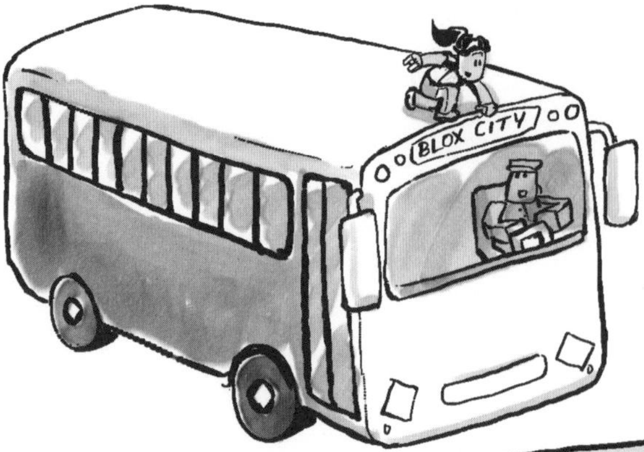
BLOX CITY

Fritz: Any luck yet?
Dash: Not yet!

Ogre: Help! A bus is trying to eat me!
Glitch: As if! If you're not going to help, Ogre, just keep quiet!

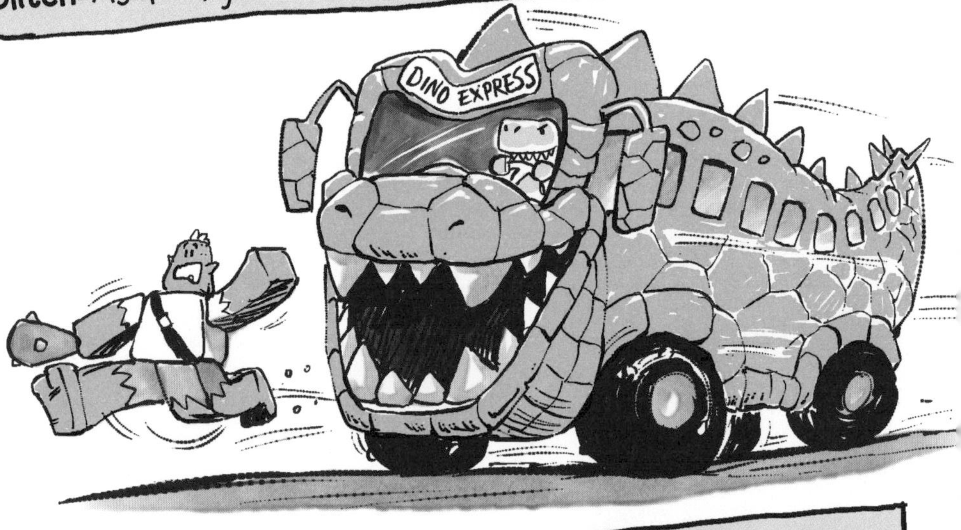
DINO EXPRESS

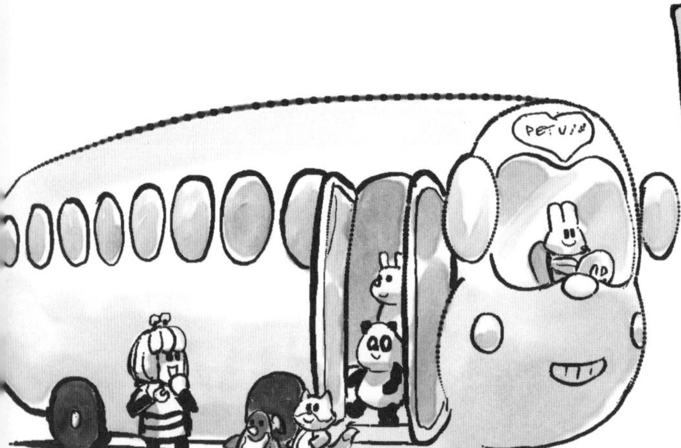

Bee: OMG! Forget the Academy. I've found a much better bus!
Dash: Focus, Bee!
Bee: But they're so cute!

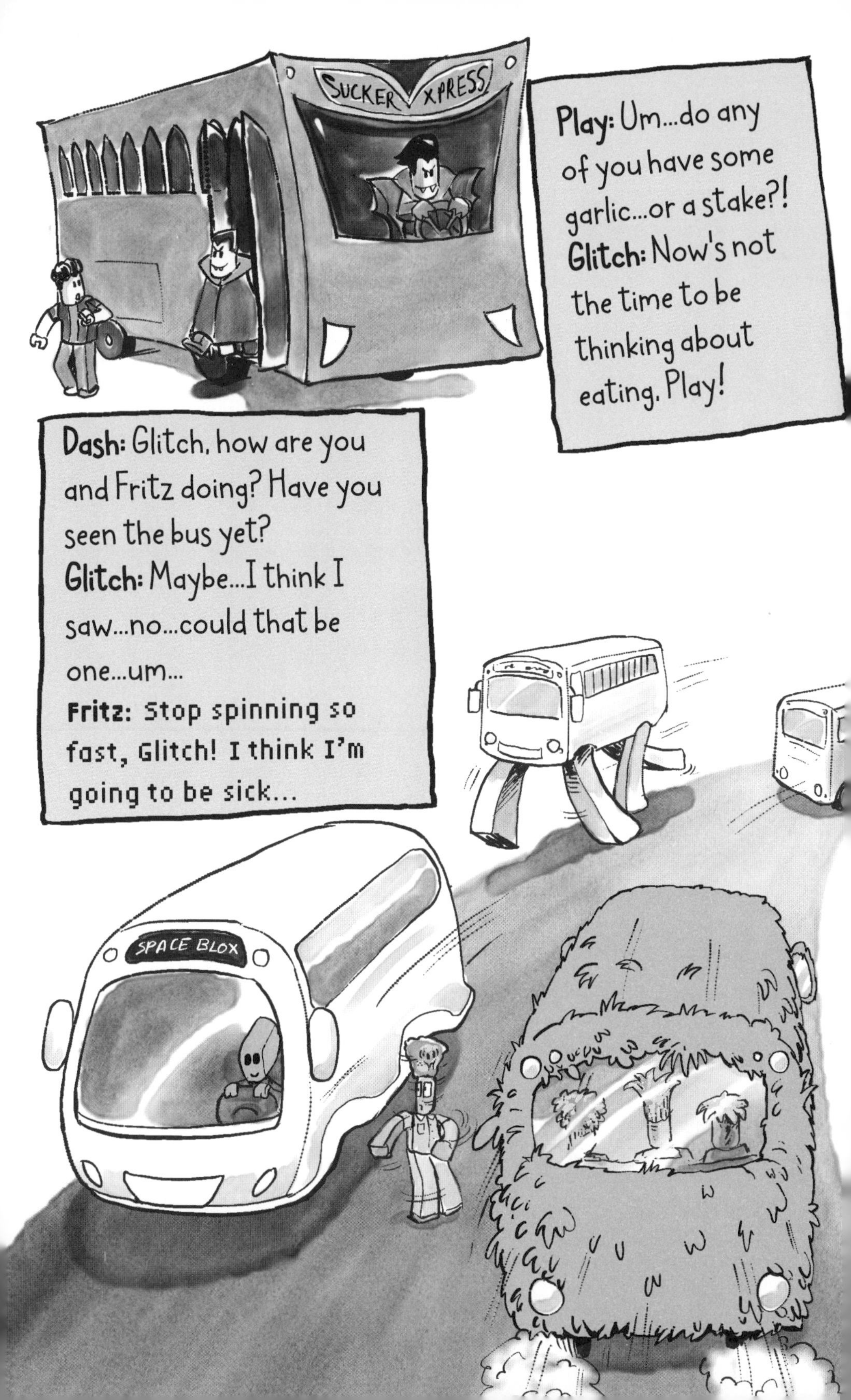
SUCKER XPRESS
Play: Um...do any of you have some garlic...or a stake?!
Glitch: Now's not the time to be thinking about eating, Play!
Dash: Glitch, how are you and Fritz doing? Have you seen the bus yet?
Glitch: Maybe...I think I saw...no...could that be one...um...
Fritz: Stop spinning so fast, Glitch! I think I'm going to be sick...
SPACE BLOX

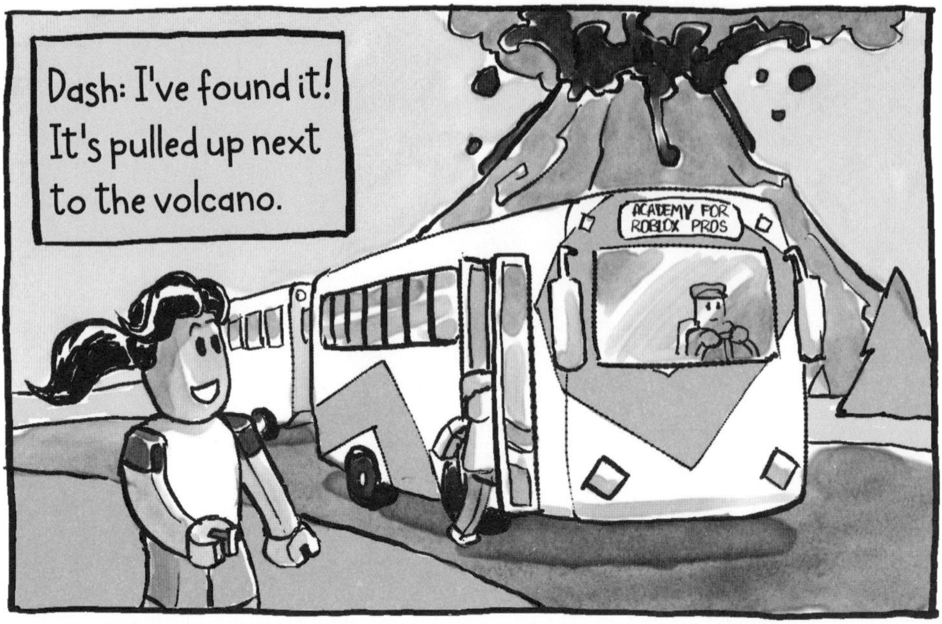
Dash: I've found it! It's pulled up next to the volcano.
ACADEMY FOR ROBLOX PROS

Bee: Awesome! I see it!

Glitch: Well done, Dash! I was starting to think we'd never find it!

Fritz: Excellent work! And may I say, what wonderful hair you have!

Ogre: Ha-ha! Fritz has a crush on Dash's hair!

Fritz: I do not! I was just remarking on how good it looked when the light was shining off her flowing, glossy...

Glitch: Shhh, Fritz! You're making it worse!

Bee: Um, when you're all finished, maybe we should get on the bus before it leaves?

Fritz: Good idea, Bee...all aboard!

Dash: Where's Play?

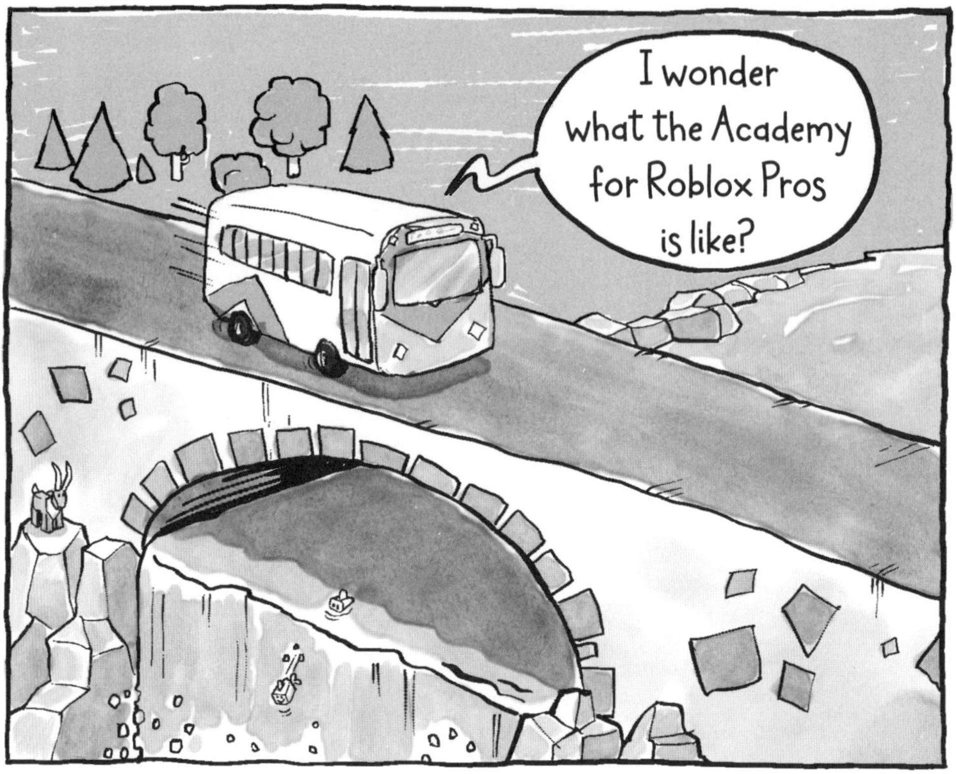
I wonder what the Academy for Roblox Pros is like?

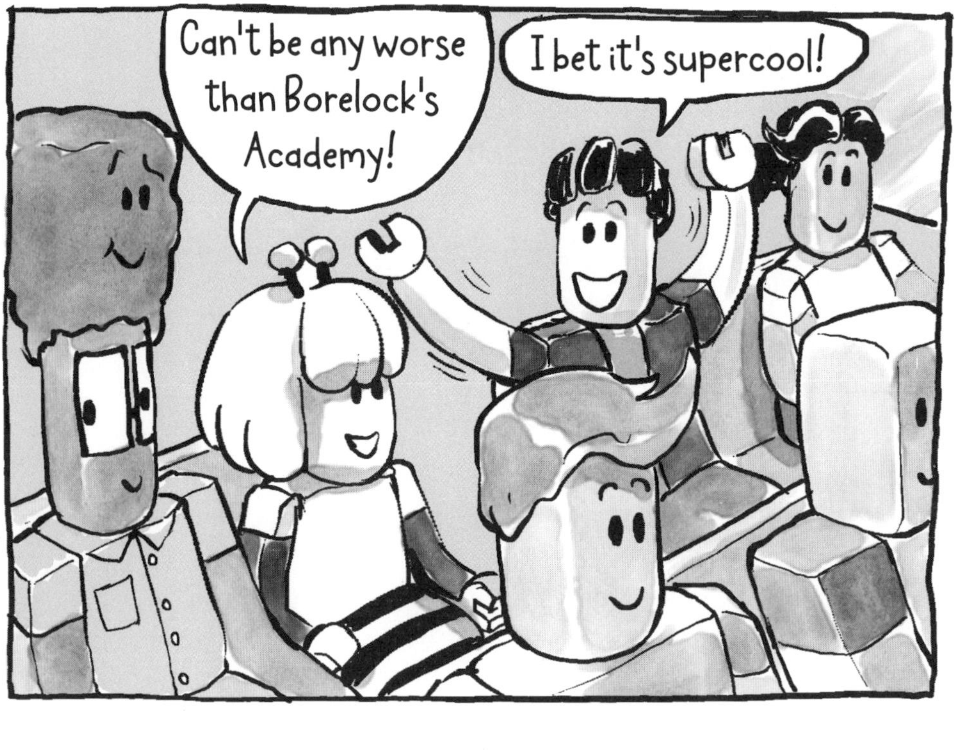
Can't be any worse than Borelock's Academy!
I bet it's supercool!

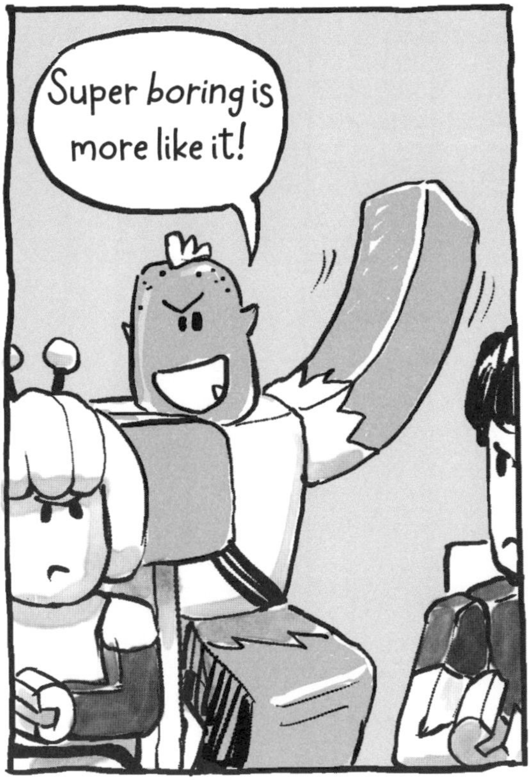
Super *boring* is more like it!

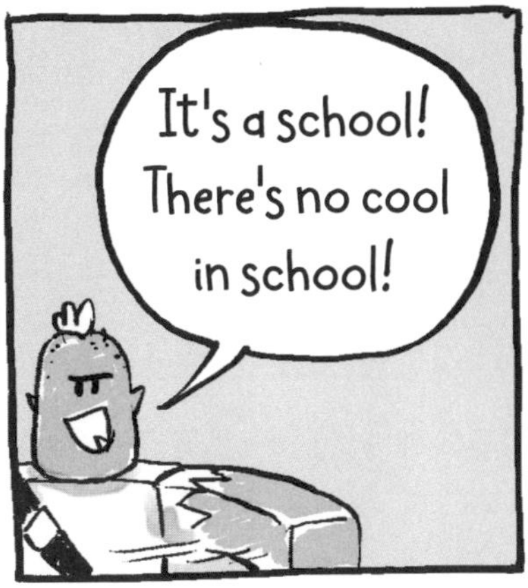
It's a school! There's no cool in school!

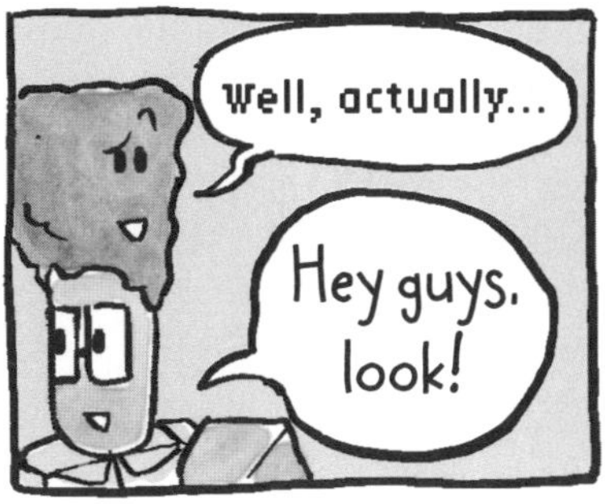
Well, actually...
Hey guys, look!

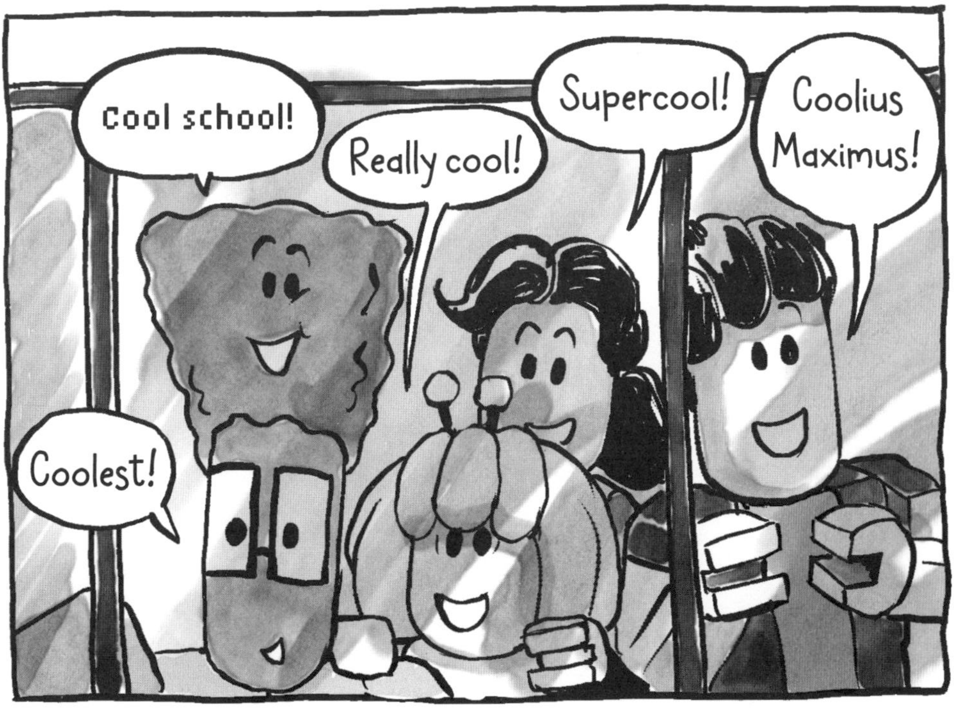
Cool school!
Really cool!
Supercool!
Coolius Maximus!
Coolest!

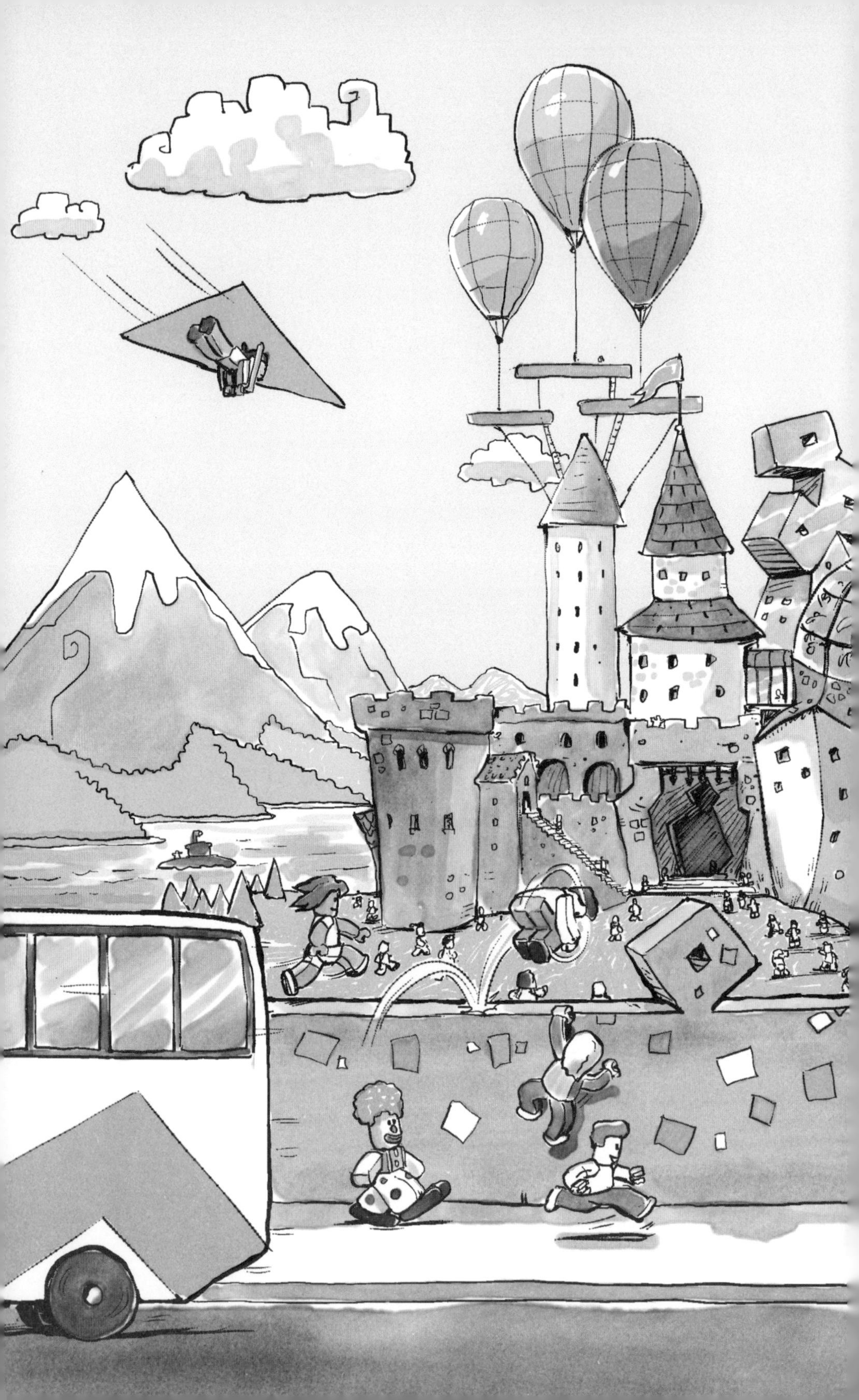

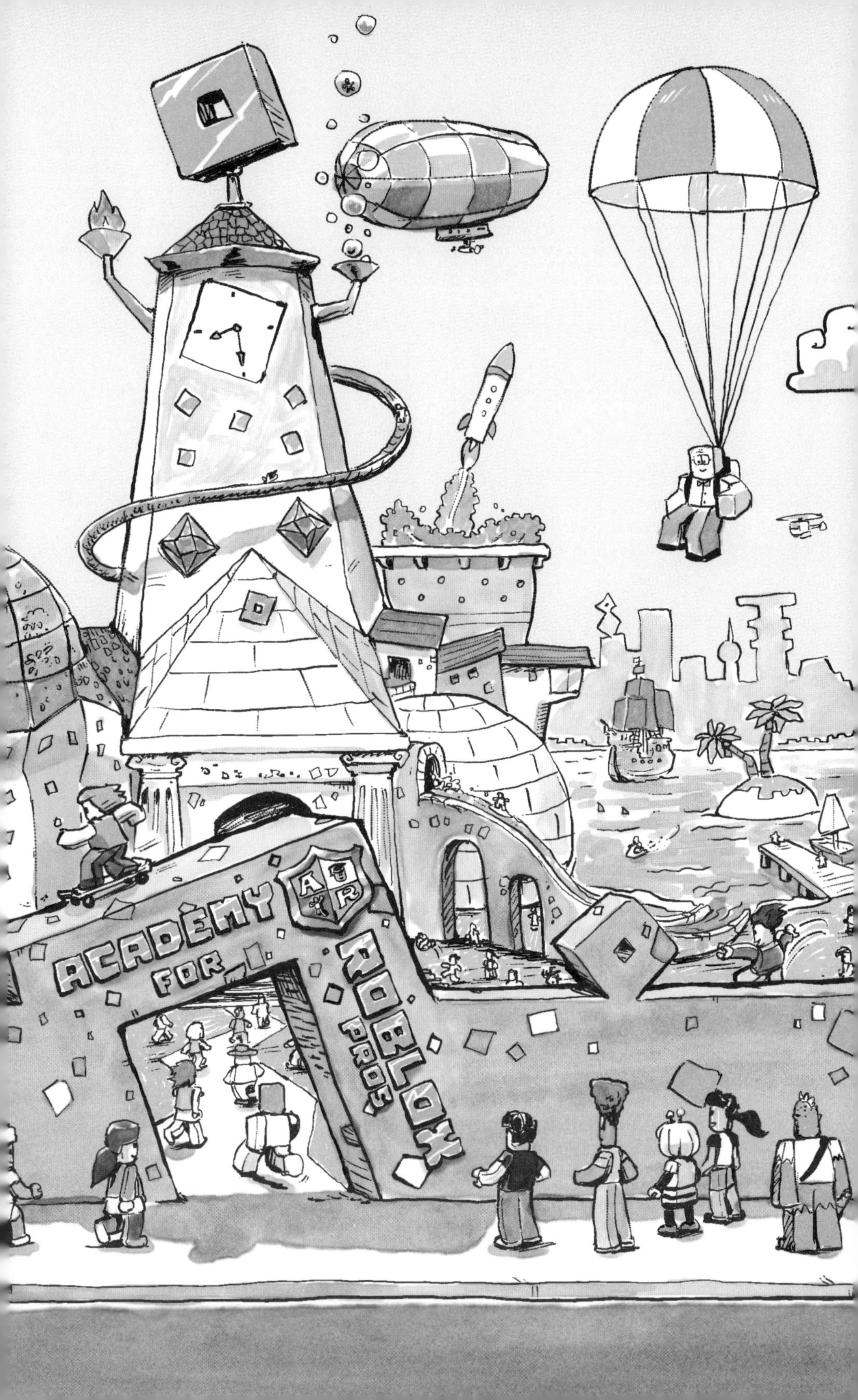
ACADEMY
FOR
ROBLOX
PROS
A R

The Academy for Roblox Pros is not your average school! While it does have the usual school things--classes, teachers, students, jocks, scary librarians...that's where the similarities end.

It was founded by Principal Blox, who was one of the original Roblox avatars--and he still sports the retro blocky old-school look!

Principal Blox wanted to create a school where new players could learn the ways of Roblox and where experienced avatars could level up their skills.

Using action-packed simulations, puzzles, role-playing, and obbys, the school teaches students to use problem-solving and teamwork as they learn and explore in the Roblox universe.

It's the only school where students want to do their homework!

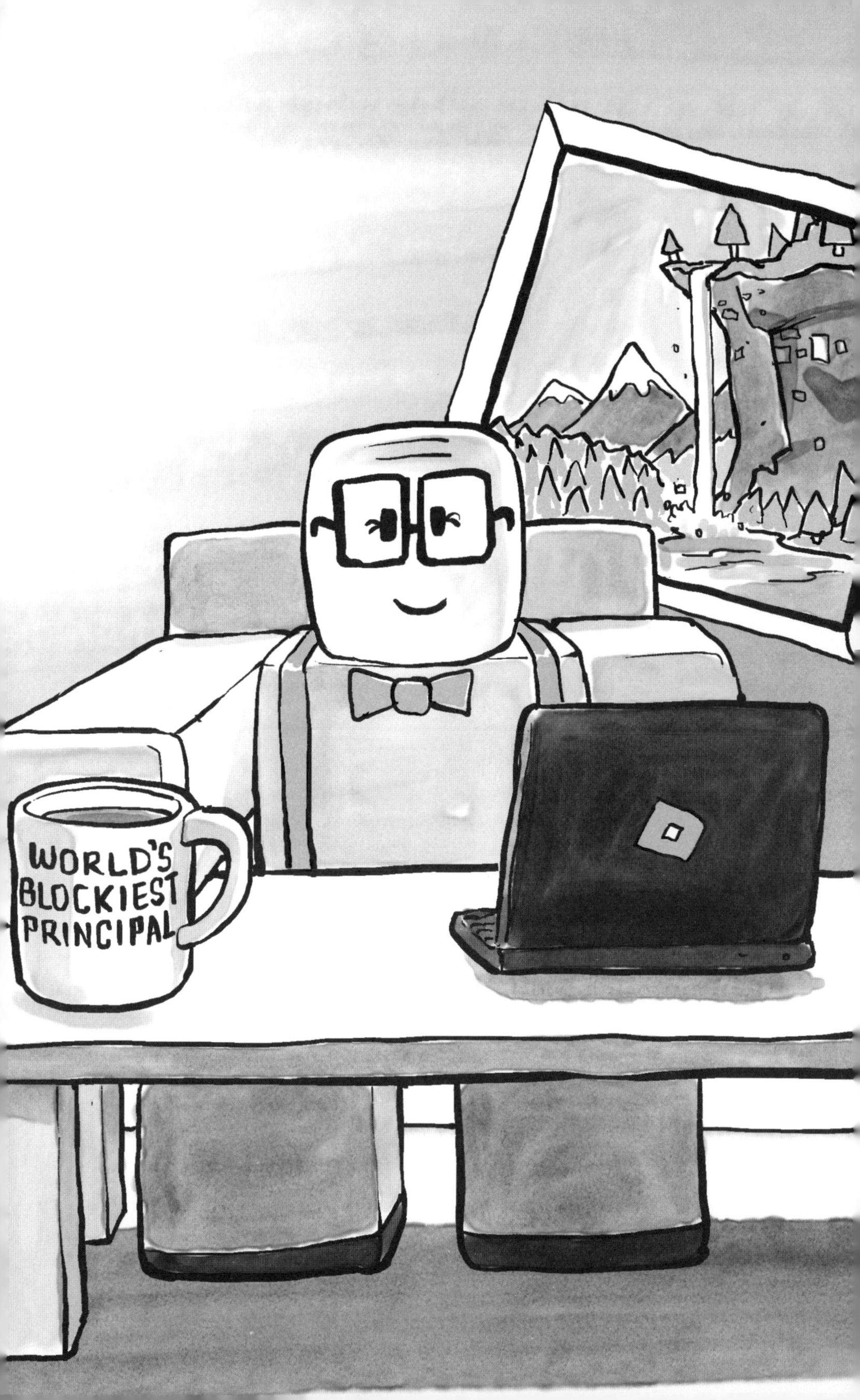
WORLD'S
BLOCKIEST
PRINCIPAL

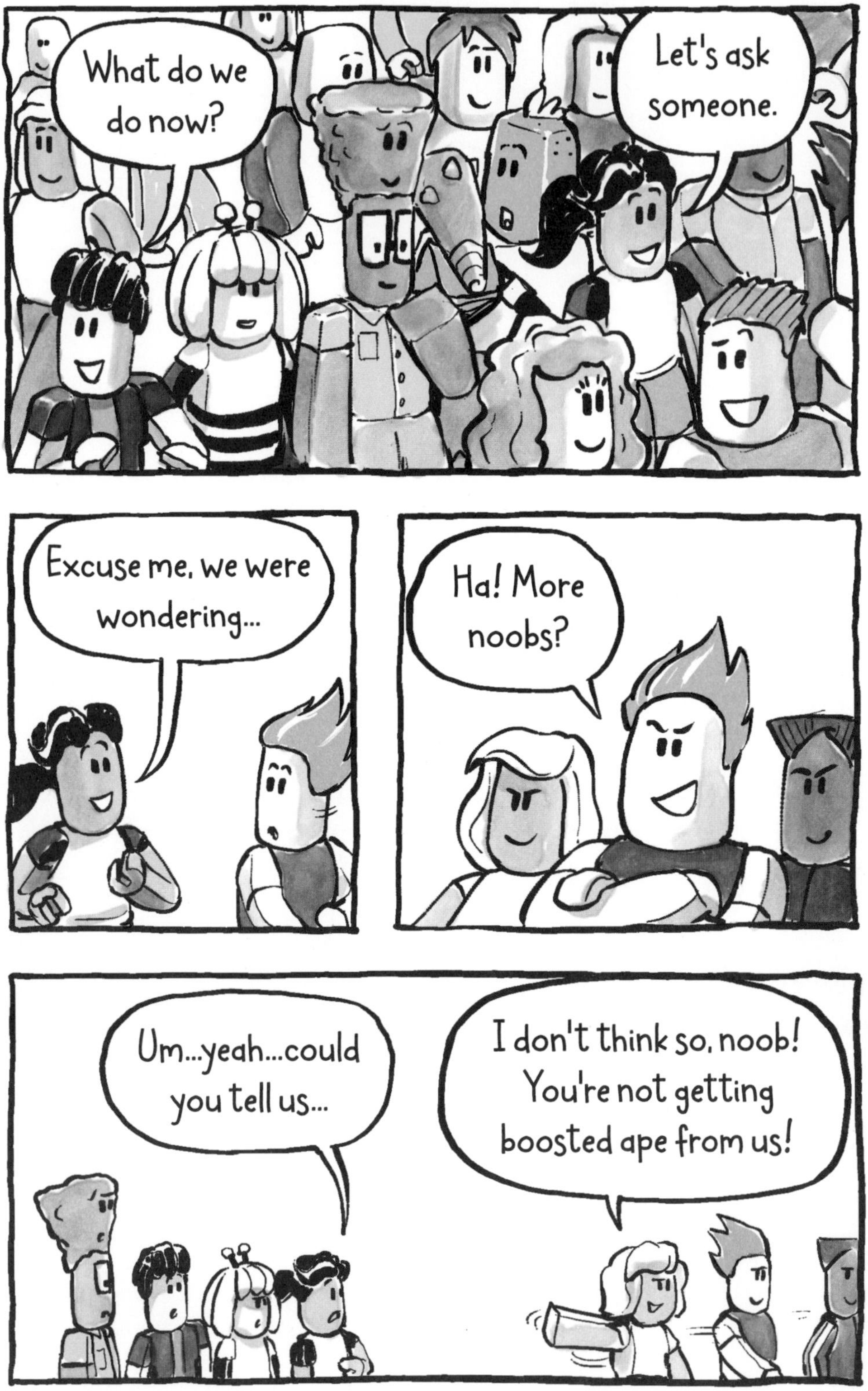
What do we do now?
Let's ask someone.
Excuse me, we were wondering...
Ha! More noobs?
Um...yeah...could you tell us...
I don't think so, noob! You're not getting boosted ape from us!

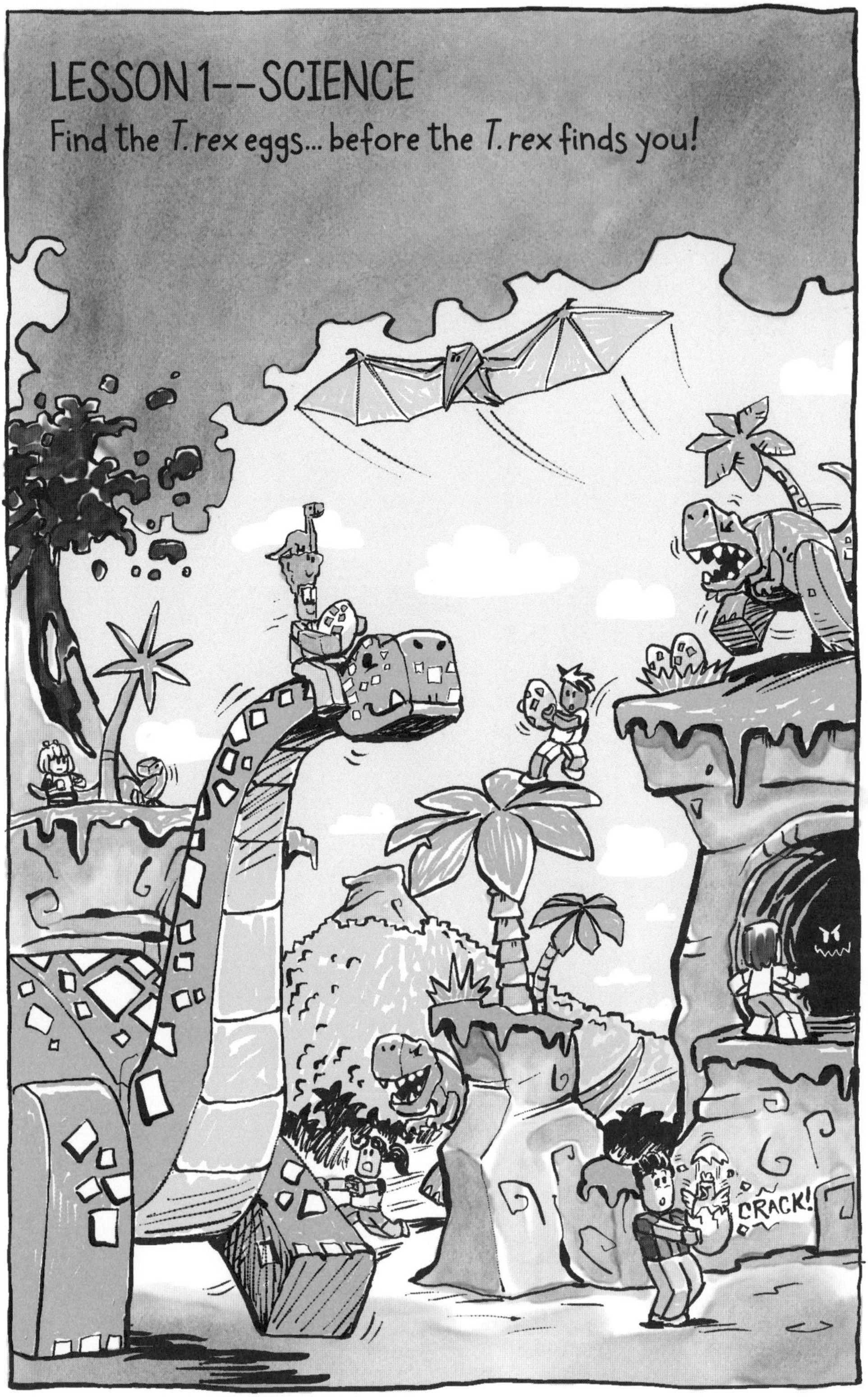
LESSON 1--SCIENCE
Find the T. rex eggs... before the T. rex finds you!
CRACK!

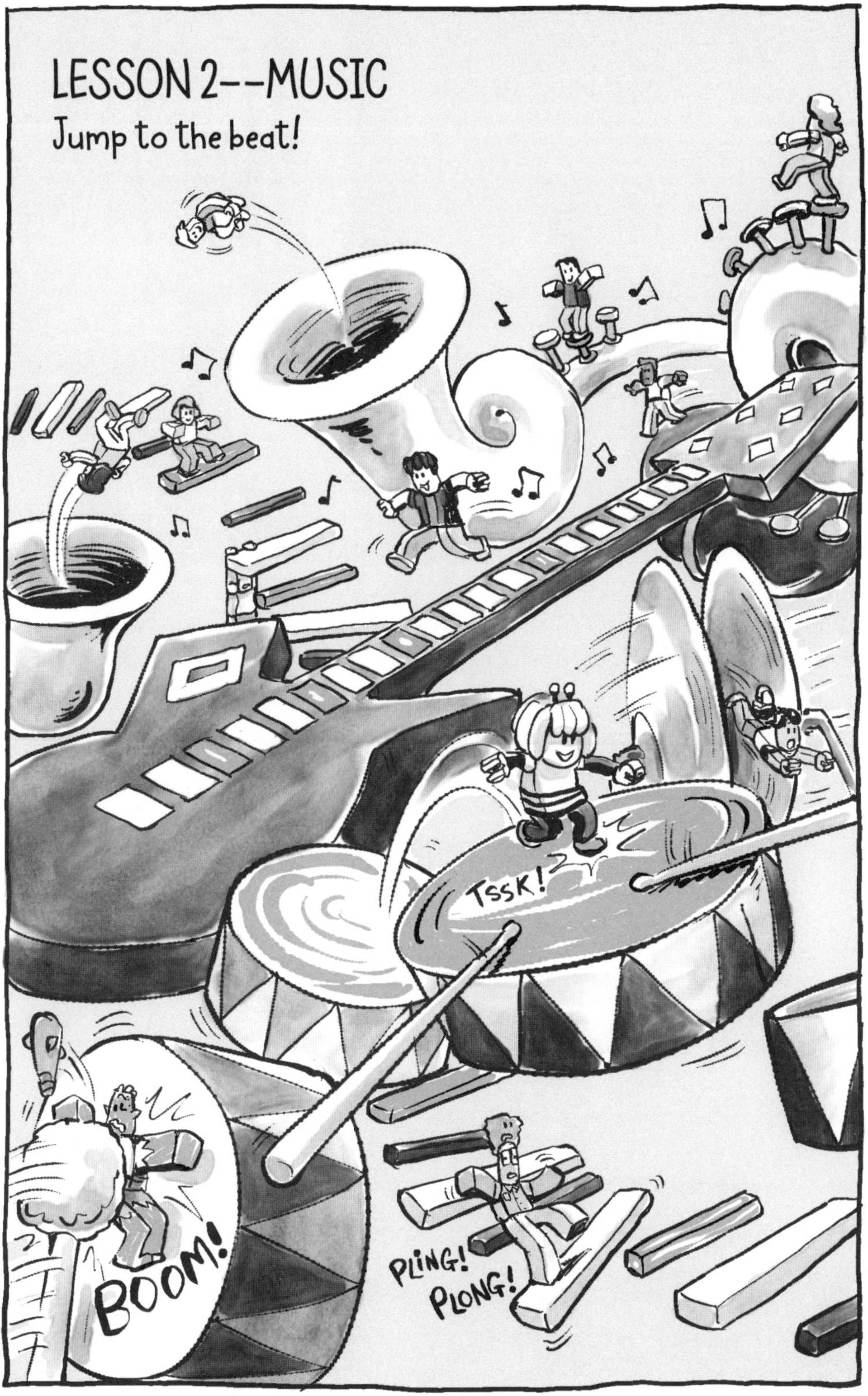
LESSON 2--MUSIC
Jump to the beat!
TSSK!
BOOM!
PLING!
PLONG!

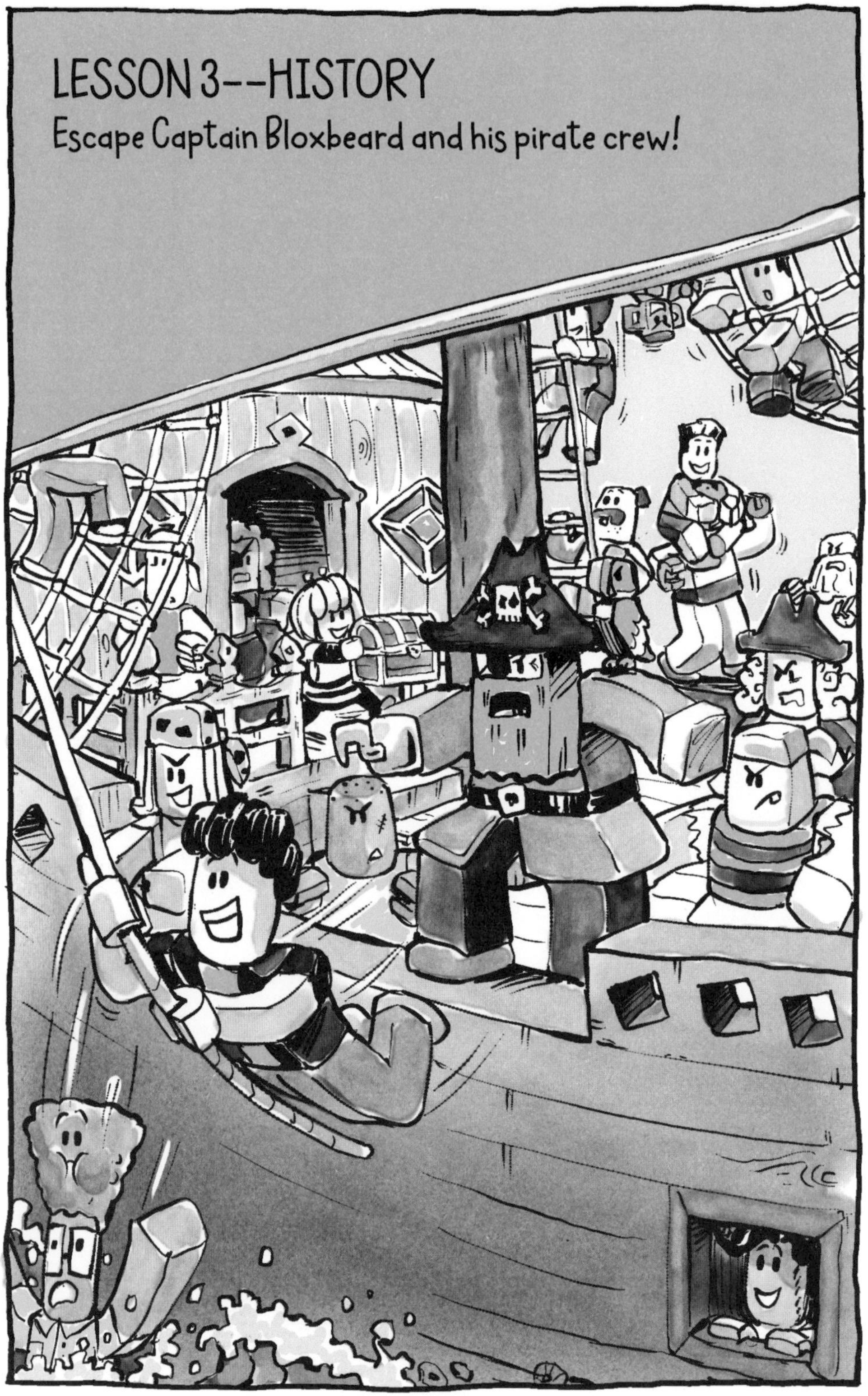
LESSON 3--HISTORY
Escape Captain Bloxbeard and his pirate crew!

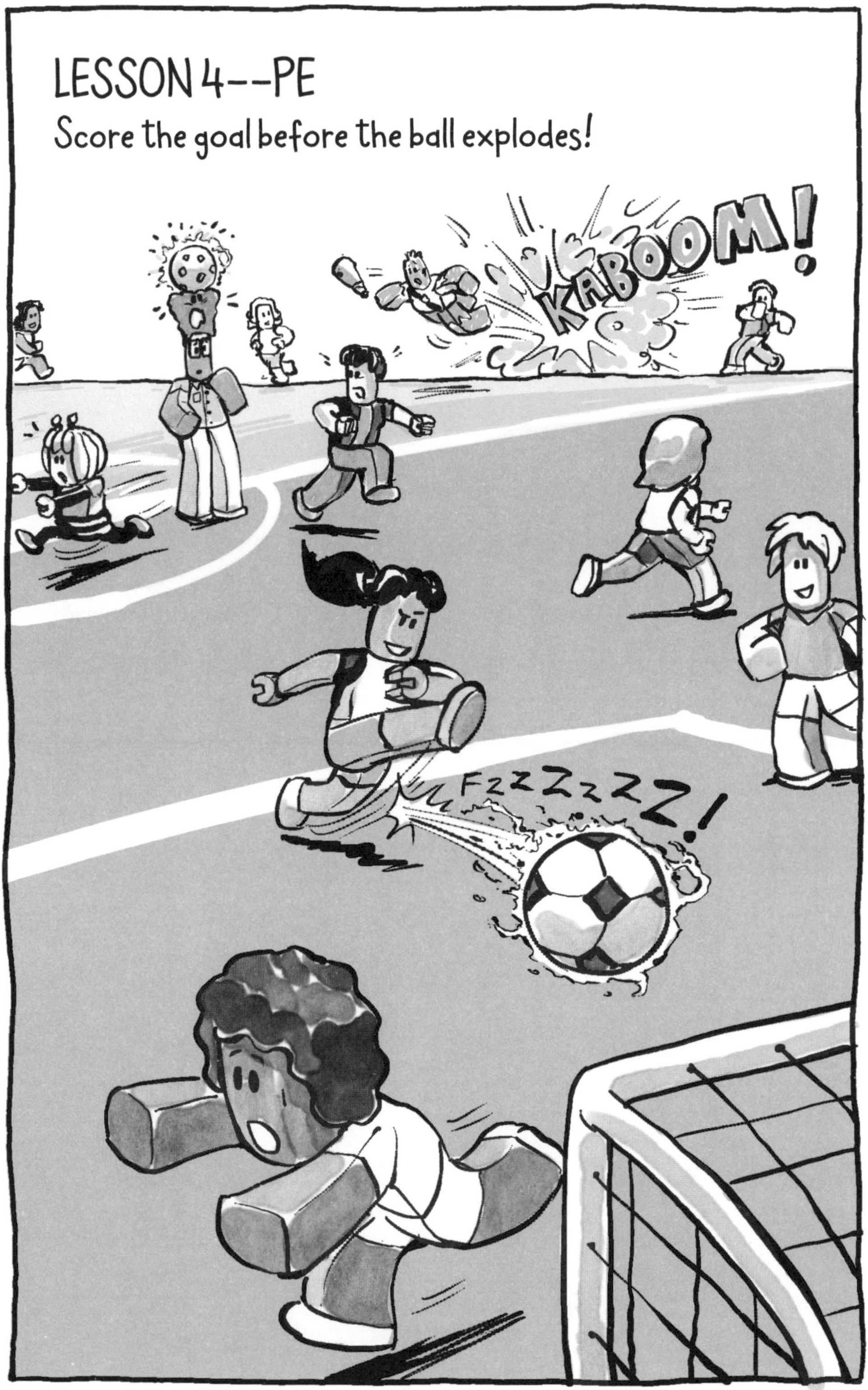
LESSON 4--PE
Score the goal before the ball explodes!
KABOOM!
FZZZZZZZ!

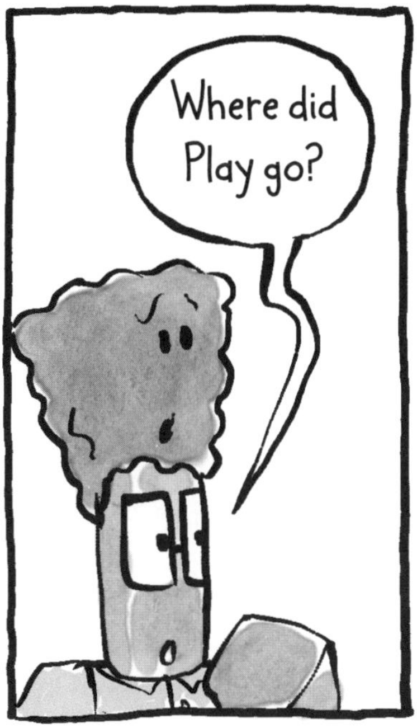
Where did Play go?

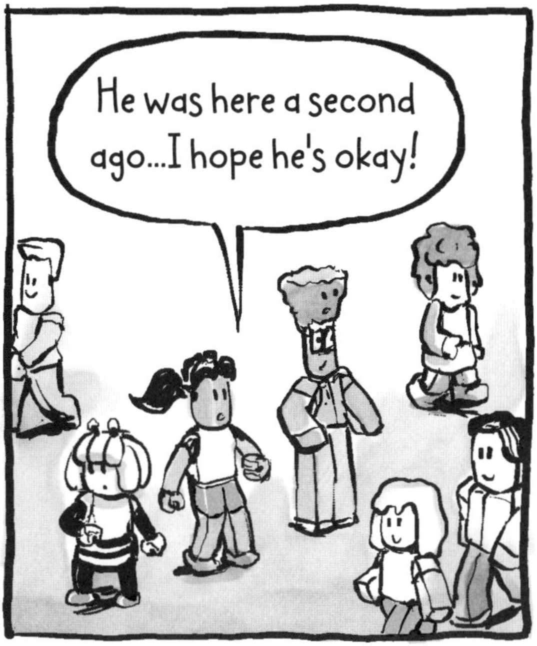
He was here a second ago...I hope he's okay!

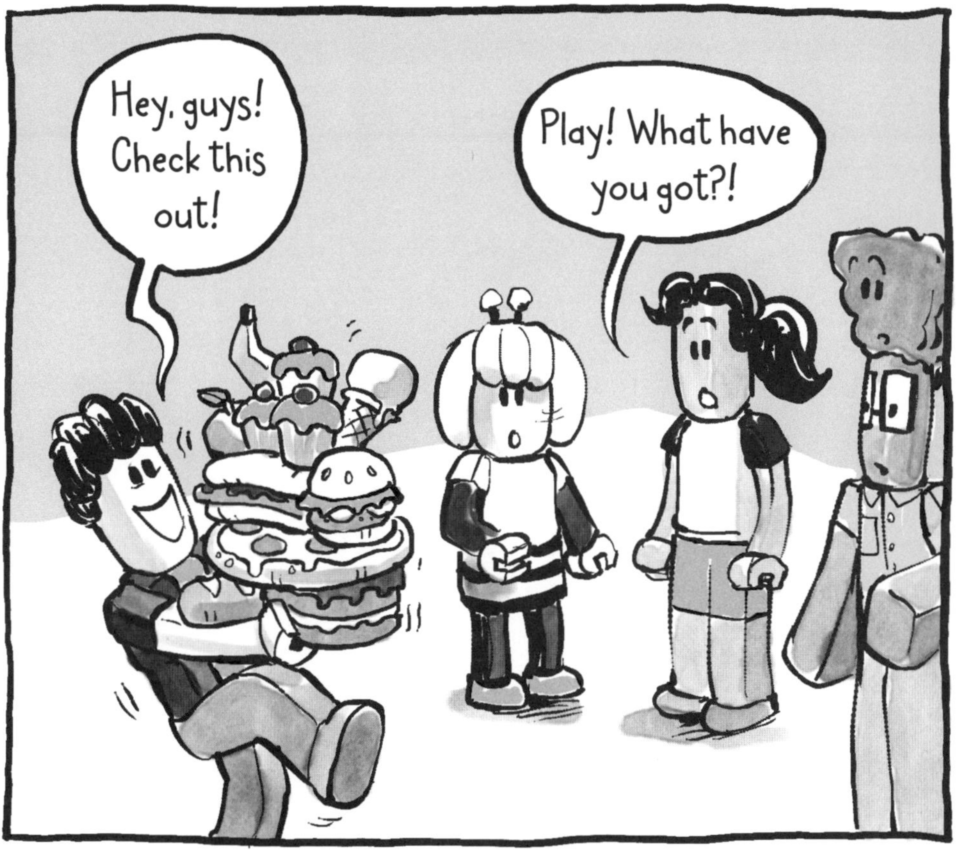
Hey, guys! Check this out!
Play! What have you got?!

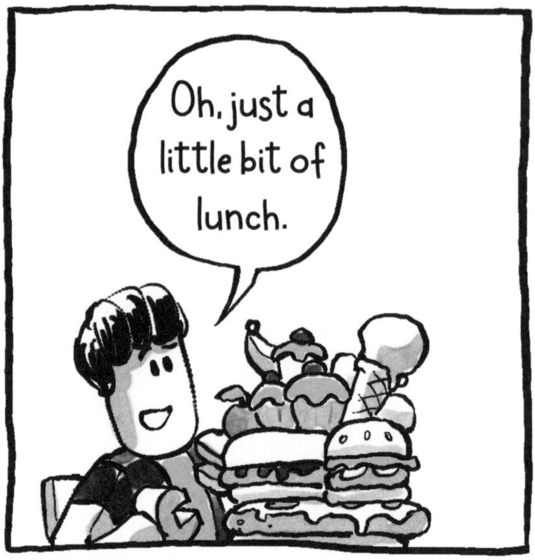
Oh, just a little bit of lunch.

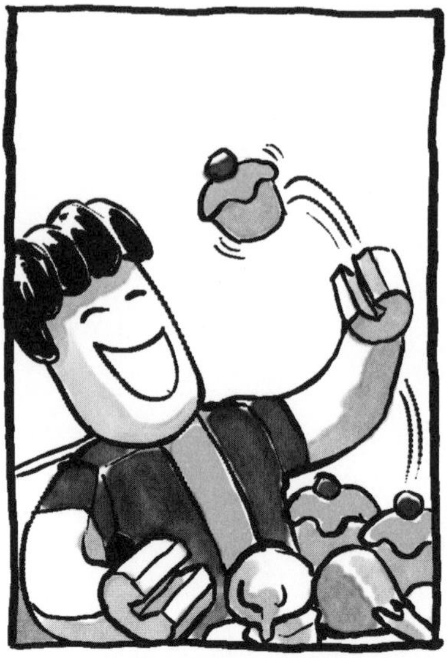

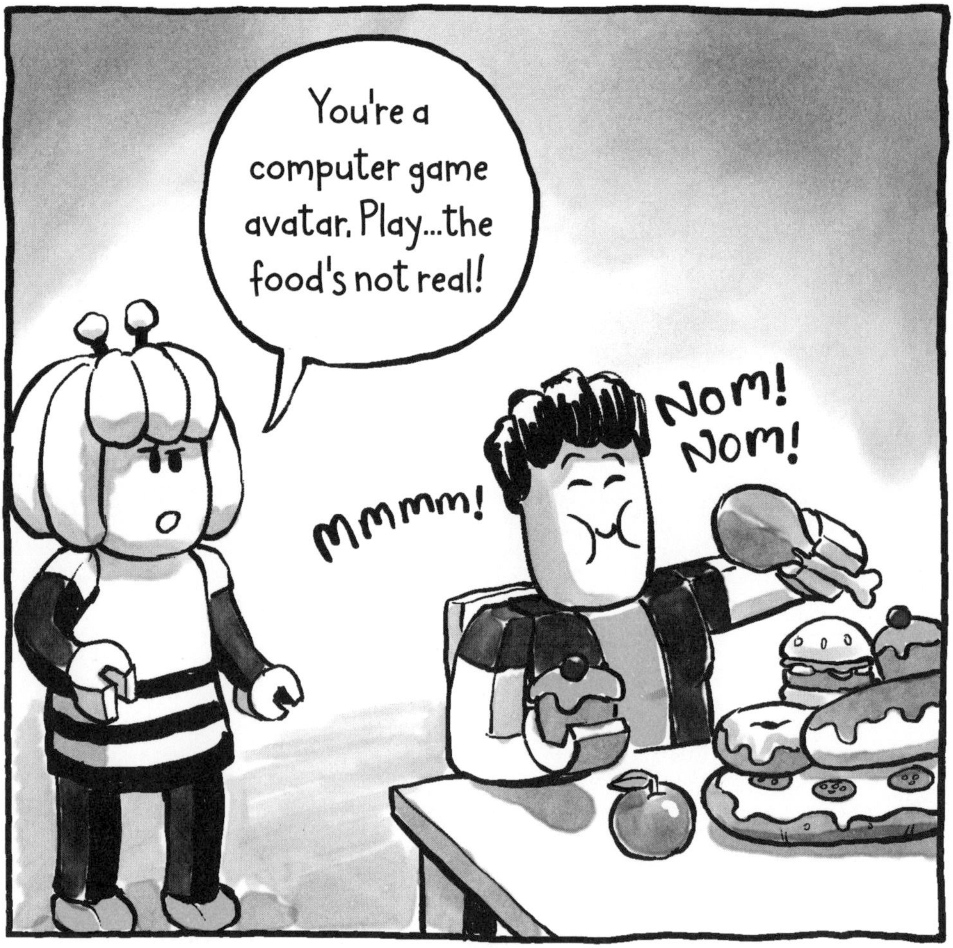
You're a computer game avatar. Play...the food's not real!
Nom! Nom!
Mmmm!

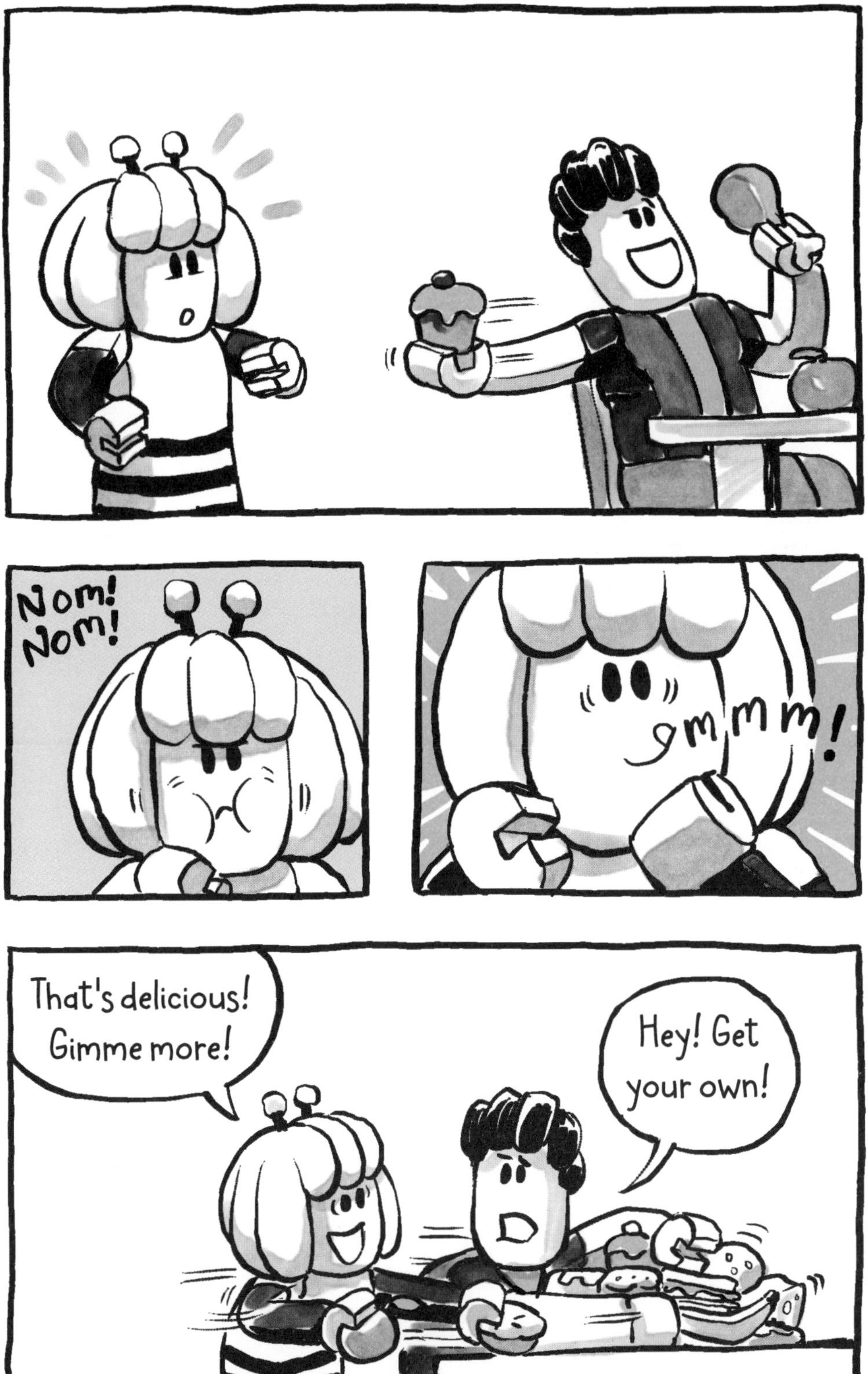
Nom!
Nom!
Mmmm!
That's delicious! Gimme more!
Hey! Get your own!

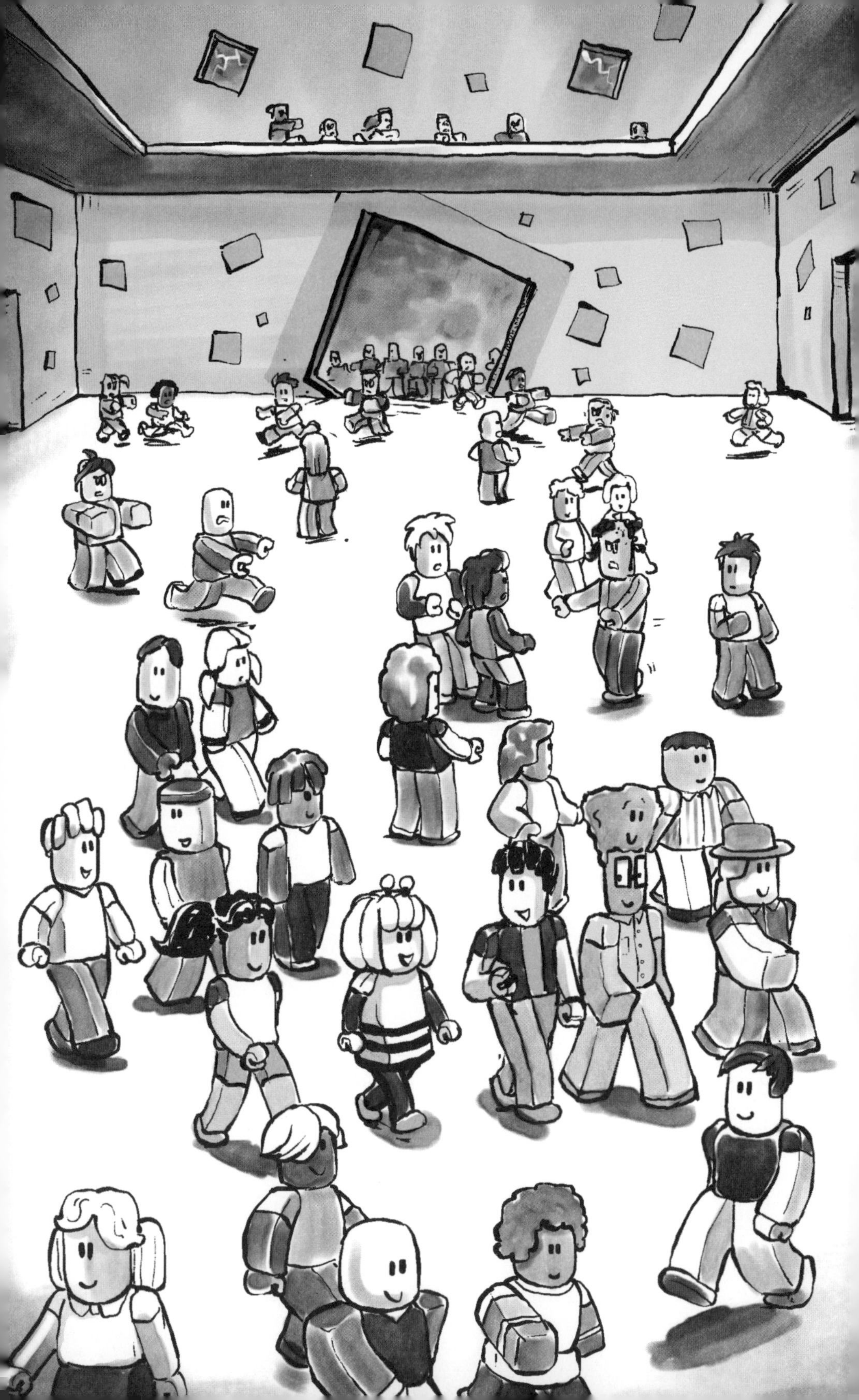

Can you get sick in Roblox?

Is that what a computer virus is?

Could math ever be fun?

Could you get brains at the cafeteria?

And if so, what do they taste like?!

These, and many other questions, were discussed by the gang as they headed excitedly off to their next class. But behind them, storm clouds were brewing at the Academy for Roblox Pros. Students were beginning to behave strangely...well, more strangely than usual.

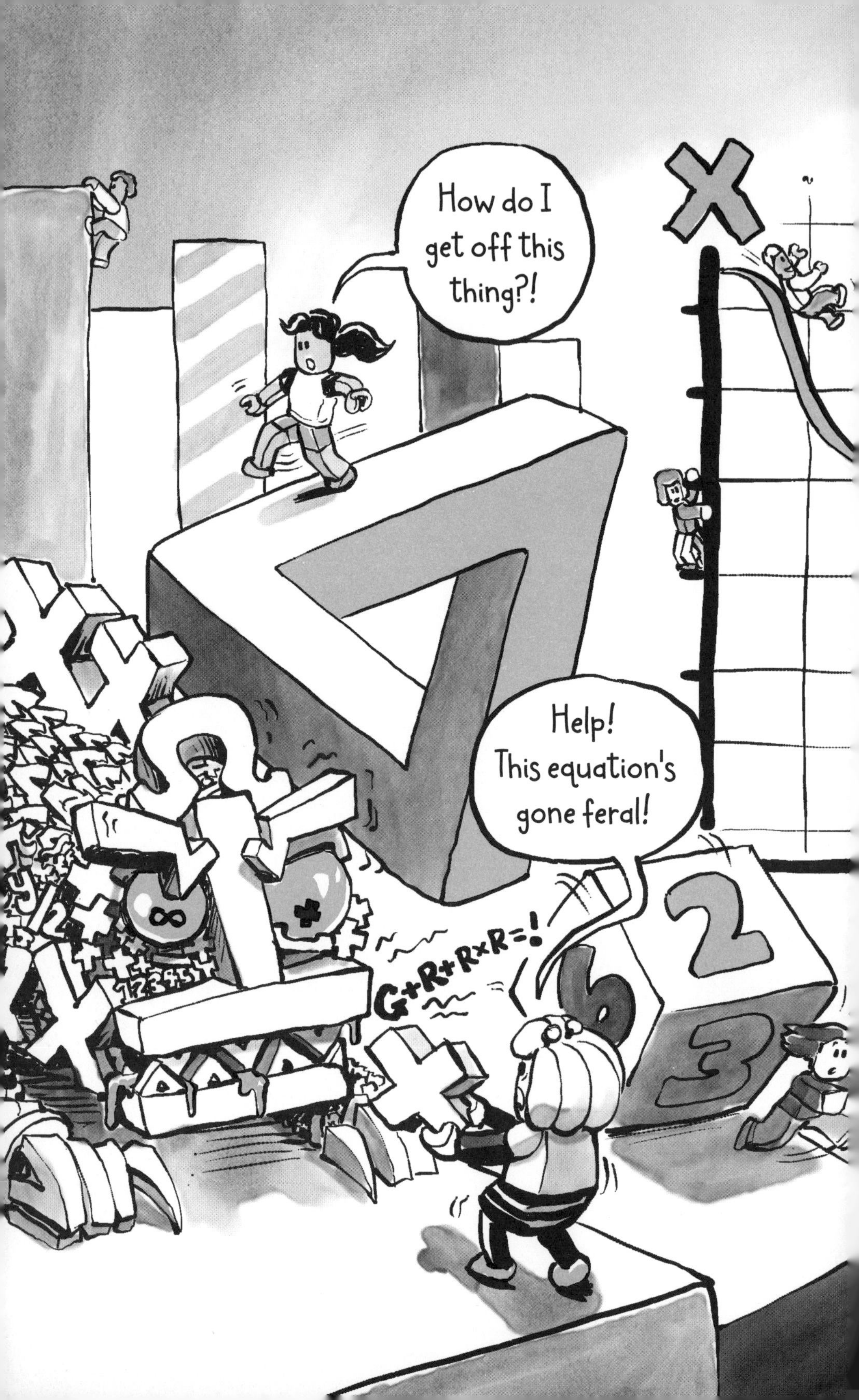
How do I get off this thing?!
Help! This equation's gone feral!
G+R+R×R=!

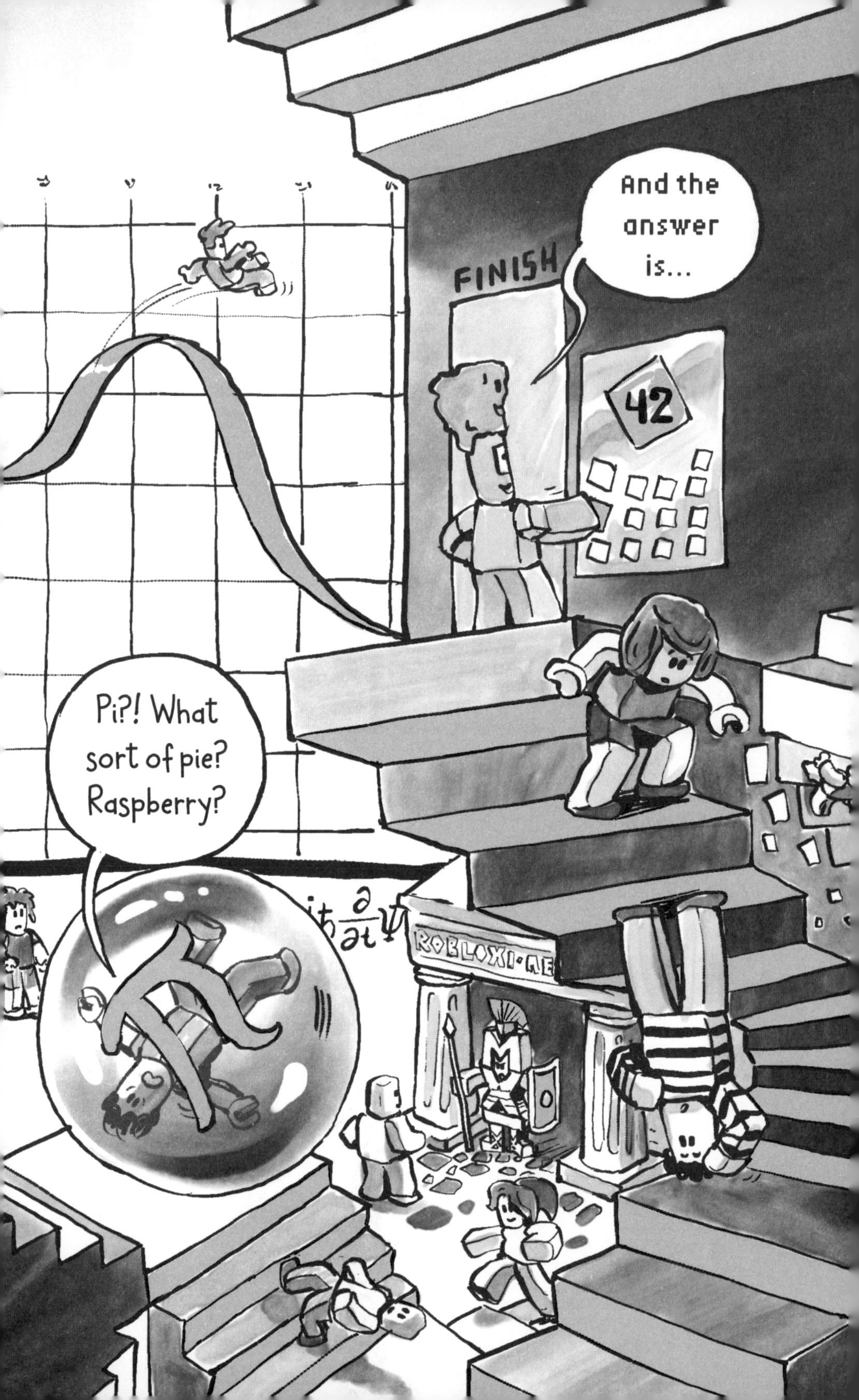
FINISH
And the answer is...
42
Pi?! What sort of pie? Raspberry?
ROBLOXI·AE

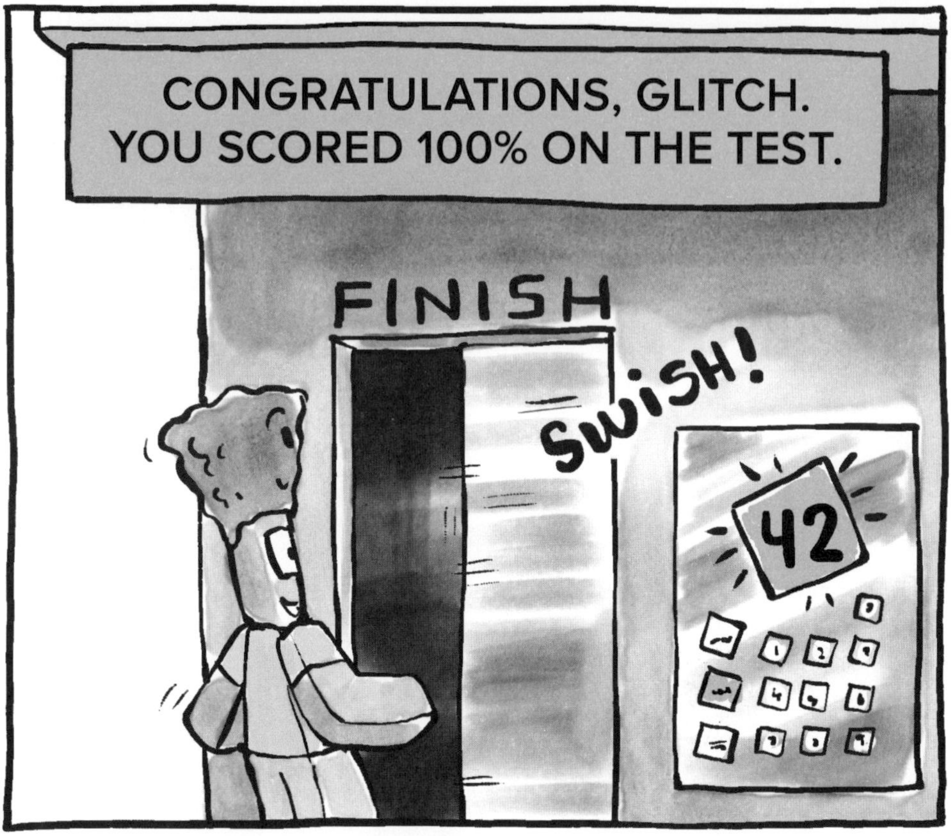
CONGRATULATIONS, GLITCH.
YOU SCORED 100% ON THE TEST.
FINISH
SWISH!
42

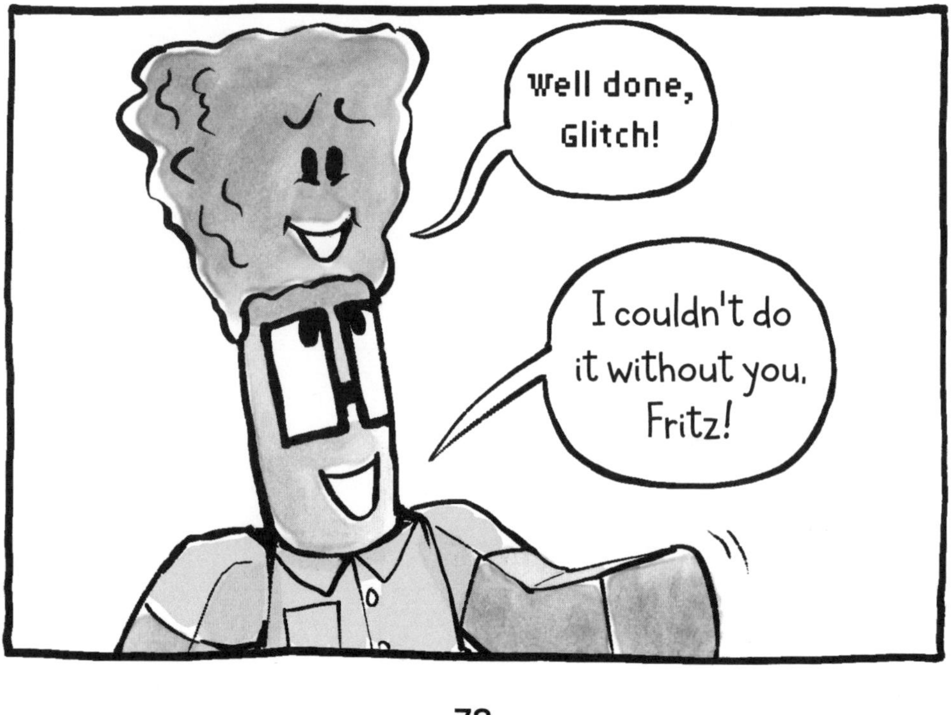
Well done, Glitch!
I couldn't do it without you, Fritz!

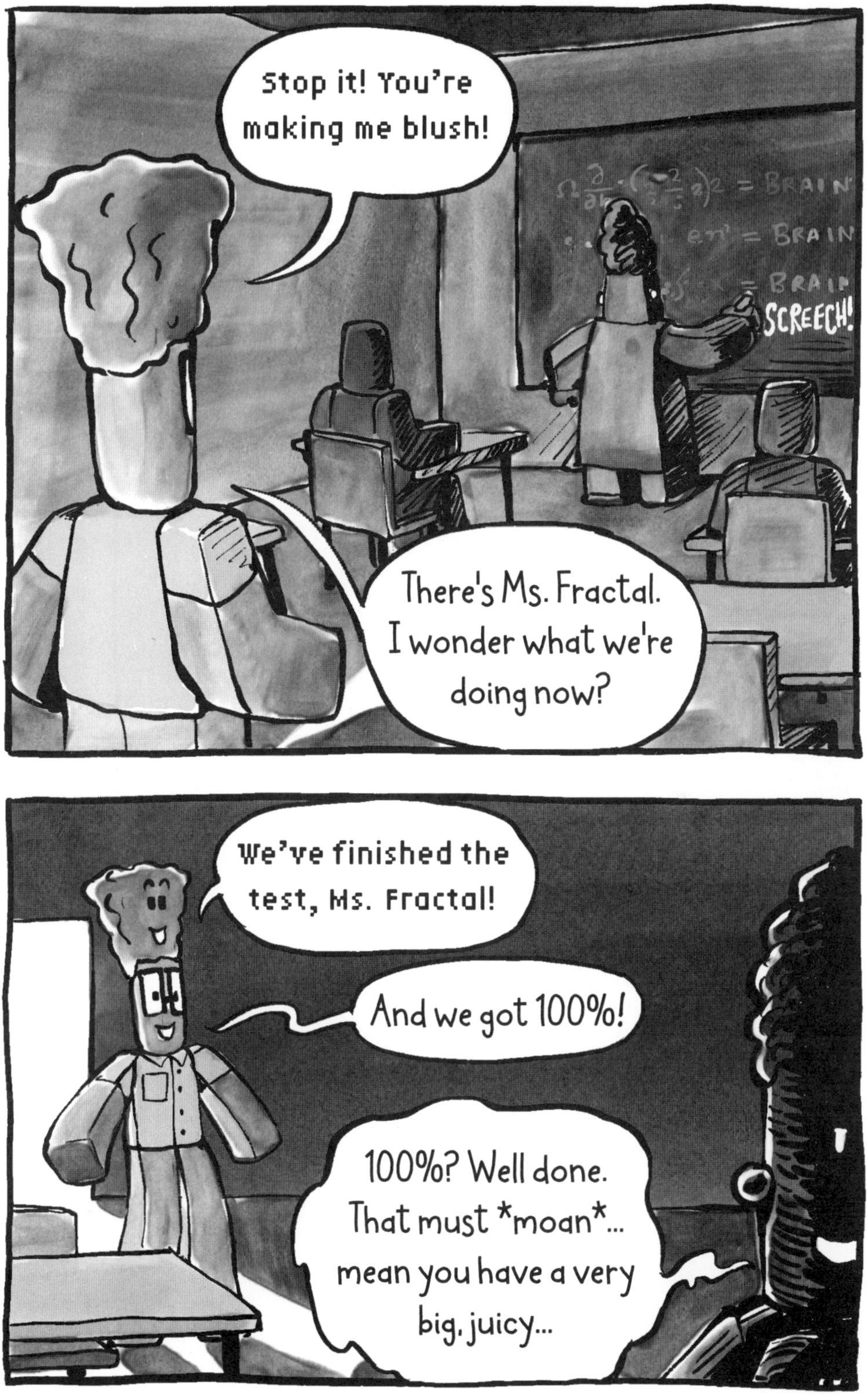
Stop it! You're making me blush!
SCREECH!
There's Ms. Fractal. I wonder what we're doing now?
We've finished the test, Ms. Fractal!
And we got 100%!
100%? Well done. That must *moan*... mean you have a very big, juicy...

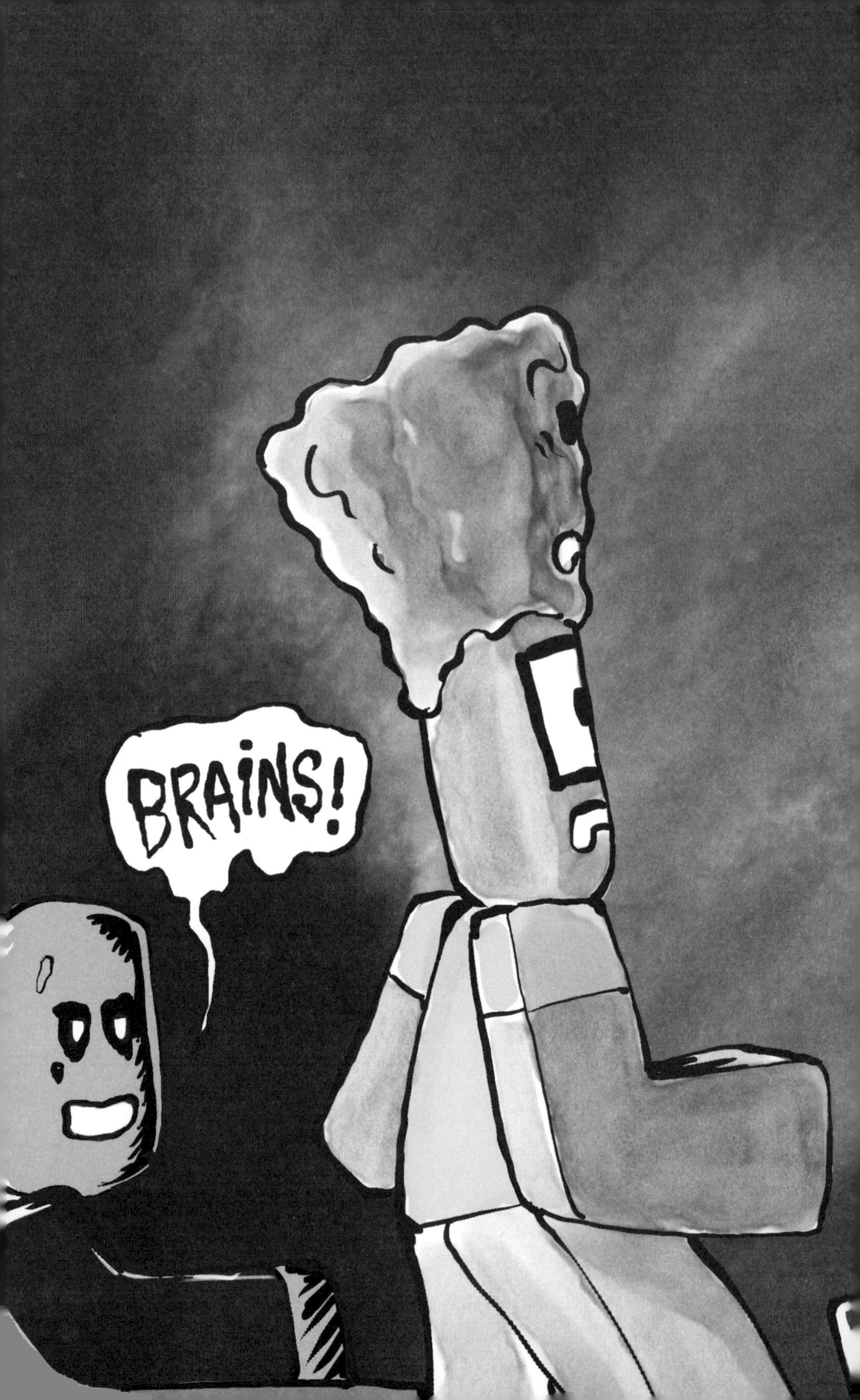
BRAINS!

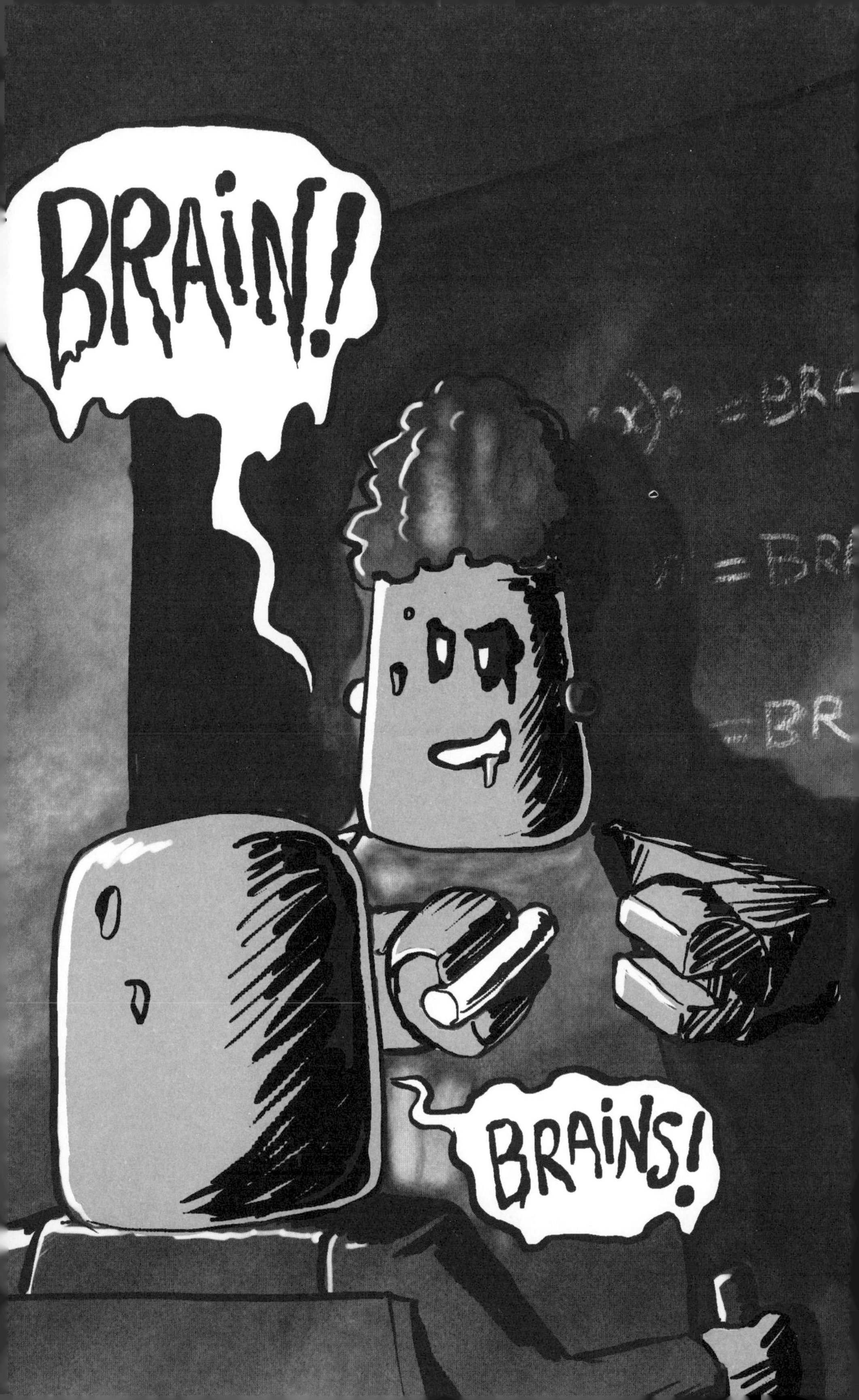
BRAIN!
BRAINS!

Meanwhile, Play, Dash, and Bee were having problems of their own...

"Where's Glitch when you need him?!" shouted Play as he dove out of the way of another killer equation.

"I don't know," replied Bee warily as she eyed two hungry sums that were approaching from the shadows.

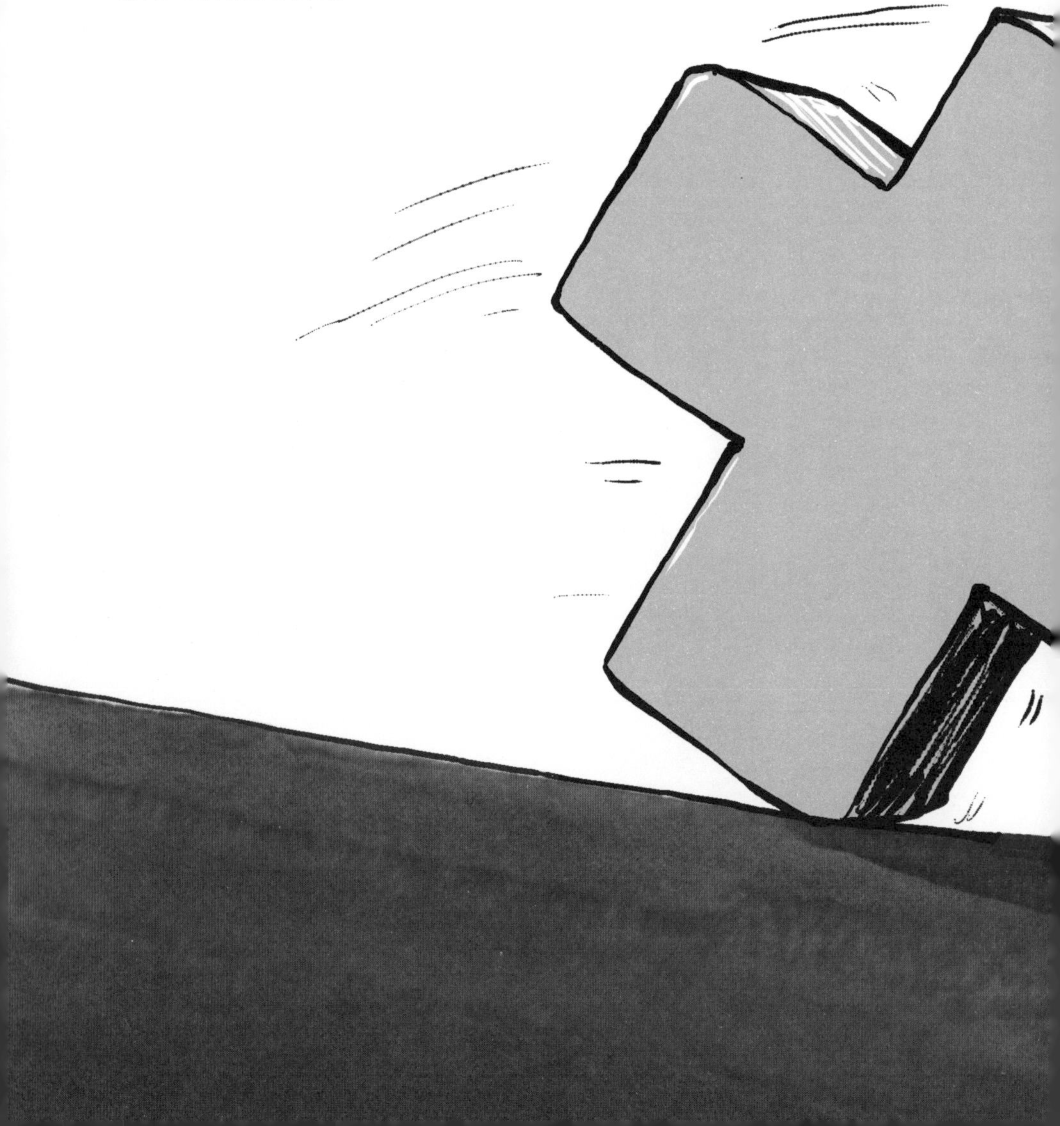

"I think we'll just have to do this without the help of Glitch's big brain," said Dash. "Let's team up and get out of here! Play, you take down that multiplication table. Bee, you deal with that sneaky statistic creeping up behind us, and I'm going to kick this fraction in the denominator!"

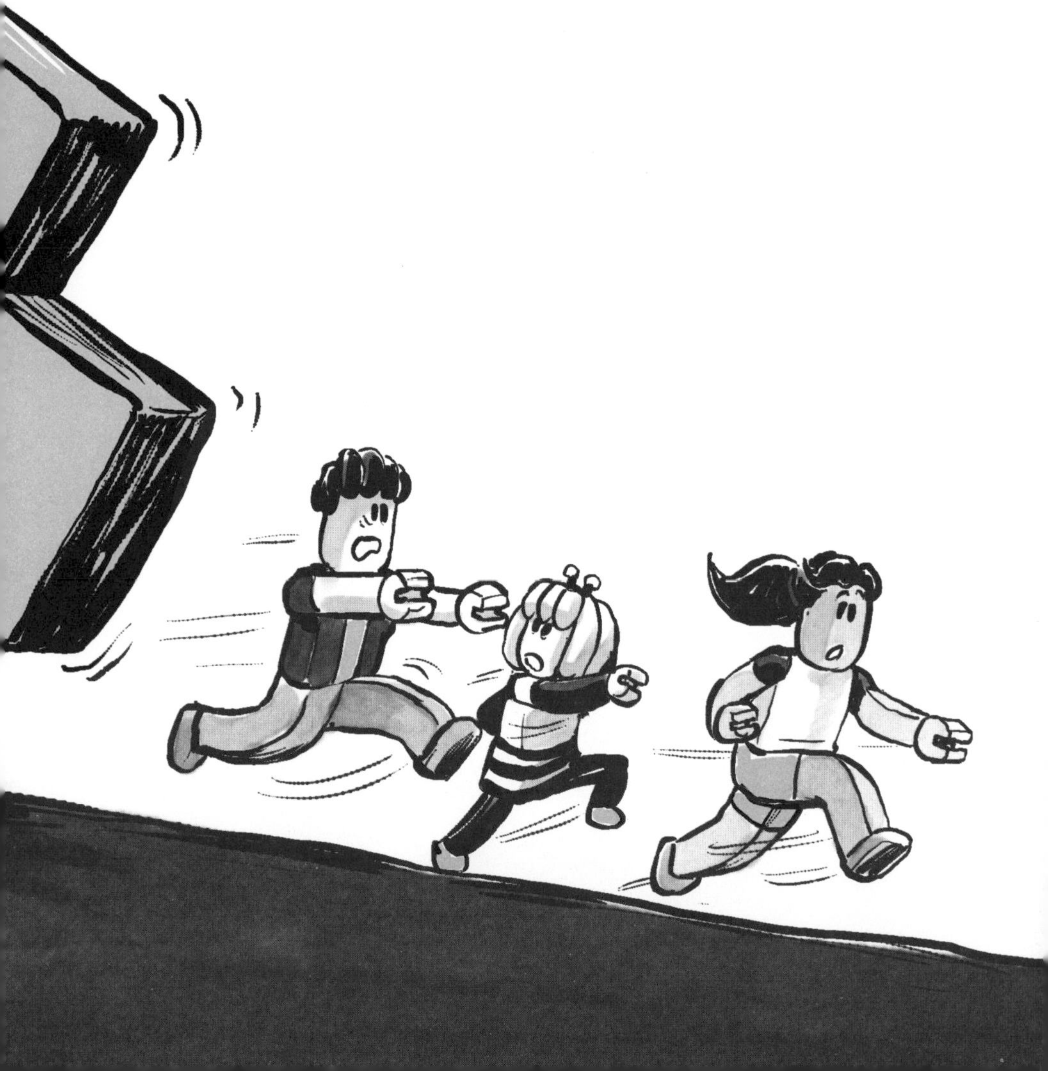

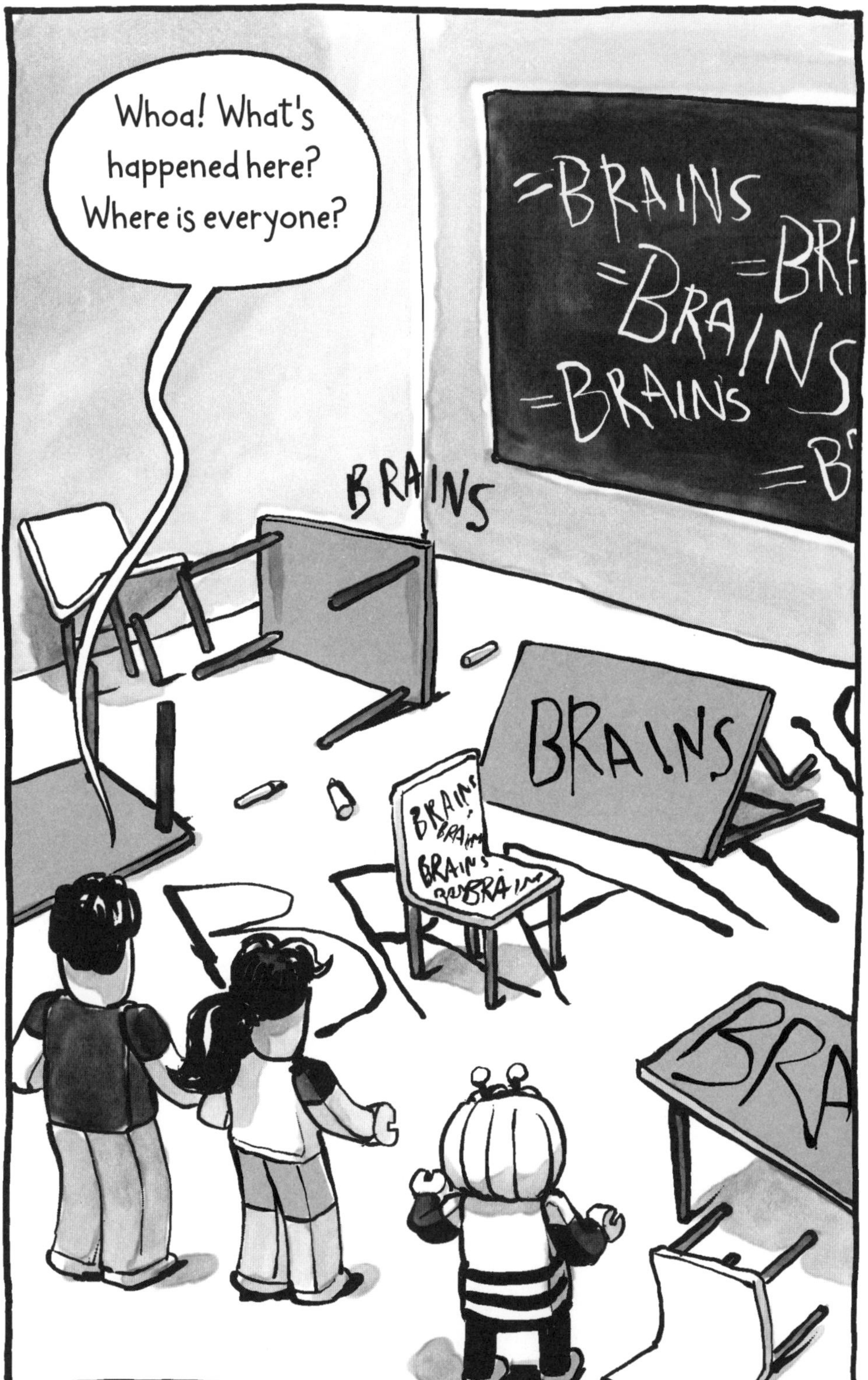
Whoa! What's happened here? Where is everyone?
=BRAINS
=BRAINS
=BRAINS
BRAINS
BRAINS

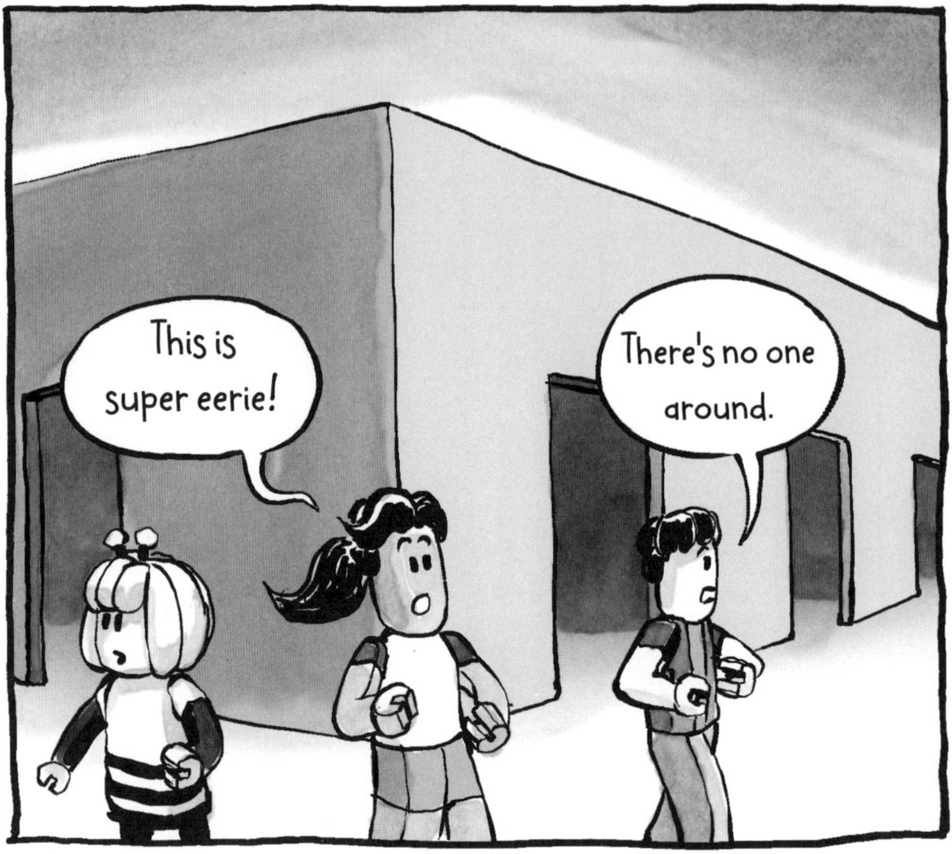
This is super eerie!
There's no one around.

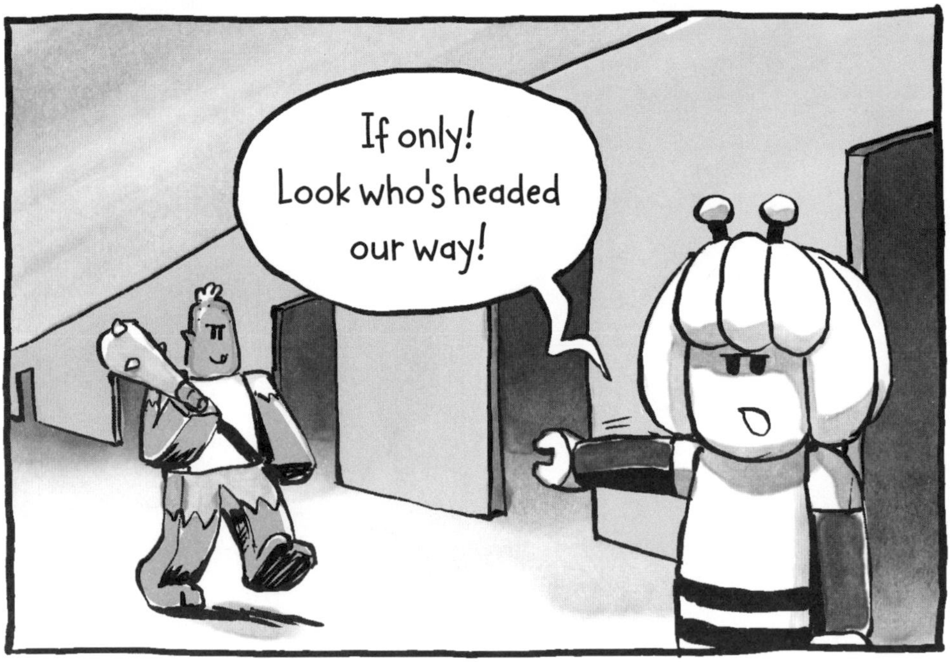
If only! Look who's headed our way!

And for the second time that day, the avatars were plunged into darkness.

"You didn't spill another slushie, did you, Ogre?" asked Play.

"Oh ha-ha," sneered Ogre. "For your information, it wasn't my fault, it was Glitch who pushed me over--"

"Shhh!" whispered Dash. "I think I can hear something..."

Eventually, after a lot of muttering from Ogre, they all fell silent. As they did, they became aware of a low moaning sound all around them.

Slowly, the noise got closer and louder.

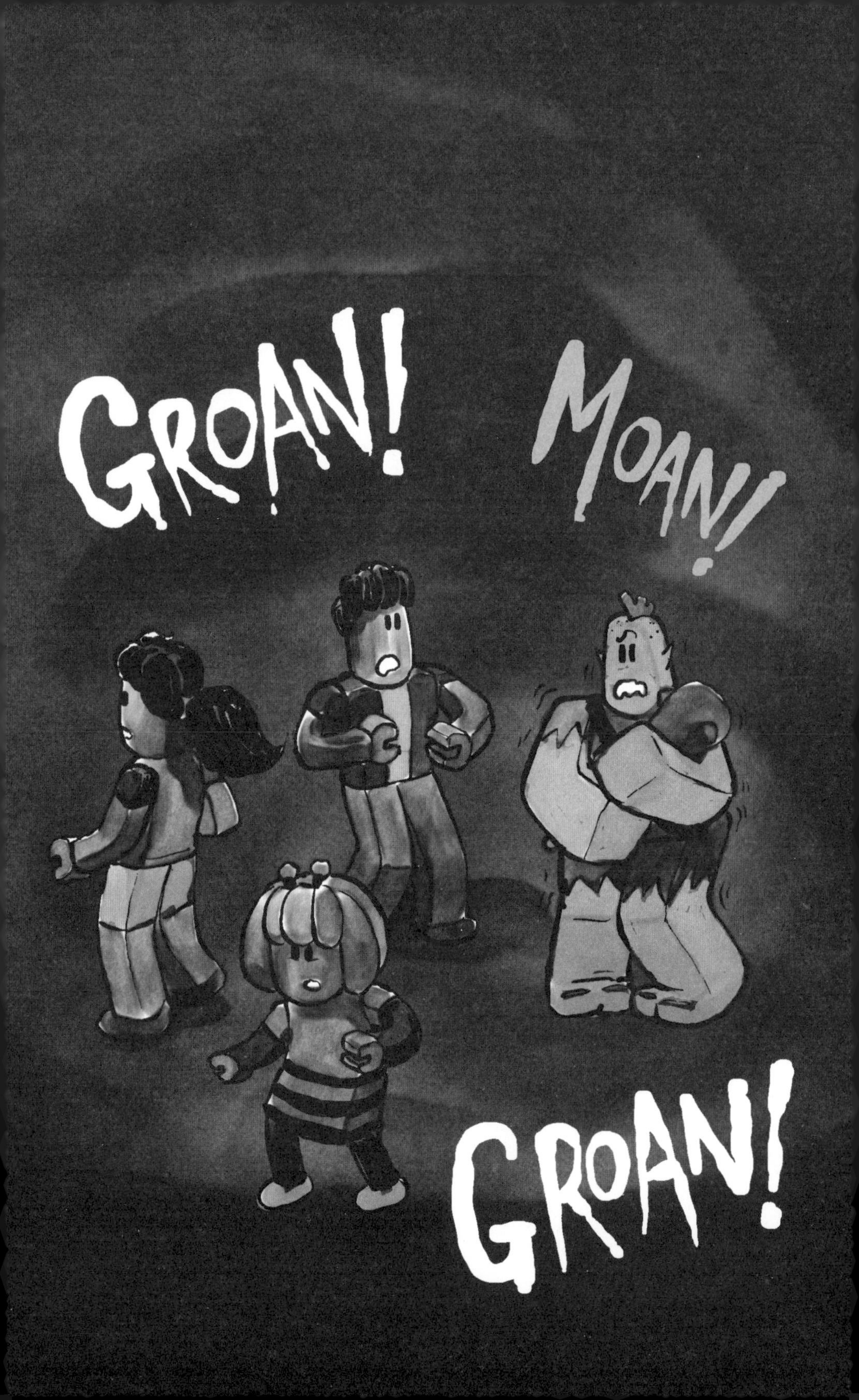
GROAN!
MOAN!
GROAN!

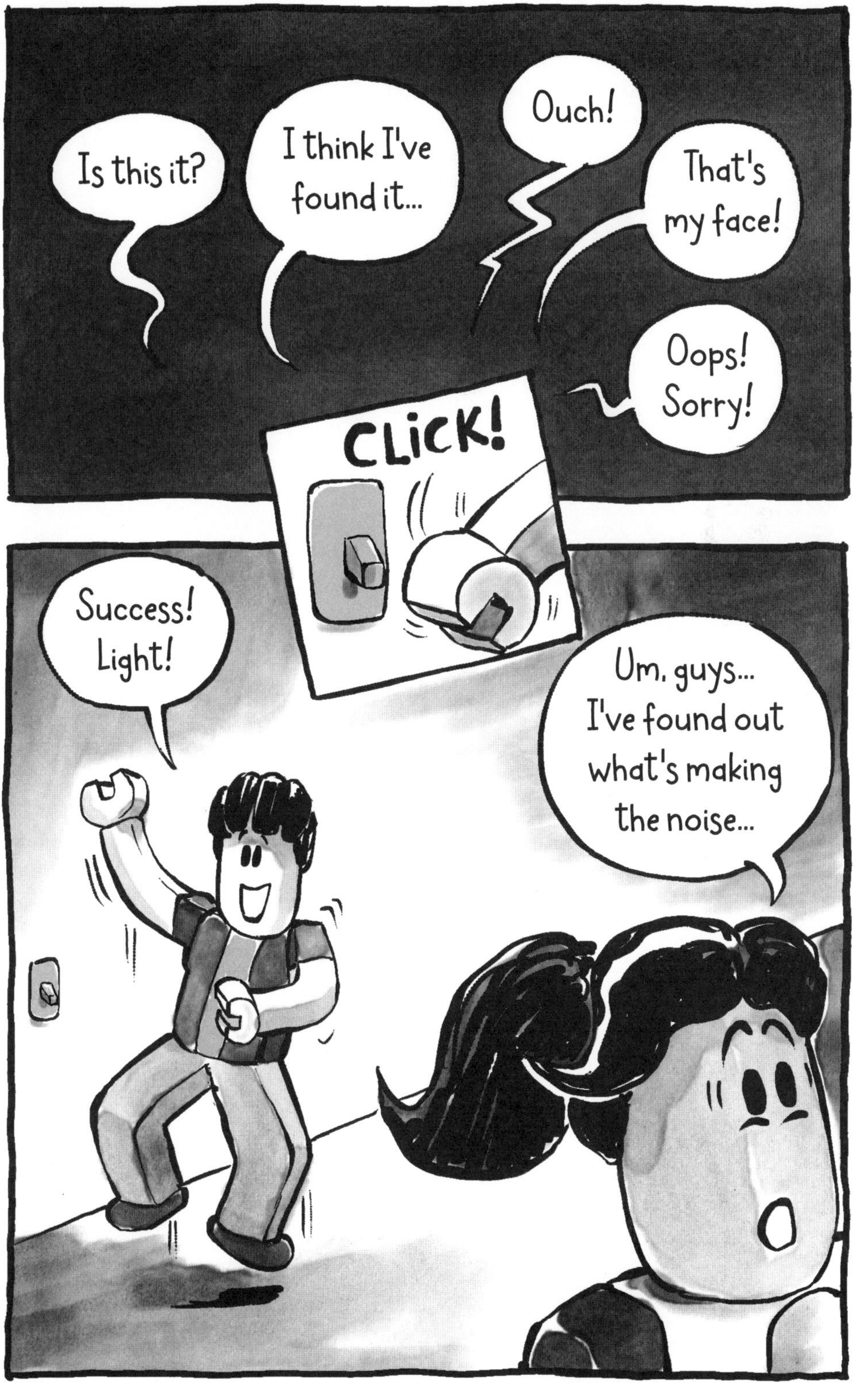
Is this it?
I think I've found it...
Ouch!
That's my face!
Oops! Sorry!
CLICK!
Success! Light!
Um, guys... I've found out what's making the noise...

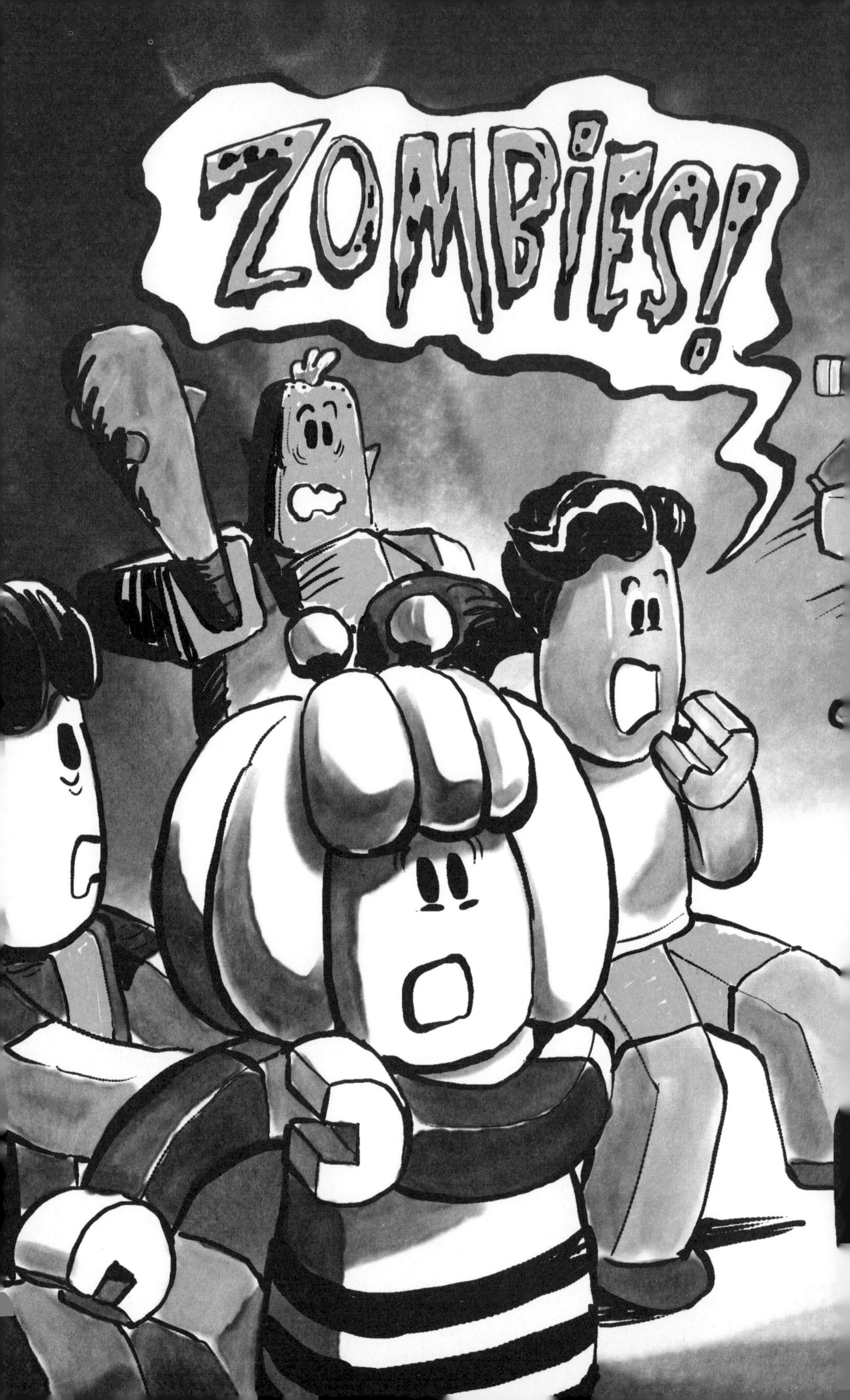
ZOMBIES!

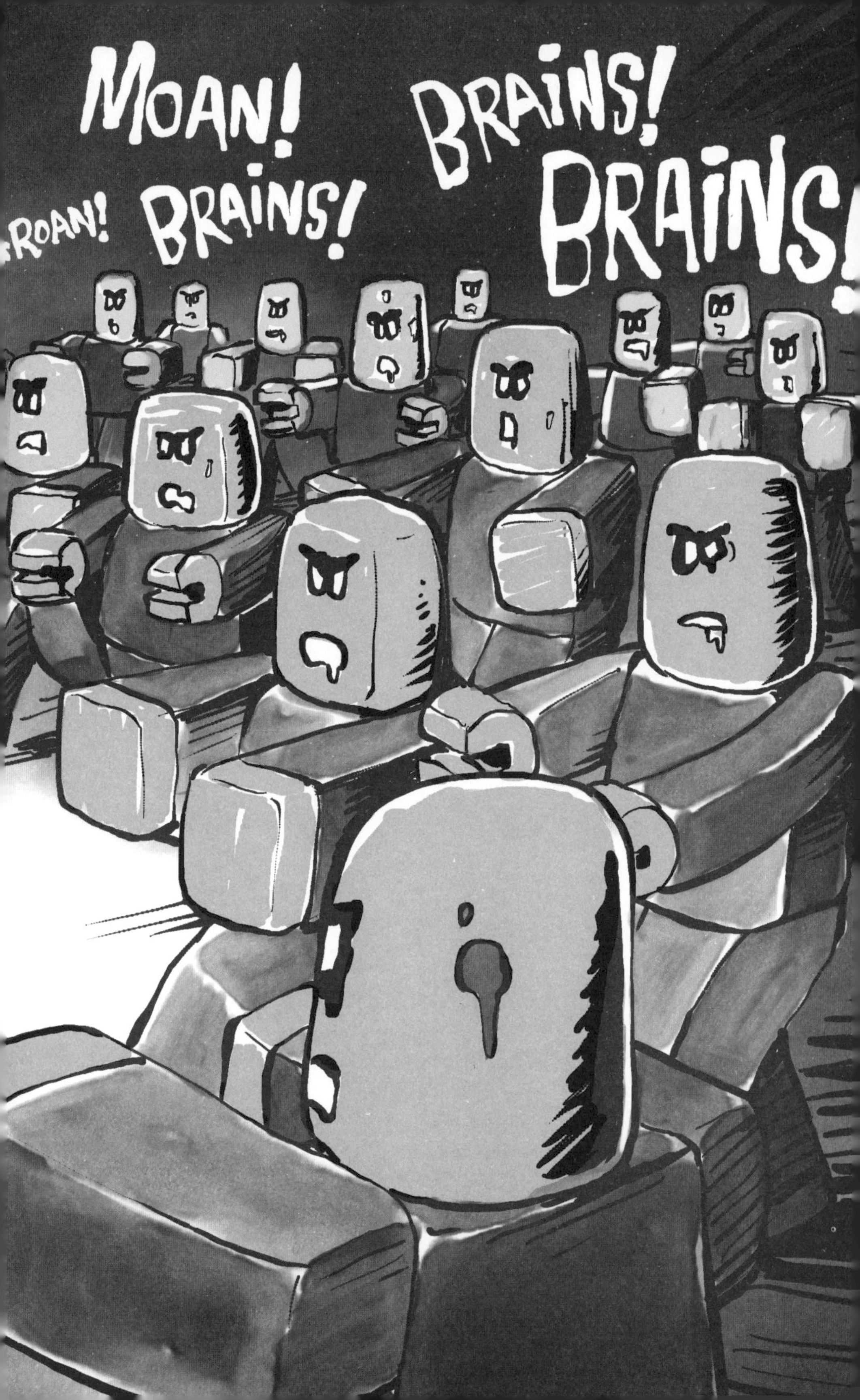
MOAN!
BRAINS!
ROAN!
BRAINS!
BRAINS!
BRAINS!

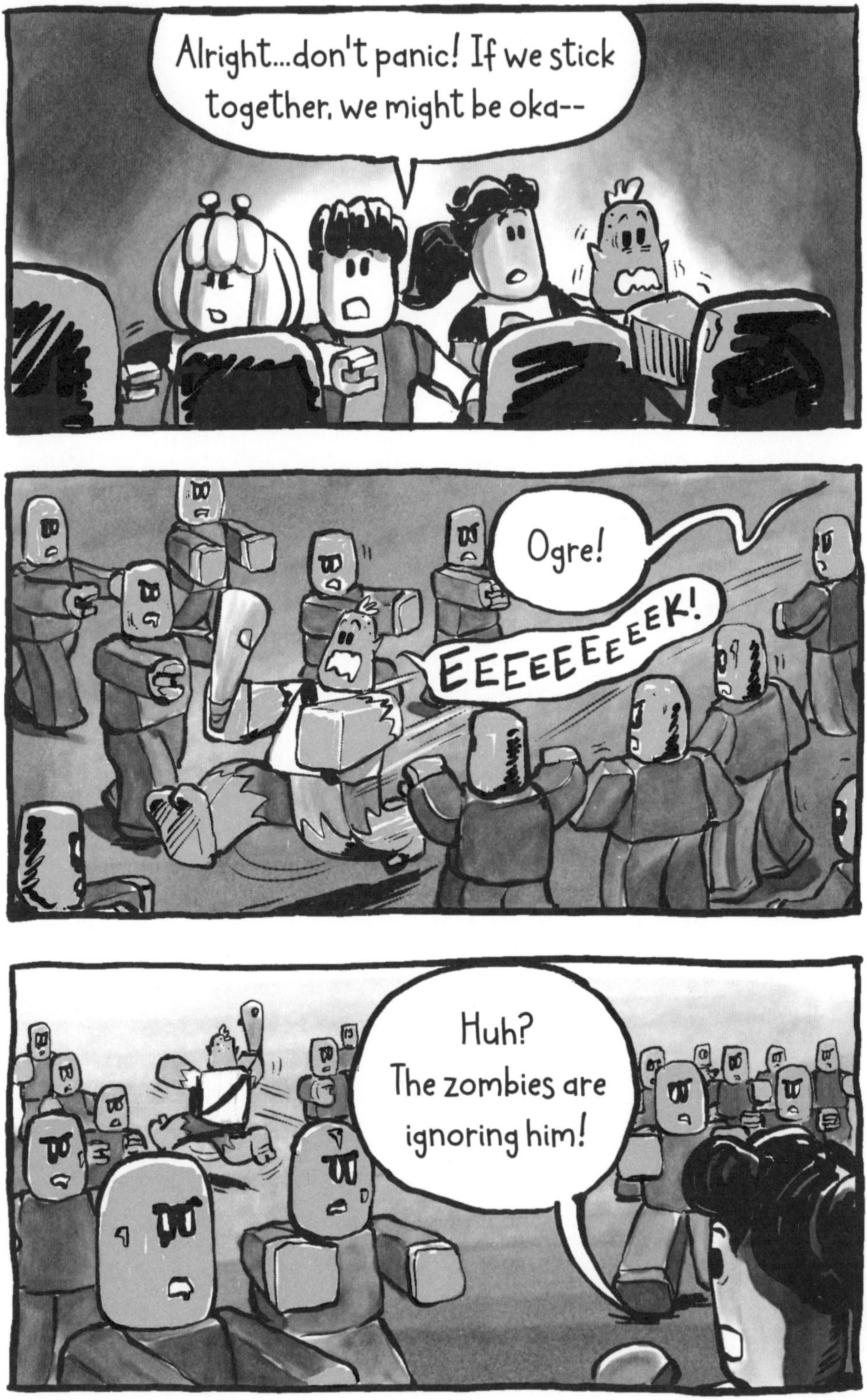
Alright...don't panic! If we stick together, we might be oka--
Ogre!
EEEEEEEEEEK!
Huh?
The zombies are ignoring him!

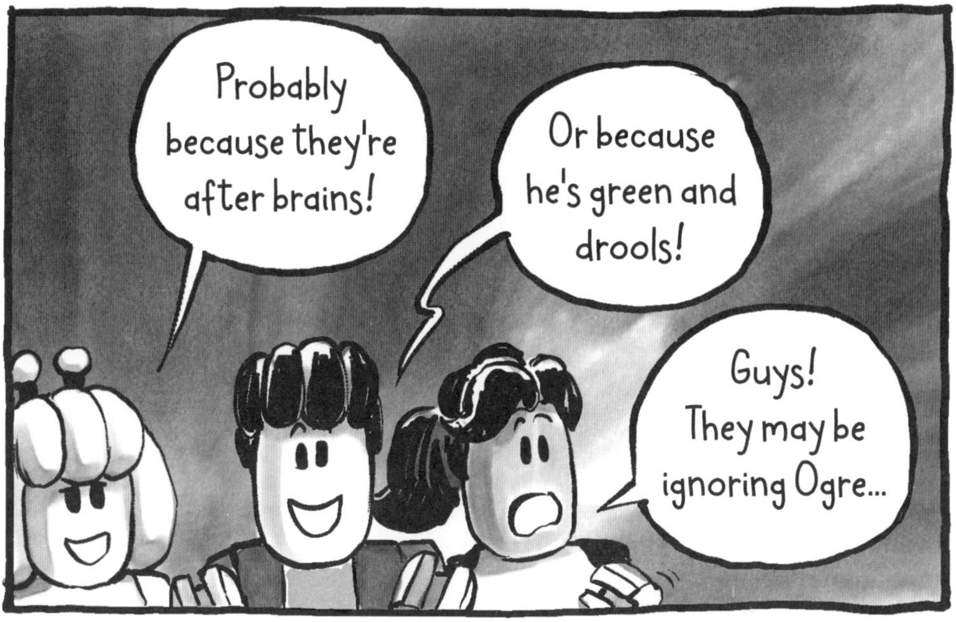
Probably because they're after brains!
Or because he's green and drools!
Guys! They may be ignoring Ogre...

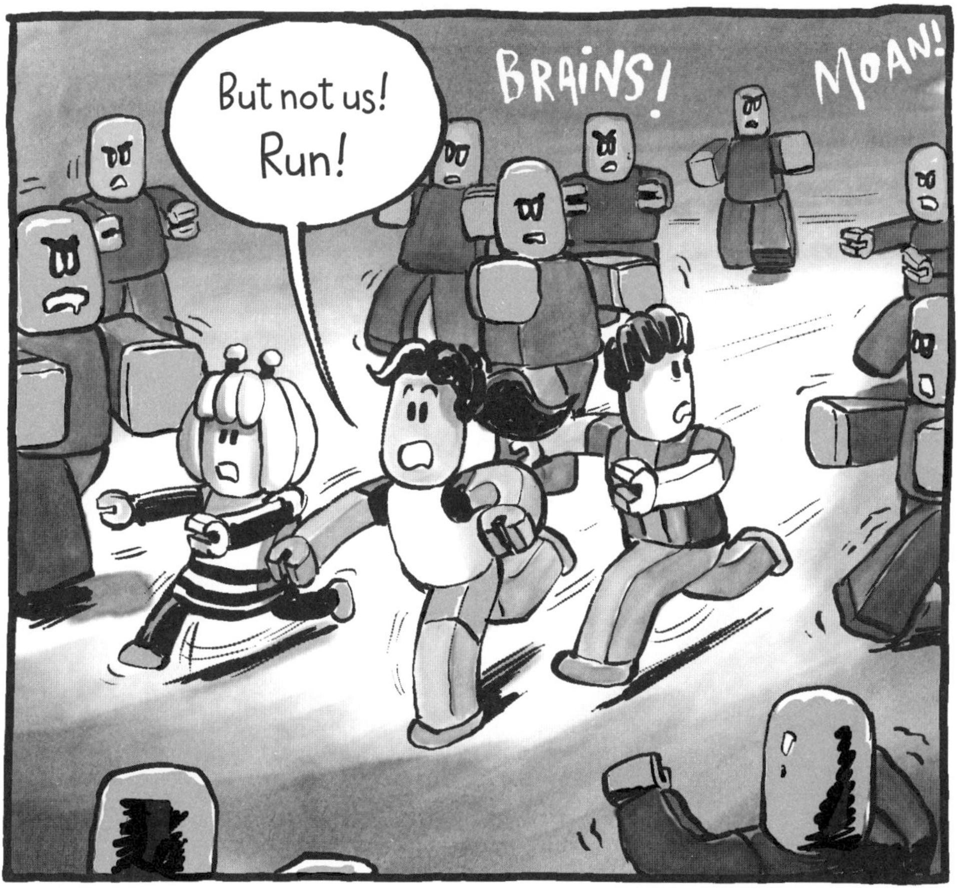
But not us! Run!
BRAINS!
MOAN!

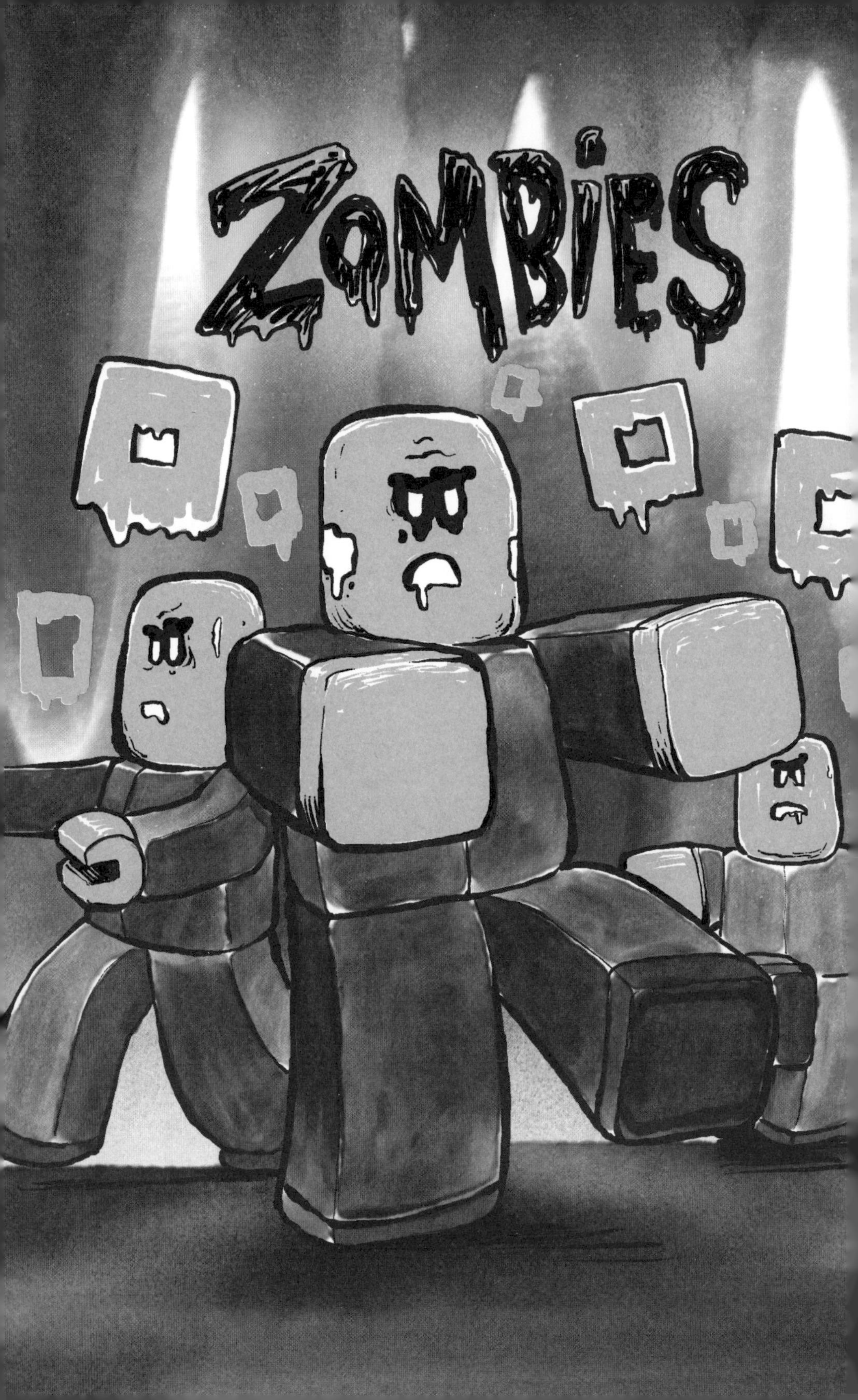
ZOMBIES

ZOMBIE STATS

- **Speed:** Slow but persistent.
- **Attack:** Will try to snack on your brains. Wearing a helmet when hanging out with a zombie is advisable.
- **Color:** They range from light snot to dark pond-scum green.
- **Smell:** A mixture of garbage, rotten fish, and unwashed gym socks.
- **Likes:** Brains, moaning, Irish dancing.
- **Dislikes:** Joggers.

HINT

How to spot a zombie

It can be extremely difficult to tell the difference between a zombie and a normal student. Both moan, drool, and smell of decay. A giveaway is that zombies are more interested in brains... and they're a bit greener.

While Bee, Dash, and Play were running away from the zombies, Glitch was walking and moaning with his new green buddies.

But Fritz, still in a state of shock, wasn't so eager to go with the flow!

When Ms. Fractal attacked them at the end of math, she hadn't noticed Fritz and had only turned Glitch into a mindless ghoul!

Fritz was saved, but now he had no choice but to follow the zombie horde.

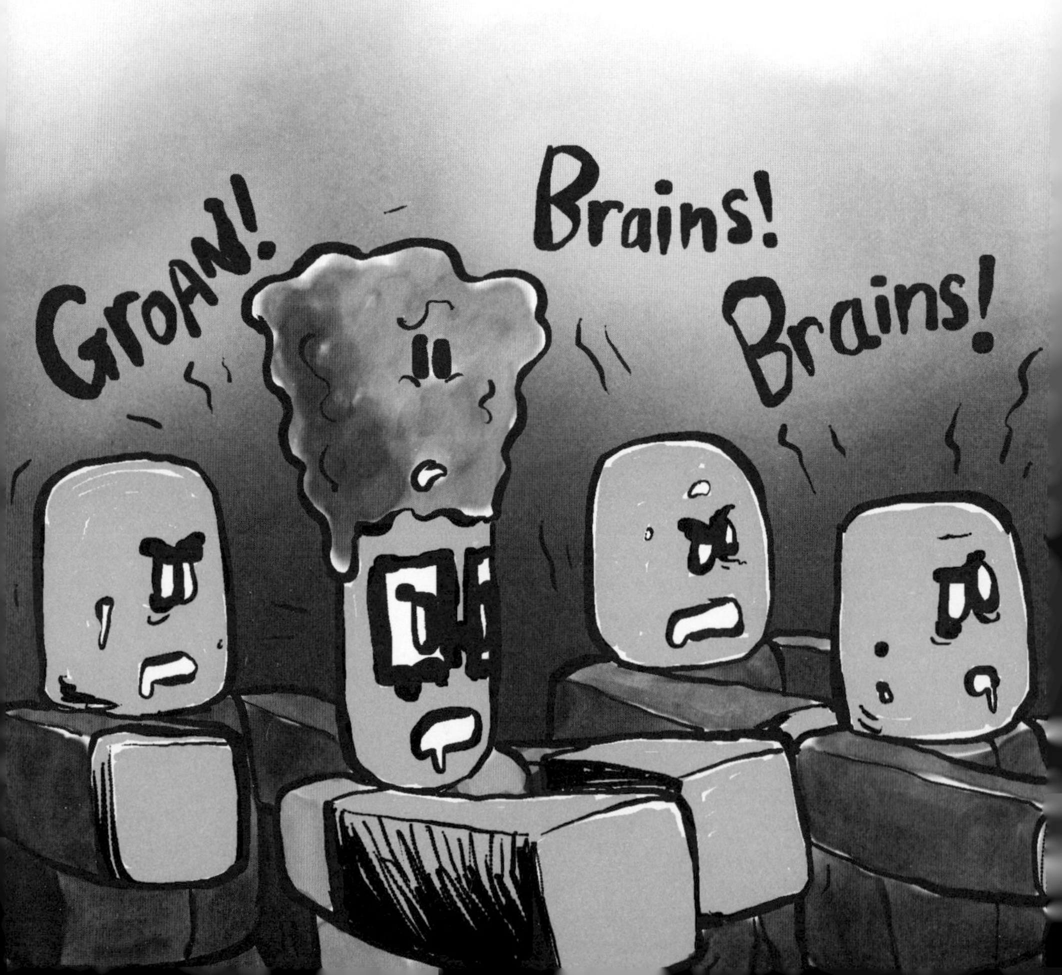
GROAN!
Brains!
Brains!

This is going from bad to worse! thought Fritz. *If only I could escape and get help...I don't think Glitch feels like a haircut though...*

As the zombie mass moved on, Fritz tried desperately to come up with a plan.

First, I need to stop Glitch from following the rest of the zombies. I don't know where they're going, but I can't imagine it's good! All this moaning and saying brains is giving me the shivers...and who is this master they keep talking about? I have to see if I can get through to Glitch...

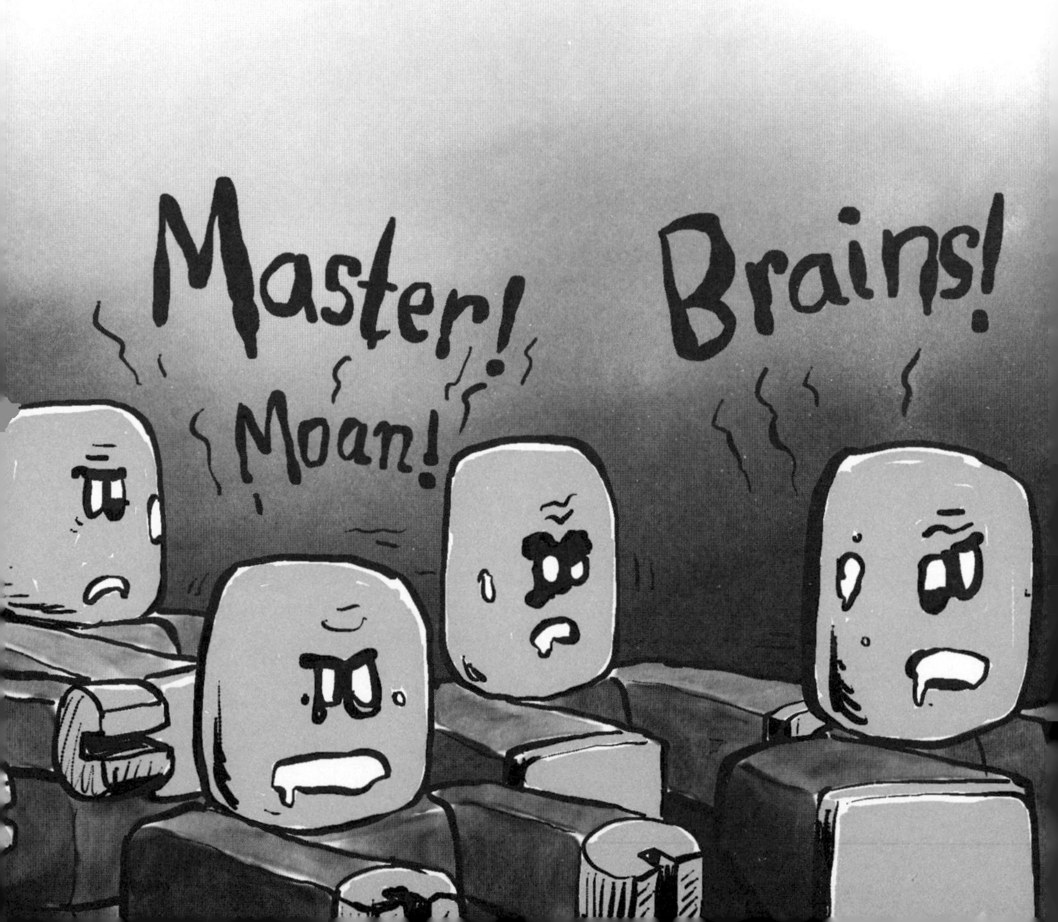
Master!
Brains!
Moan!

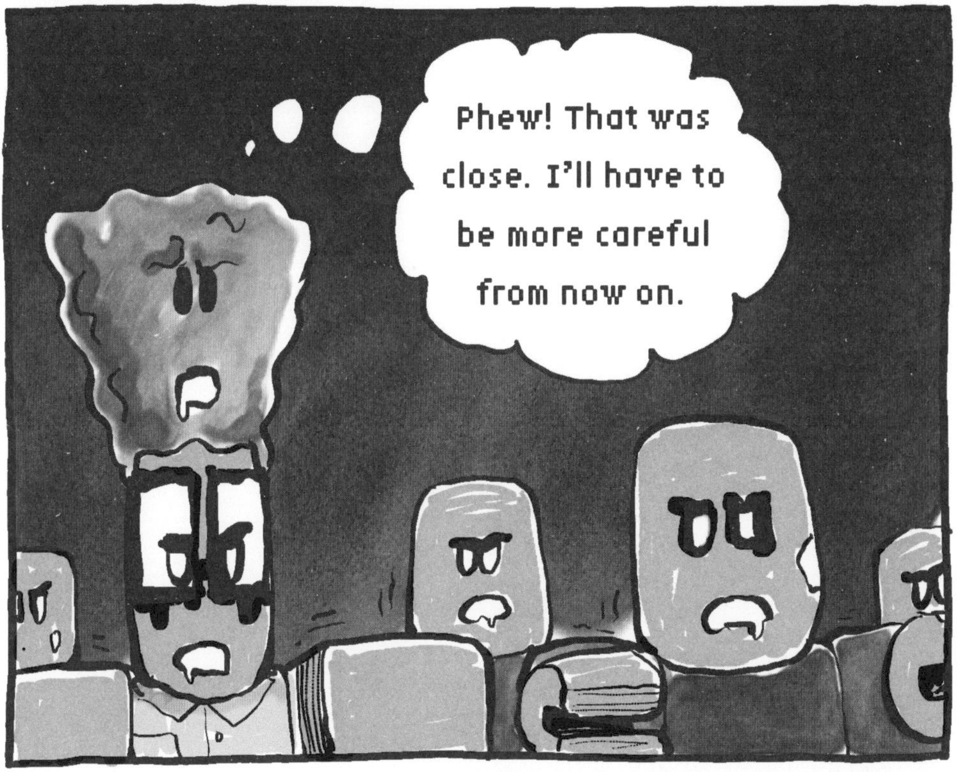
Phew! That was close. I'll have to be more careful from now on.

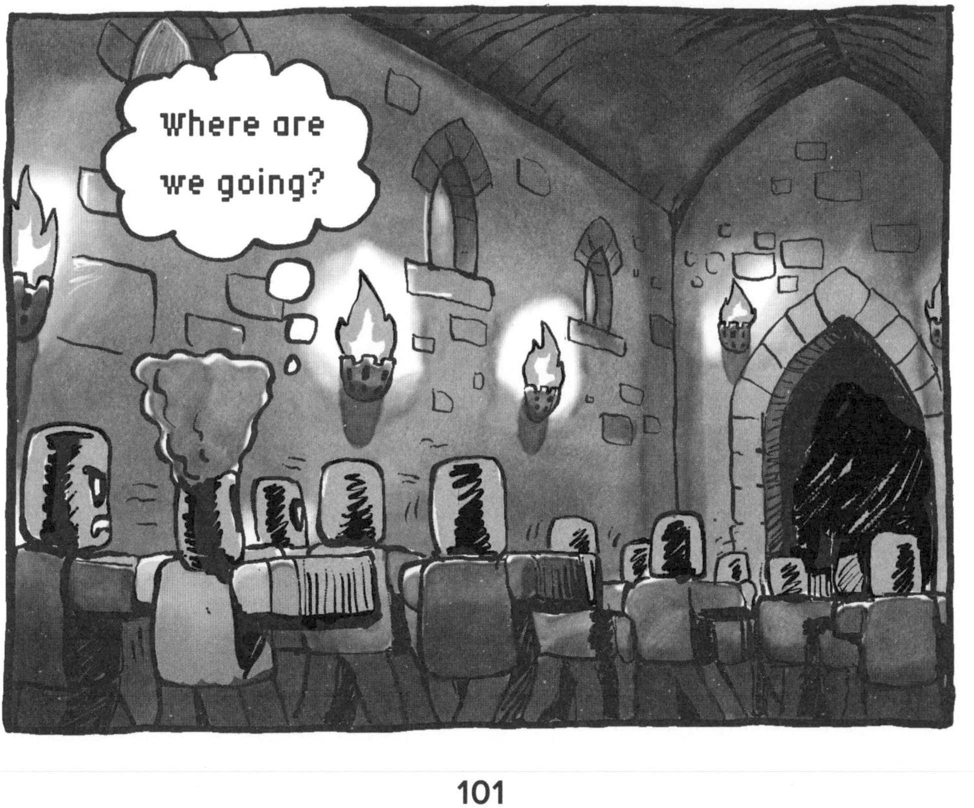
Where are we going?

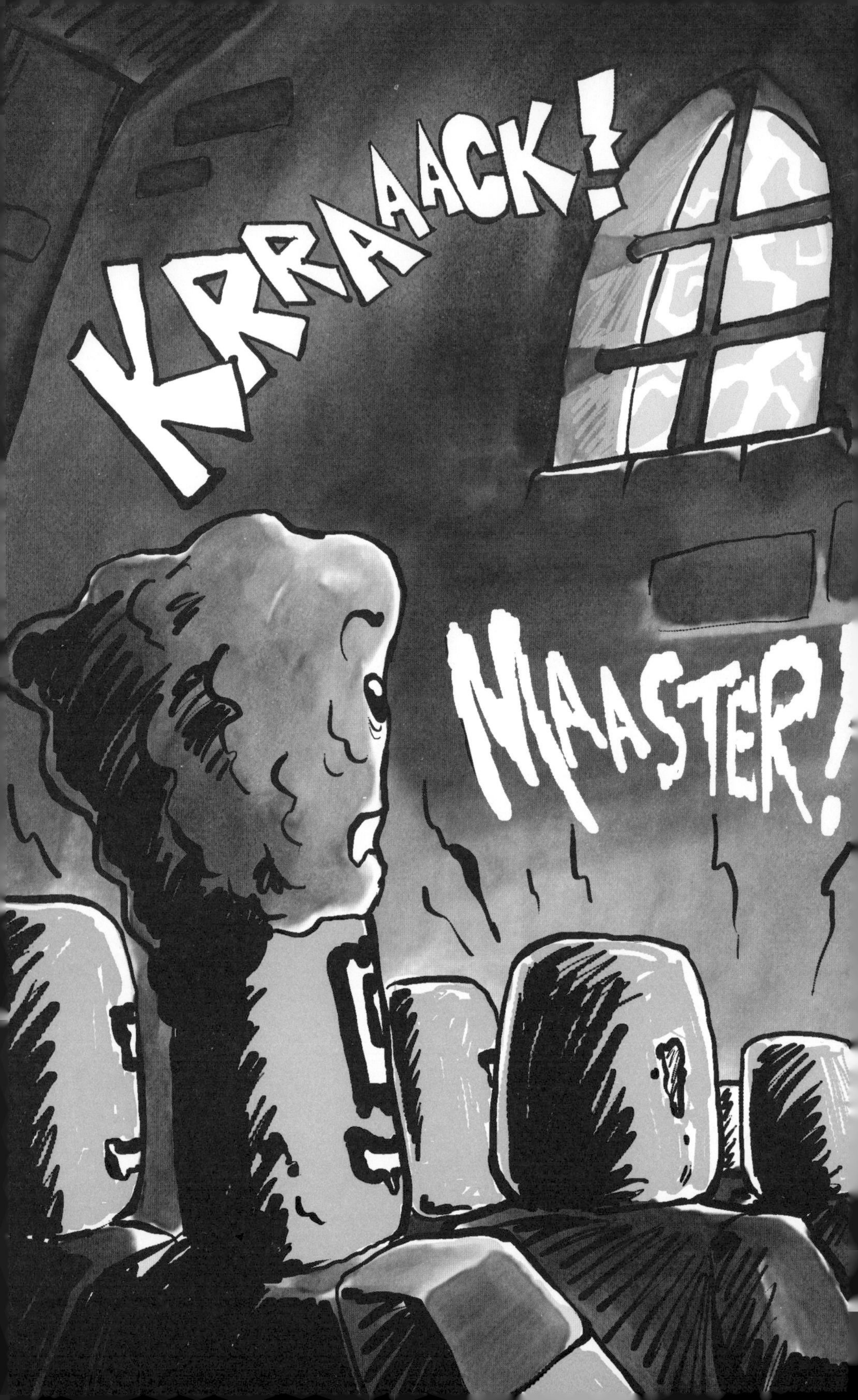
KRRAAACK!
MAASTER!

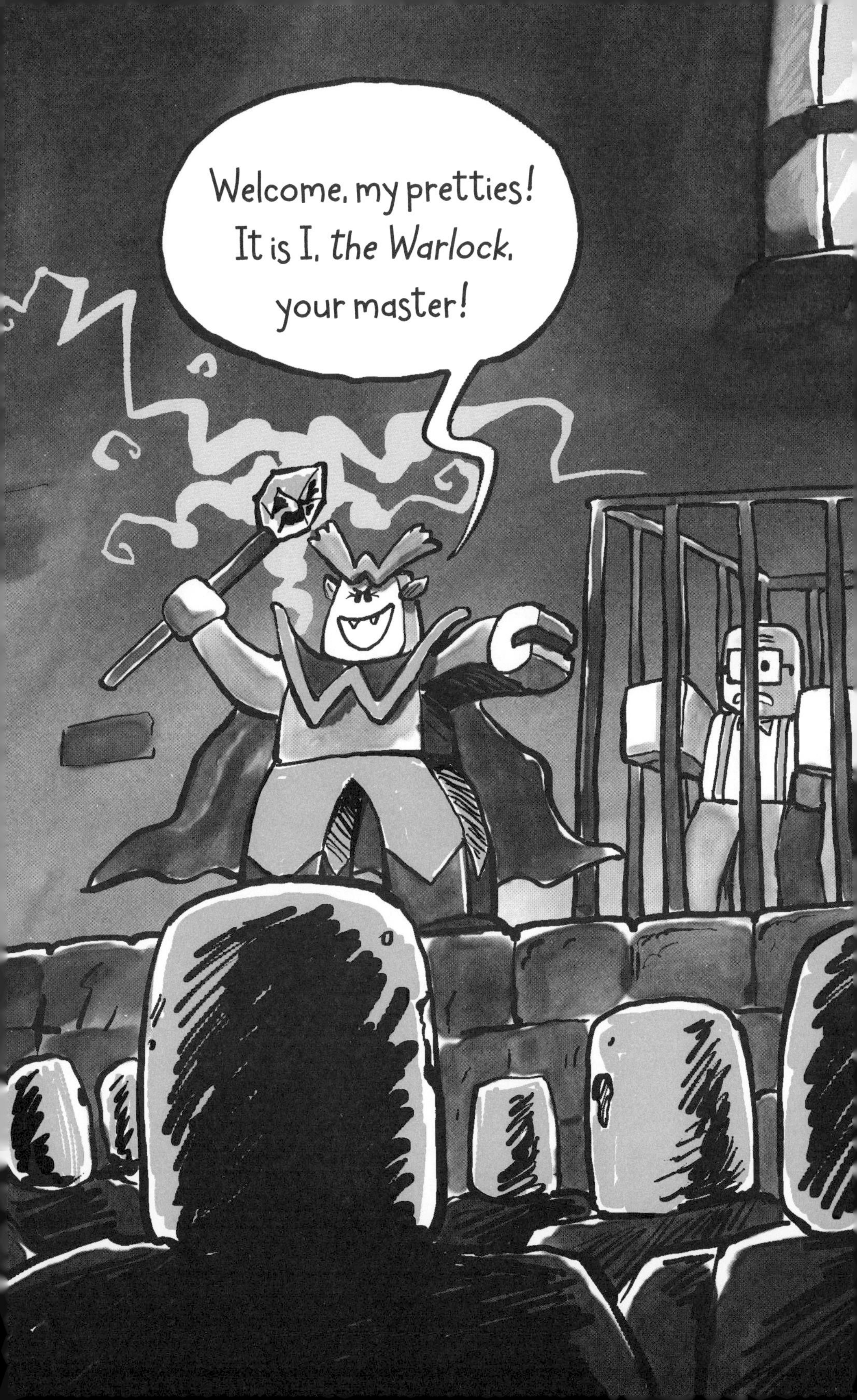
Welcome, my pretties! It is I, the Warlock, your master!

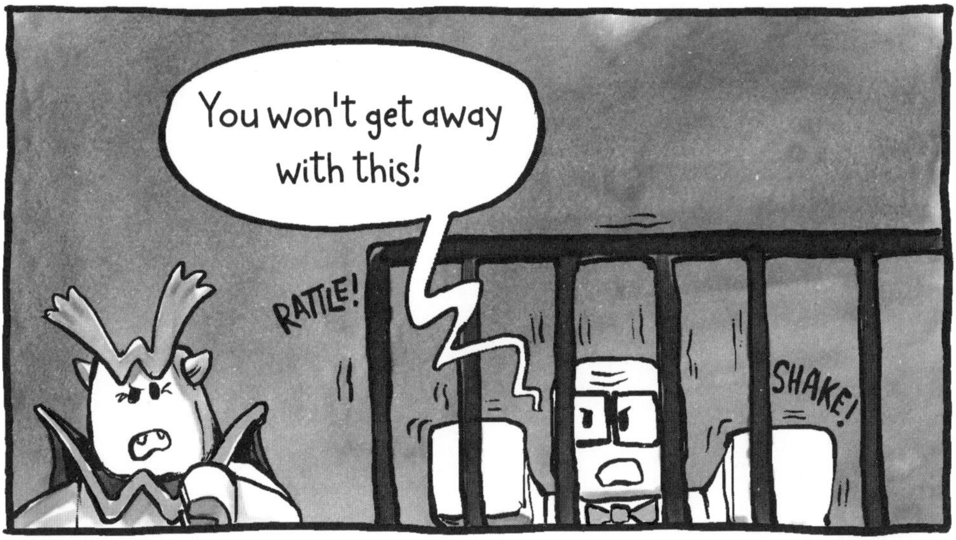
You won't get away with this!
RATTLE!
SHAKE!

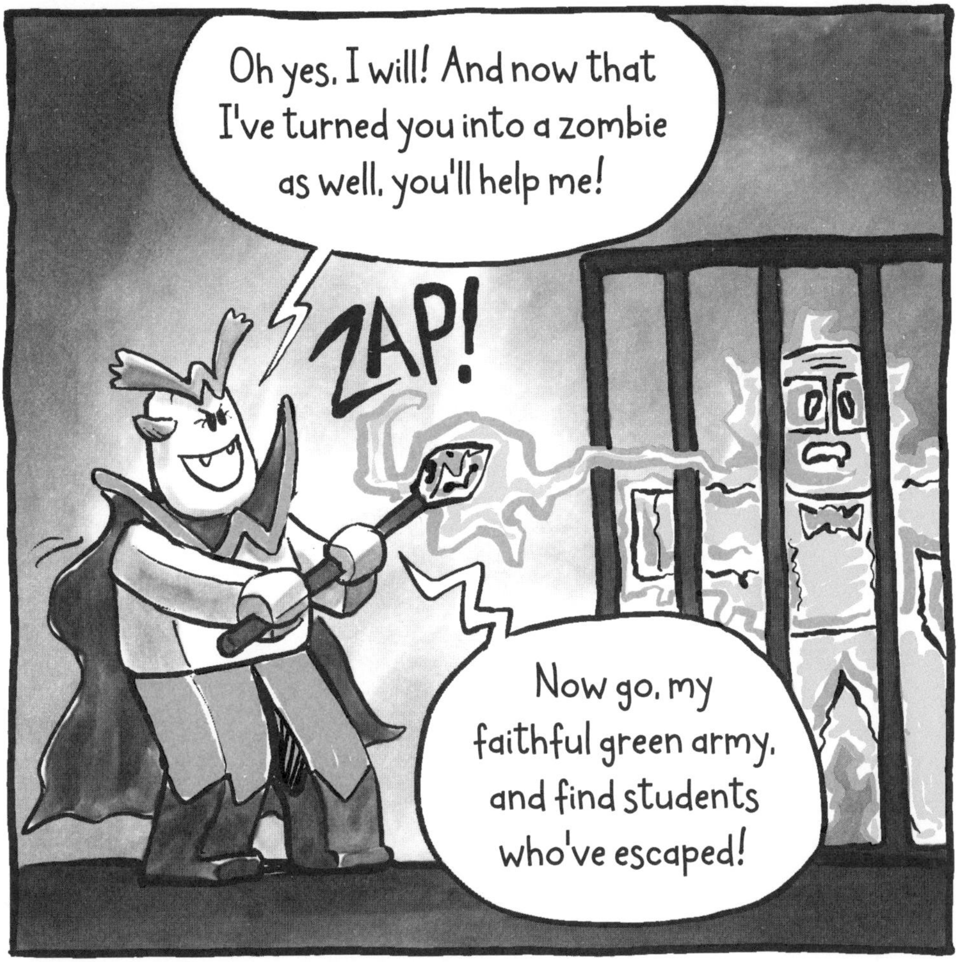
Oh yes, I will! And now that I've turned you into a zombie as well, you'll help me!
ZAP!
Now go, my faithful green army, and find students who've escaped!

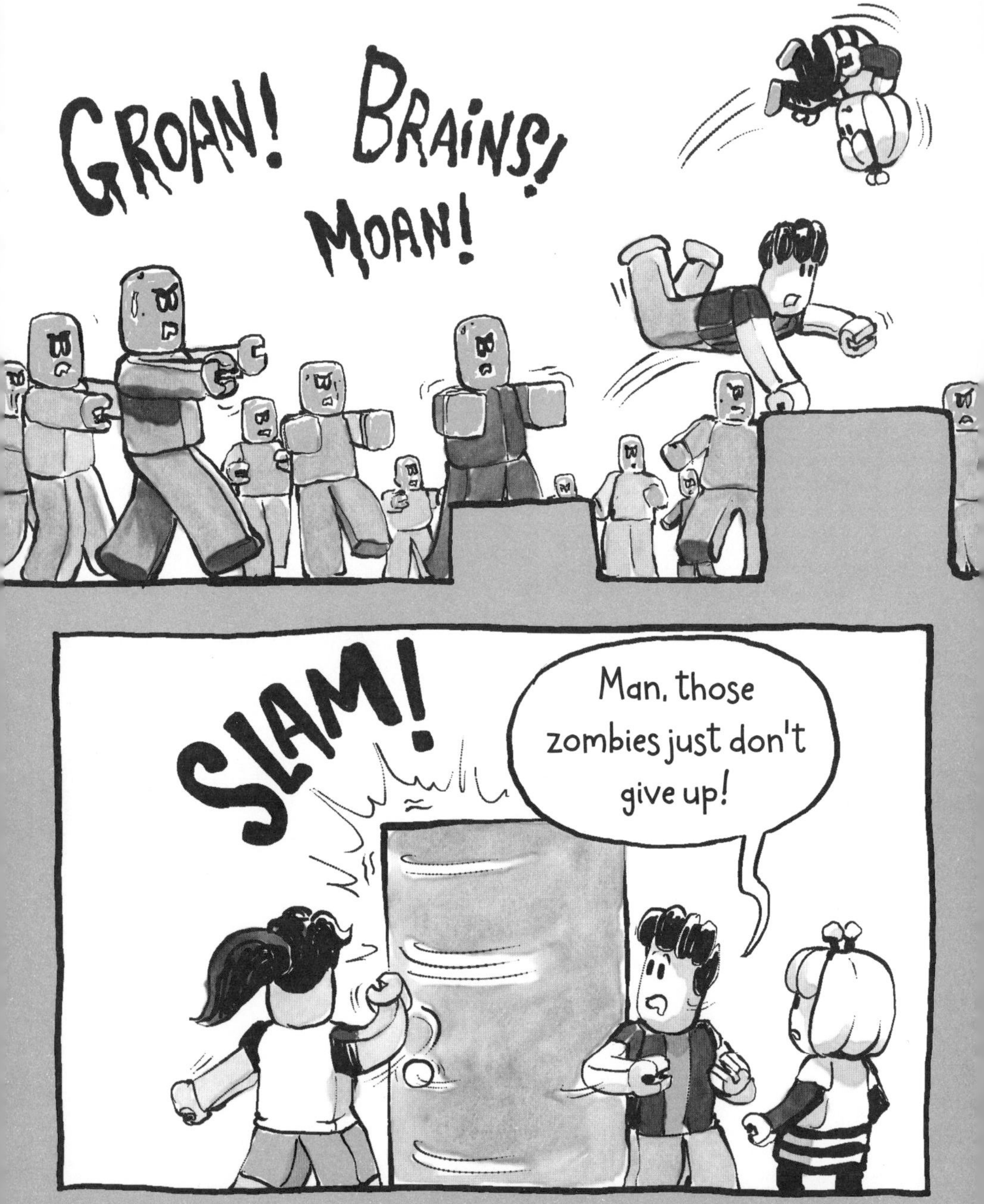
GROAN! BRAINS!
MOAN!
SLAM!
Man, those zombies just don't give up!

"I've got it!" said Bee. "We can't run, and we can't hide, but we can disguise! Follow me!" she shouted, and raced off down the corridor. Play and Dash followed as Bee led them to the Roblox art room.

"I don't think now's the time for painting," panted Play.

"That depends on what you're painting," replied Bee with a grin.

Into the classroom they went, and Bee began looking through the art supplies.

As a bewildered Dash and Play watched on, Bee found some cans of green paint and three brushes.

"Right," she said. "Time to blend in."

But Dash and Play were still confused.

"We're going to paint ourselves to look like zombies!" snapped Bee. "You both have the right expressions for a zombie at the moment, now put on the paint before they find us!"

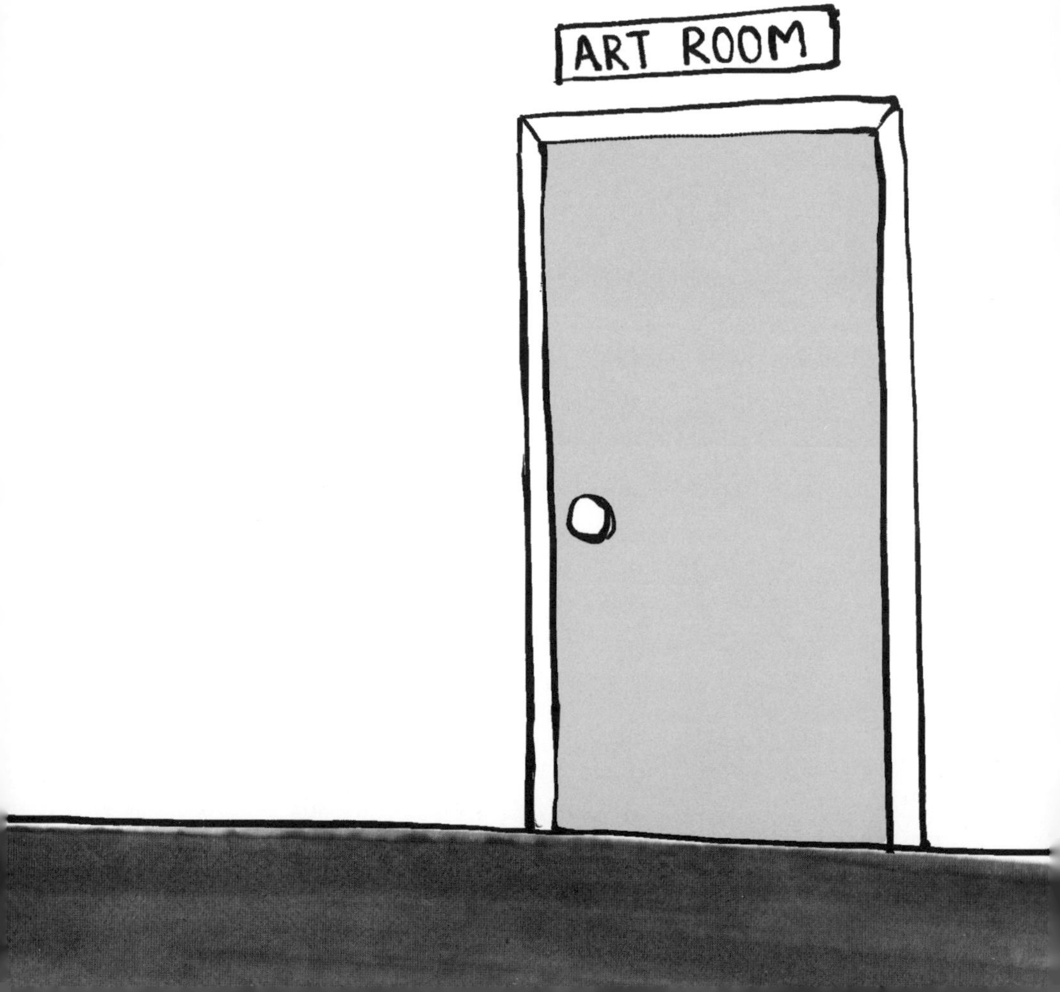
ART ROOM

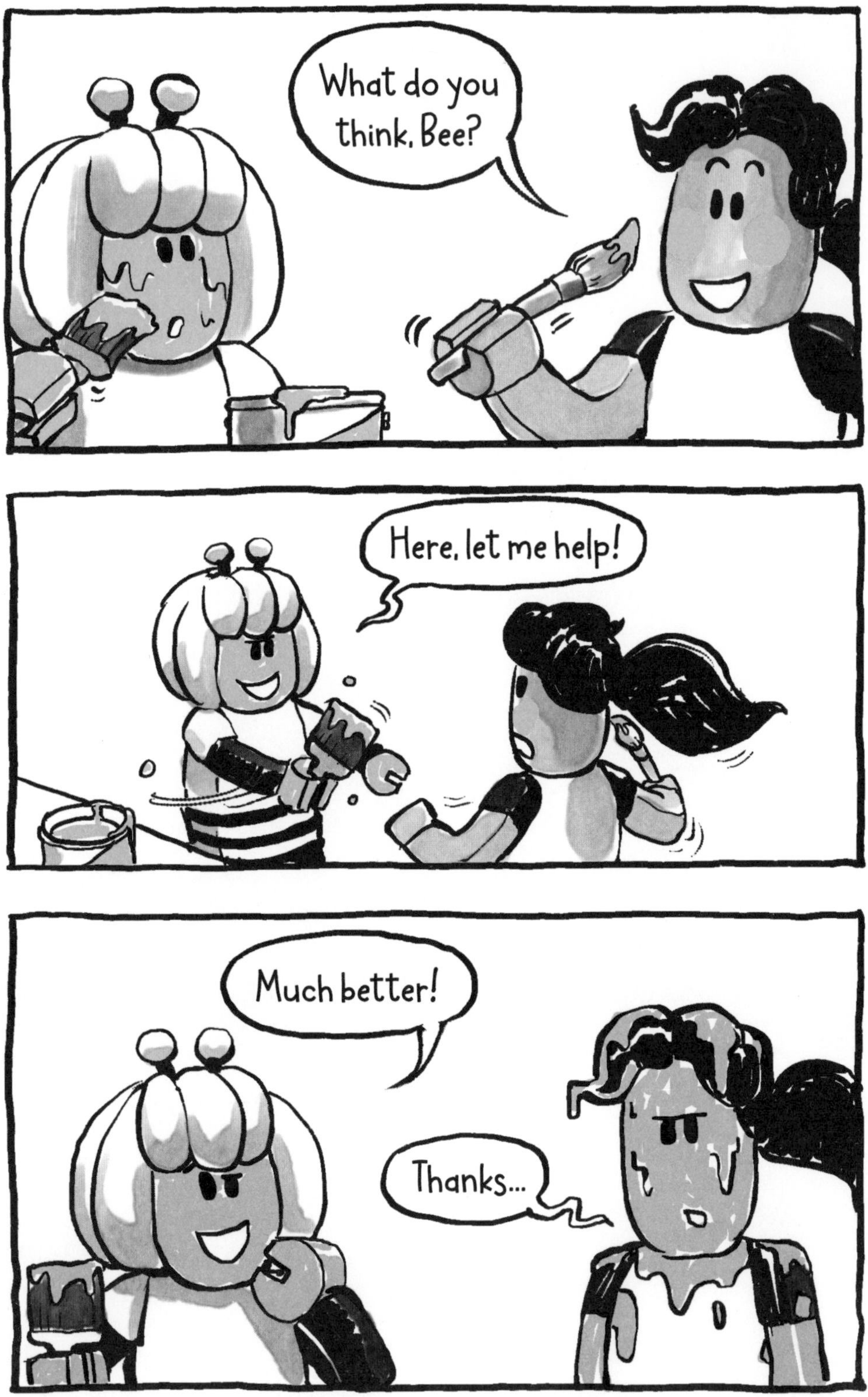
What do you think, Bee?
Here, let me help!
Much better!
Thanks...

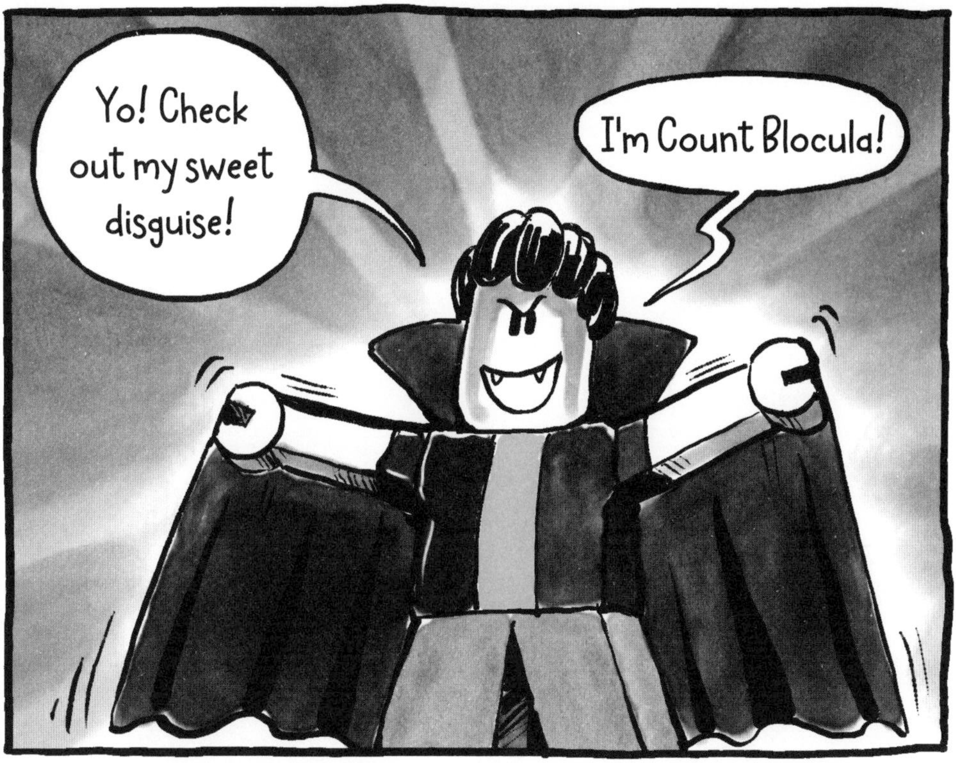
Yo! Check out my sweet disguise!
I'm Count Blocula!

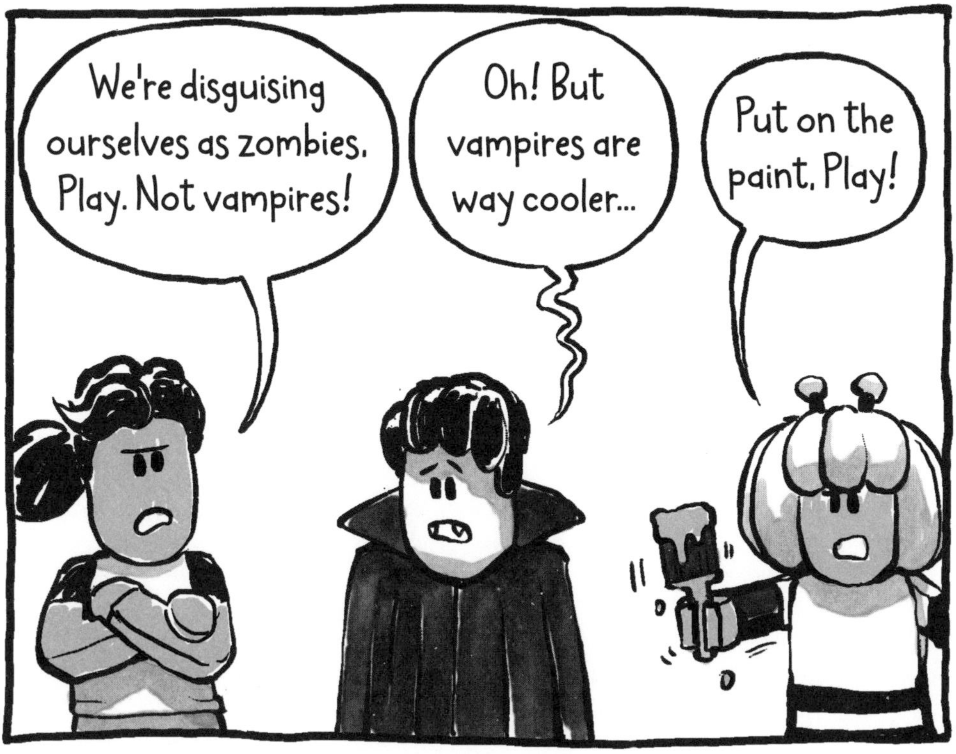
We're disguising ourselves as zombies, Play. Not vampires!
Oh! But vampires are way cooler...
Put on the paint, Play!

Cautiously, they edged out of the classroom and slid onto the back of the marching zombies. At first, they were terrified they'd be found out, but as they kept going, their confidence rose. The zombies seemed to accept them as their own!

"I can't believe it's working," mumbled Play. "What do we do now?"

"Let's just see where they're going and…look!" Bee exclaimed, pointing ahead. "I think that's… yes! It looks like Glitch!"

"Oh no!" cried Dash. "He's a zombie!"

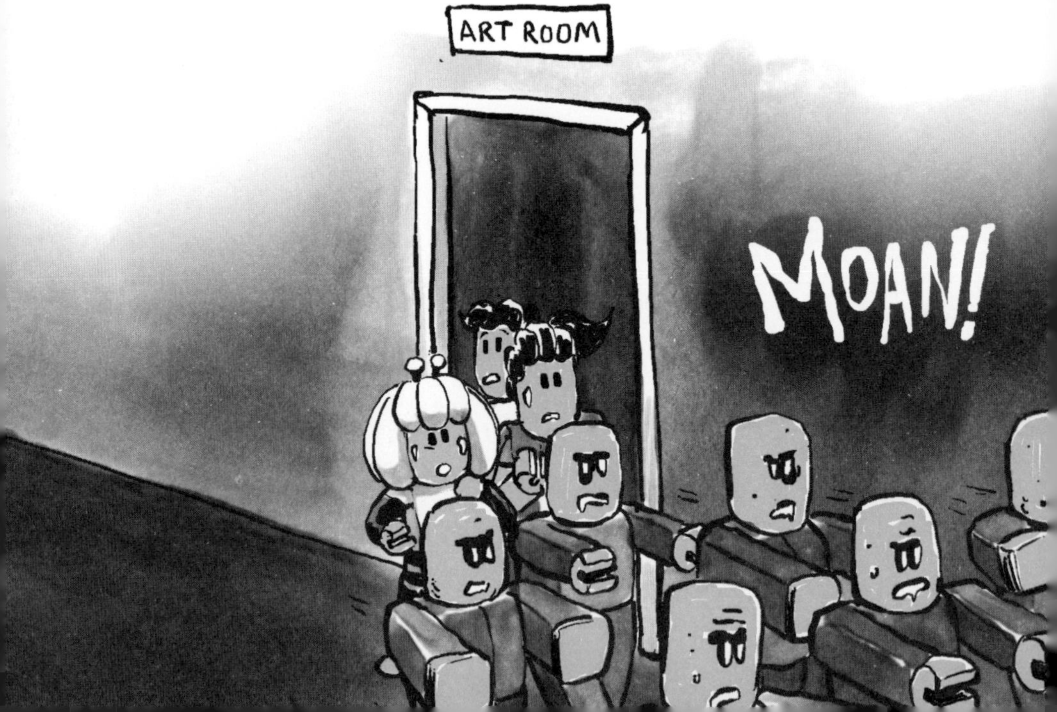
ART ROOM
MOAN!

"Yeah..." said Play hesitantly. "But he's still got hair...like us. Maybe he's pretending, too?"

"Or he's only part zombie...can you be part zombie?" asked Dash.

"We need to get him away from the rest of the zombies and find out," said Bee. "But how?"

"Leave that to me," said Play as he began shouldering his way through the mass of green.

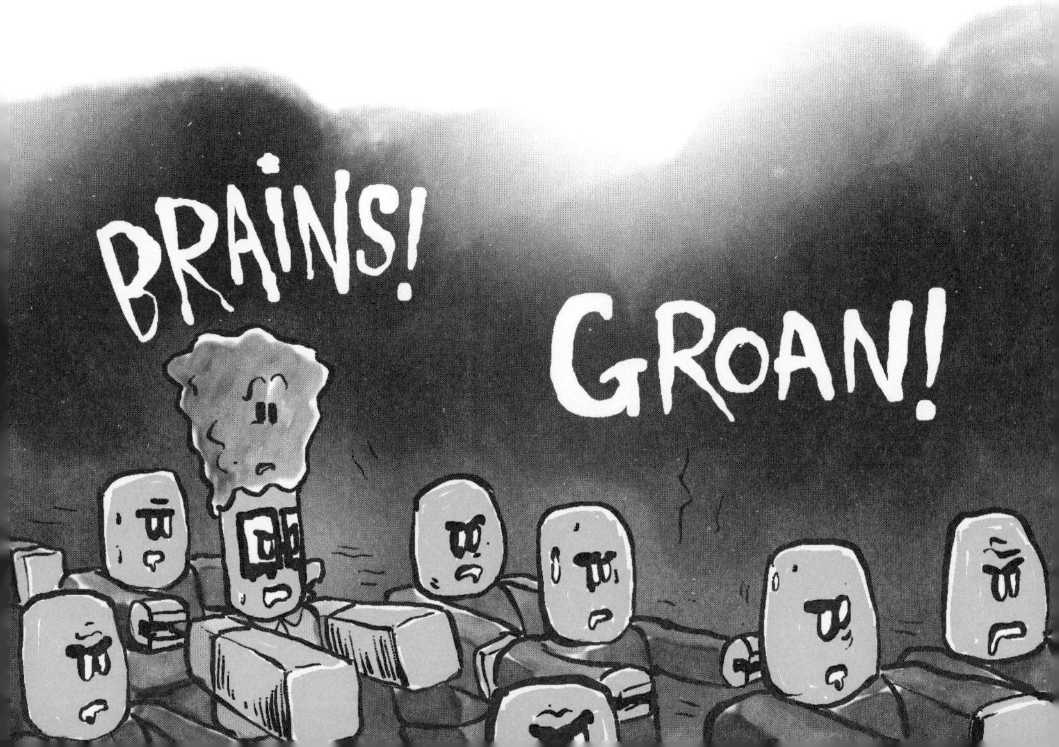
BRAINS!
GROAN!

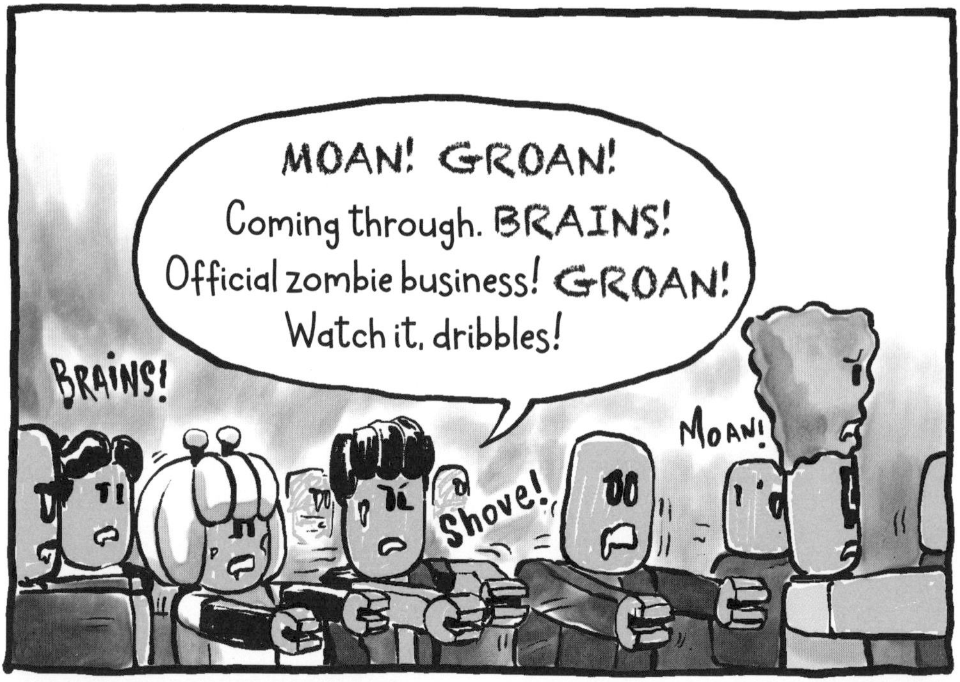
MOAN! GROAN!
Coming through. BRAINS!
Official zombie business! GROAN!
Watch it, dribbles!
BRAINS!
Shove!
MOAN!

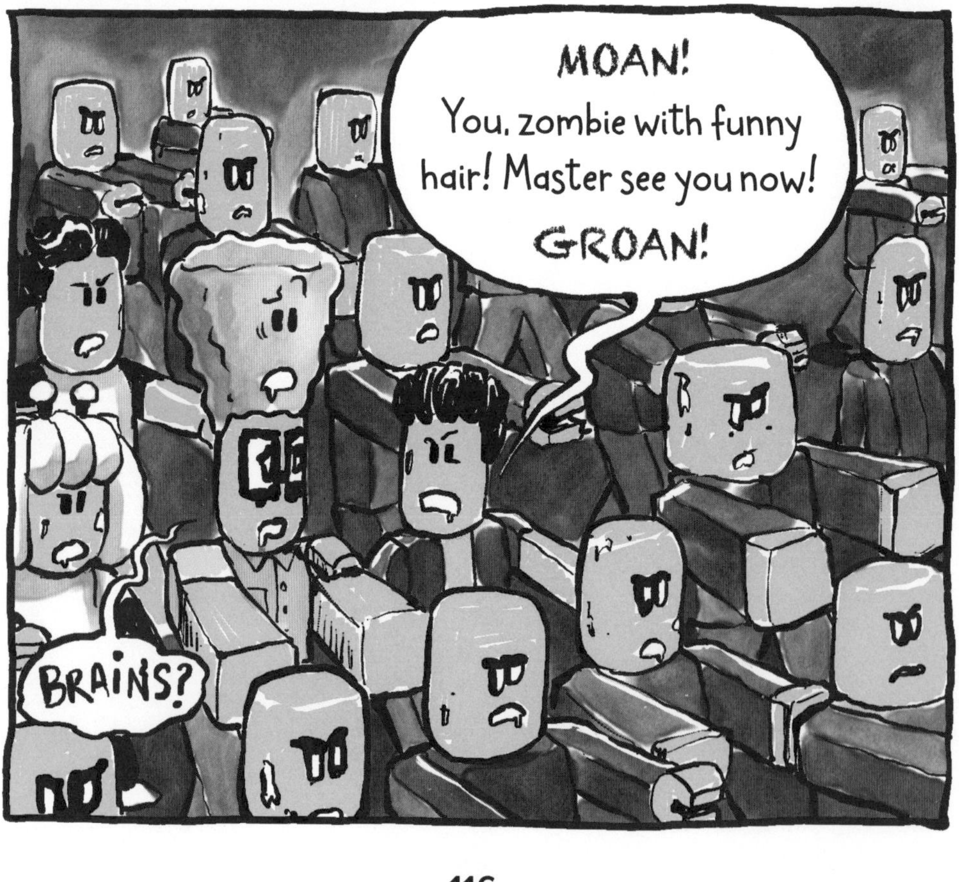
MOAN!
You, zombie with funny hair! Master see you now!
GROAN!
BRAINS?

Fritz told them about the Warlock and how he had a magic staff that could transform avatars into zombies. He then explained Warlock's fiendish plan to take over the school and then unleash his zombie army on the rest of Roblox.

"We have to stop him!" exclaimed Dash.

"Yeah," agreed Play. "This is the best school ever! I'm not letting this Warlock ruin everything!"

"We have to find a way to get that staff off him," said Bee. "If it can turn avatars into zombies, then it can probably turn them back."

Bee, Play, Dash, and Fritz, intent on saving the school and their friend Glitch, set about formulating a way to take down the Warlock. A little later, they had the beginnings of a clever plan...

"I think it might just work," said Fritz. "But I'm not going to be able to help you at all... Unfortunately, zombie Glitch has a mind of his own!"

At that moment, the kids heard a muffled, whimpering noise. They crept cautiously toward the sound and found Ogre, curled up and shaking in the corner of the room.

"Aargh! Zombies!" he screamed as he saw them. "Please don't eat my brains!"

"It's okay, Ogre," said Dash soothingly. "It's us, Bee, Play, and Dash. We're only disguised as zombies. No one's going to eat your brains!"

"Wouldn't be much of a meal, anyway," snickered Bee.

"N--nn--not zombies?" He sniffed. "What are you doing then?"

"We're going to save the school!" said Play. "And you're going to help us!"

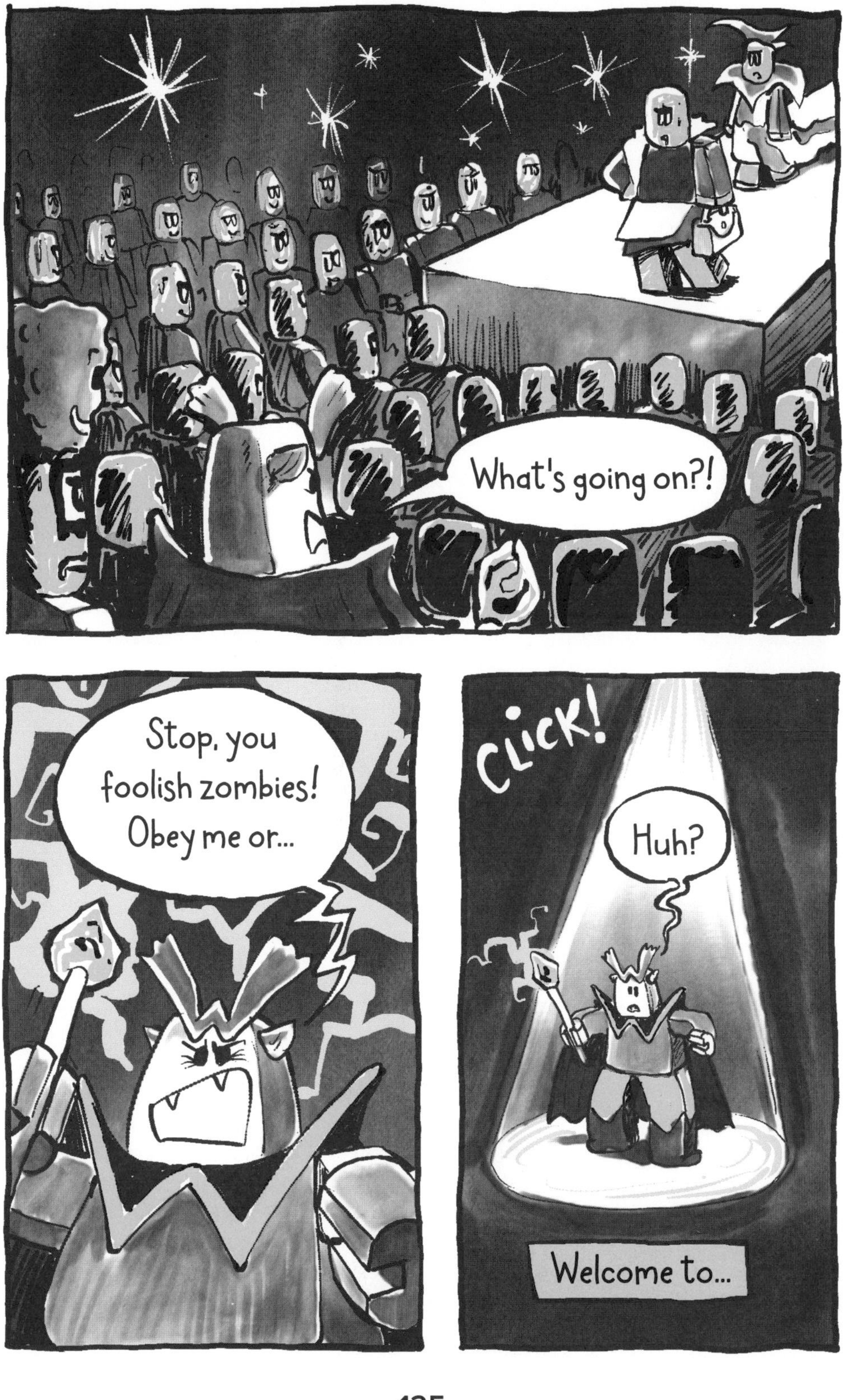
What's going on?!
Stop, you foolish zombies! Obey me or...
CLICK!
Huh?
Welcome to...

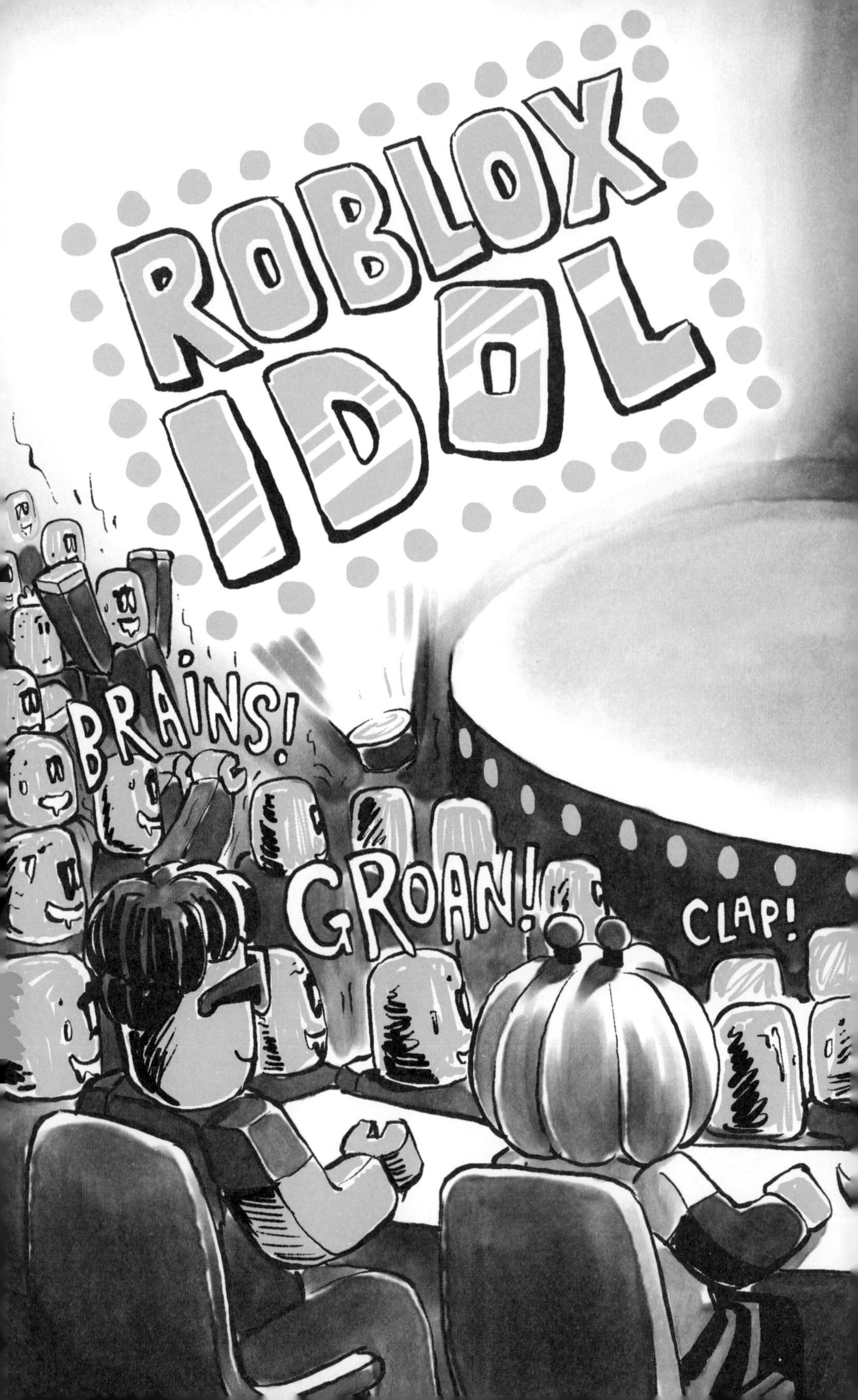
ROBLOX IDOL
BRAINS!
GROAN!
CLAP!

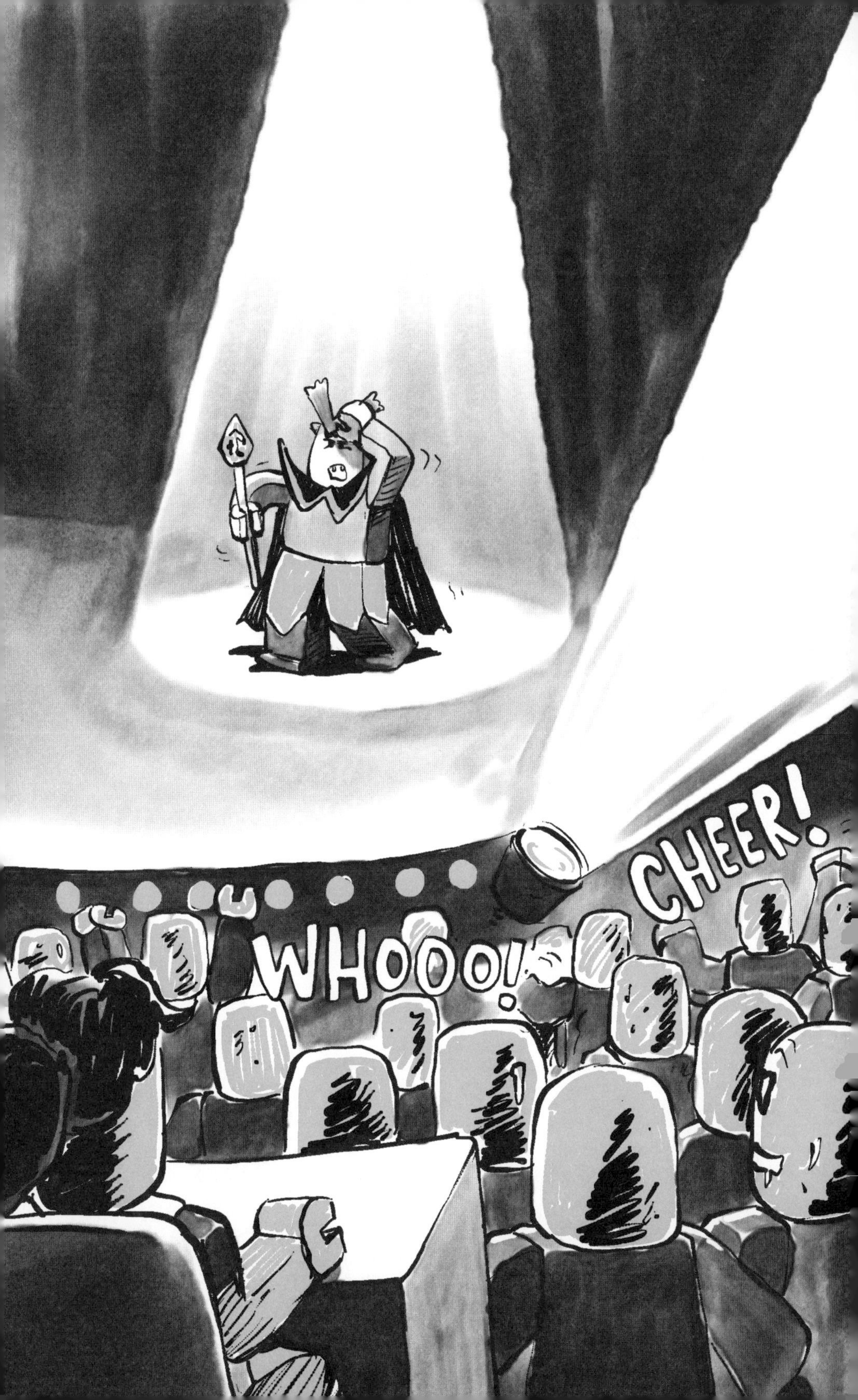
CHEER!
WHOOO!

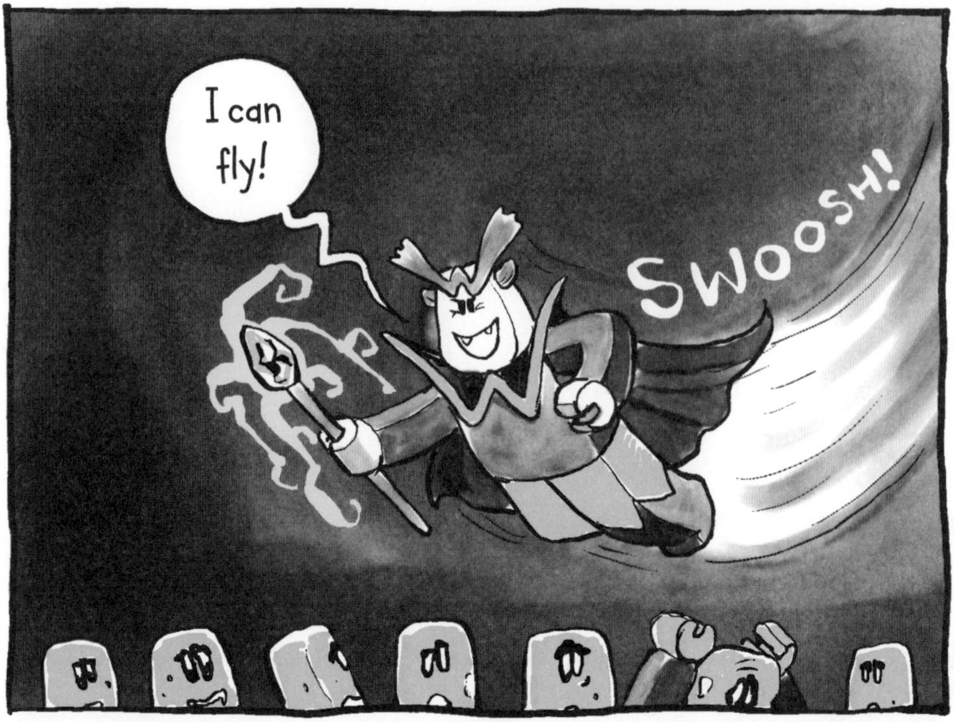
I can fly!
SWOOSH!

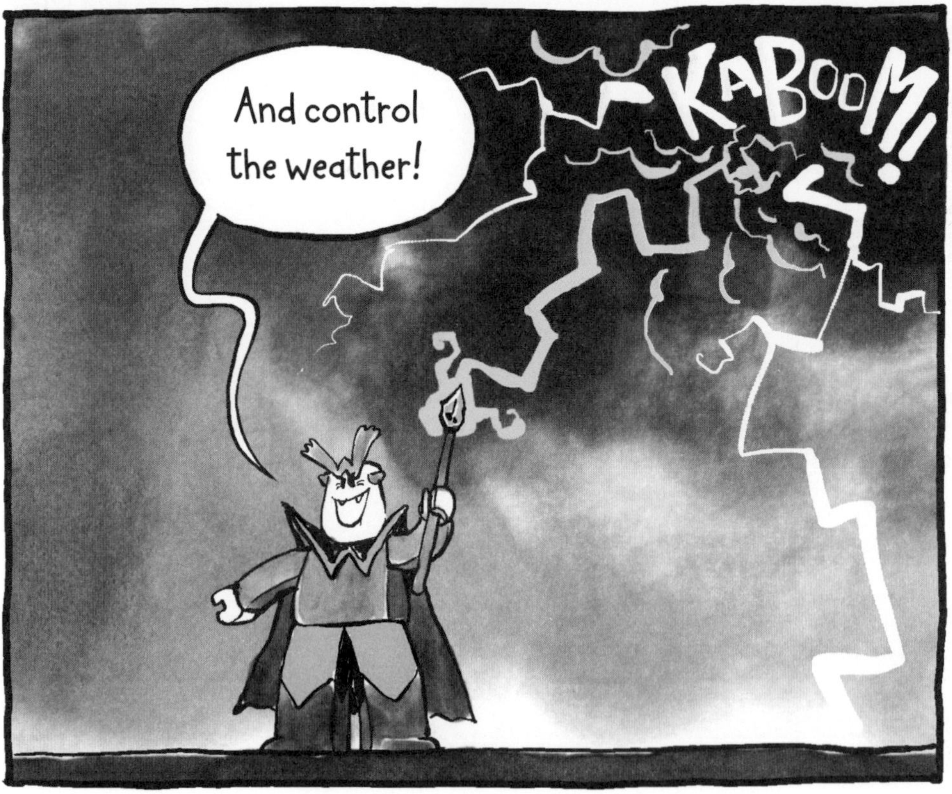
And control the weather!
KABOOM!!

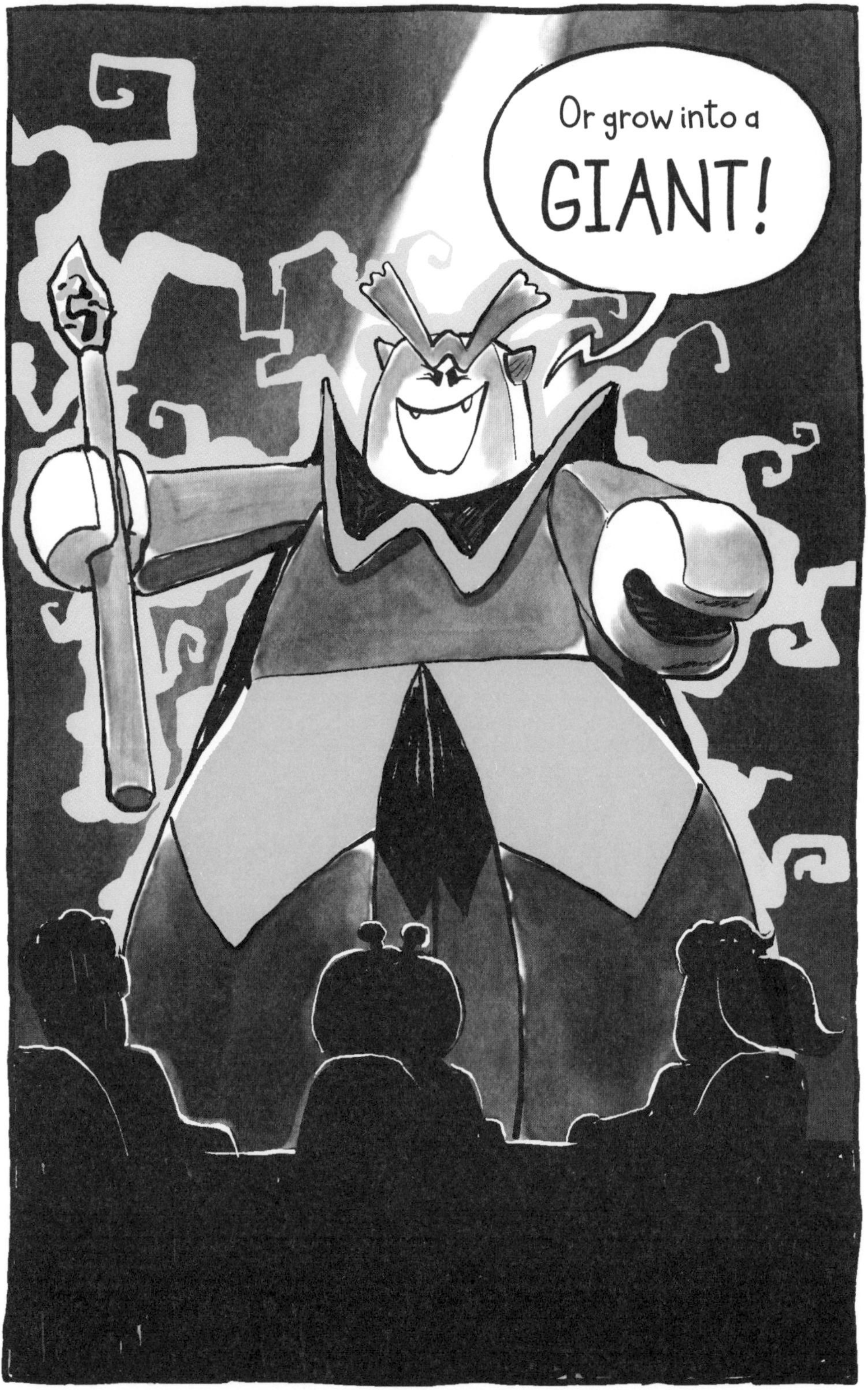
Or grow into a
GIANT!

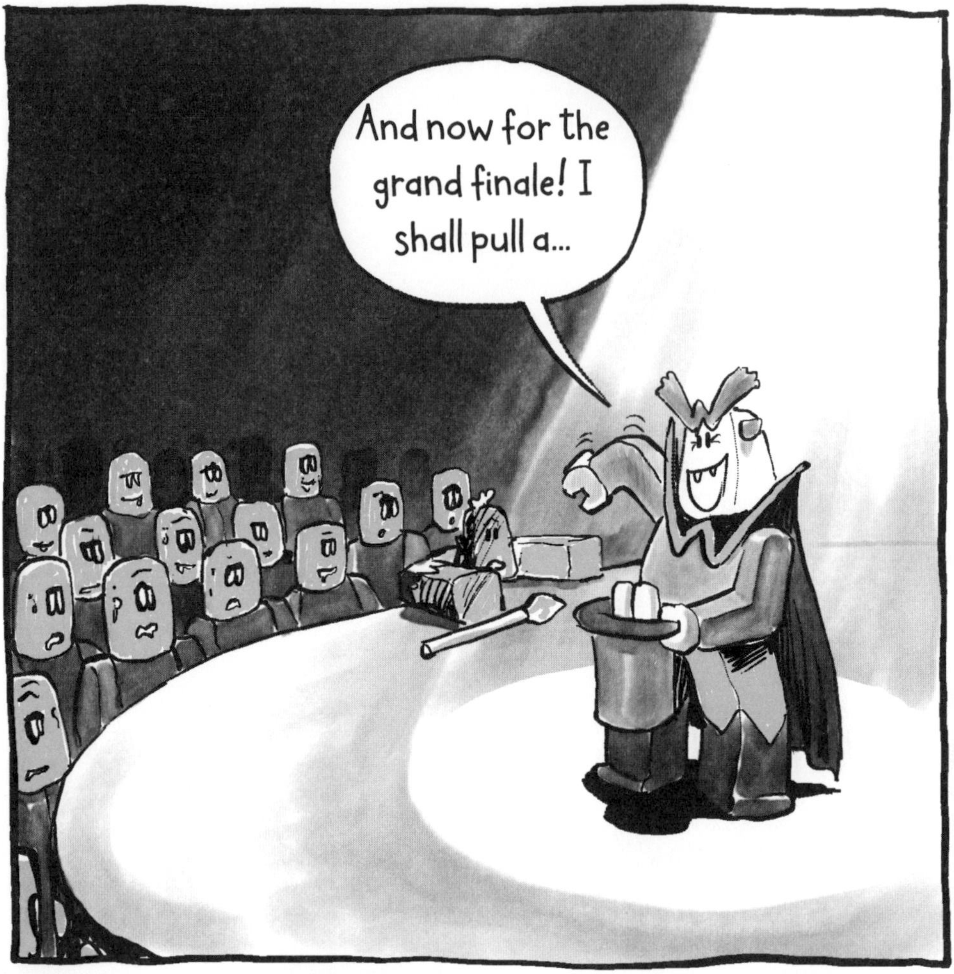
And now for the grand finale! I shall pull a...

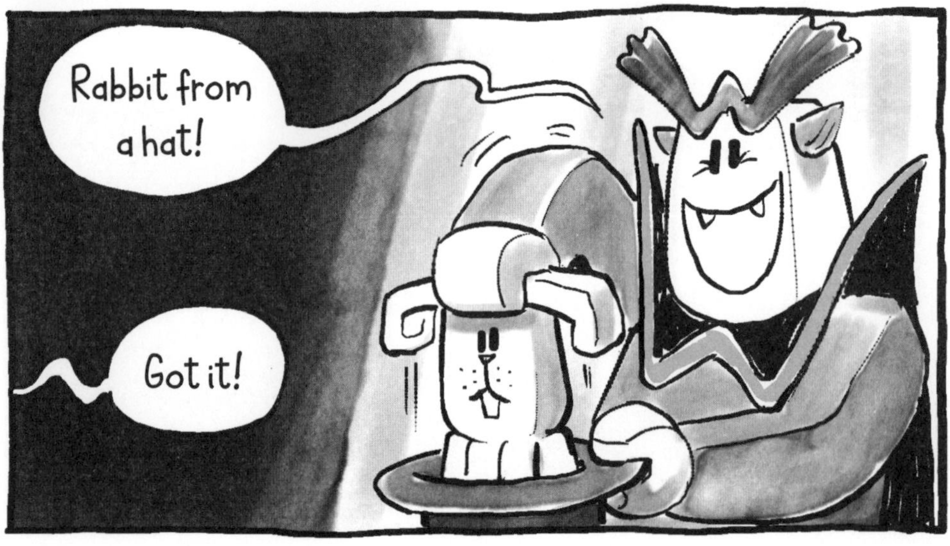
Rabbit from a hat!
Got it!

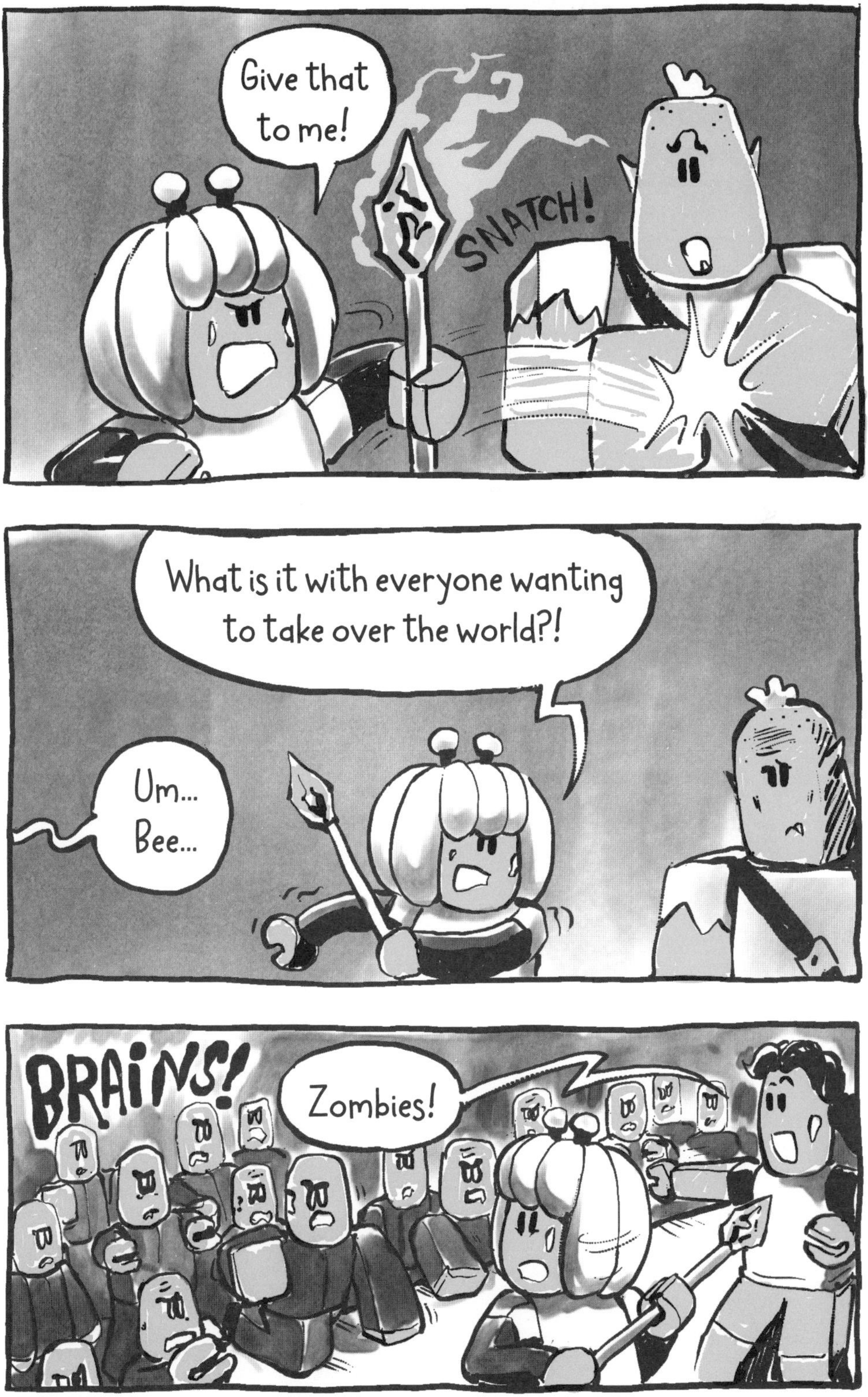
Give that to me!
SNATCH!
What is it with everyone wanting to take over the world?!
Um... Bee...
BRAINS!
Zombies!

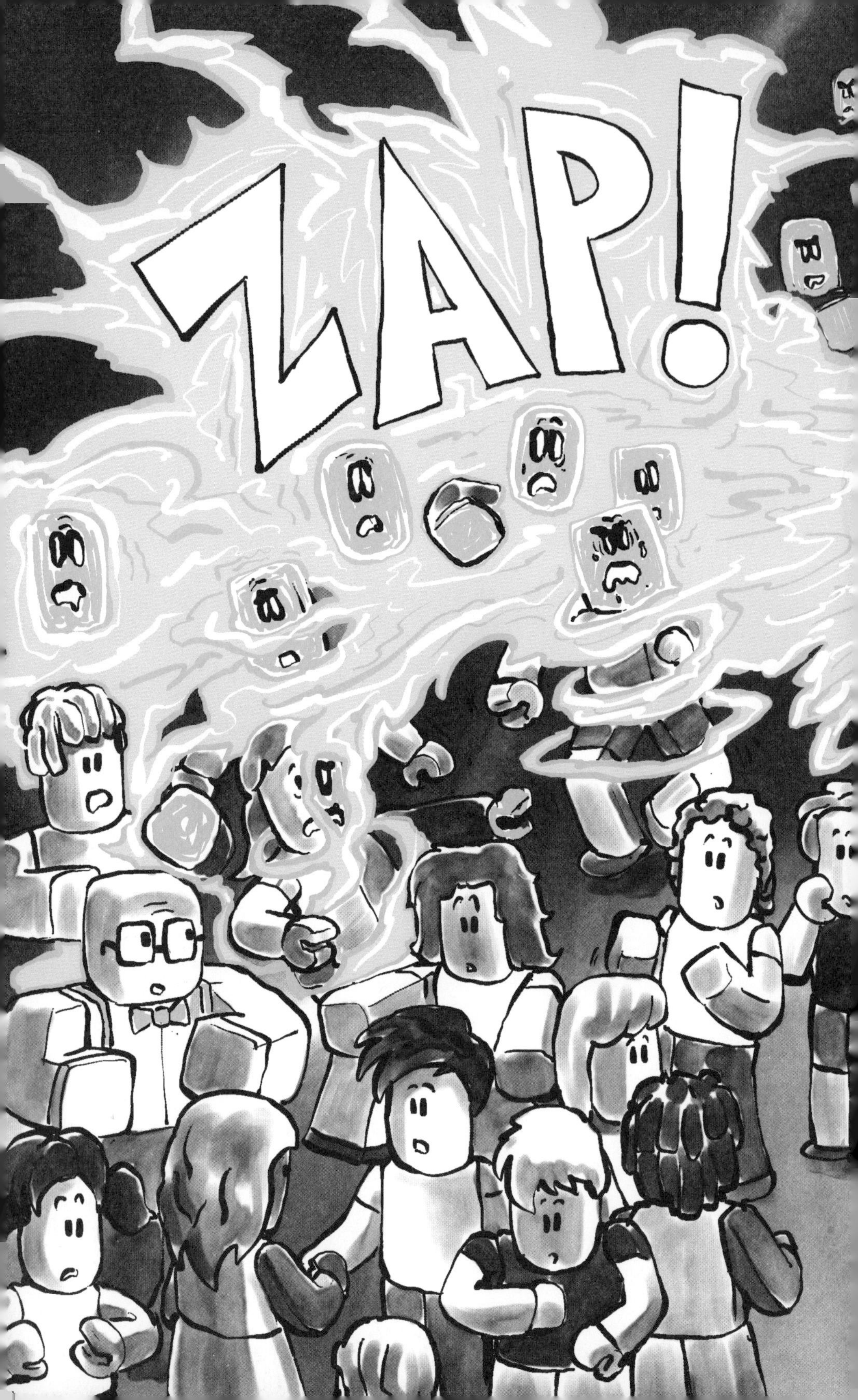
ZAP!

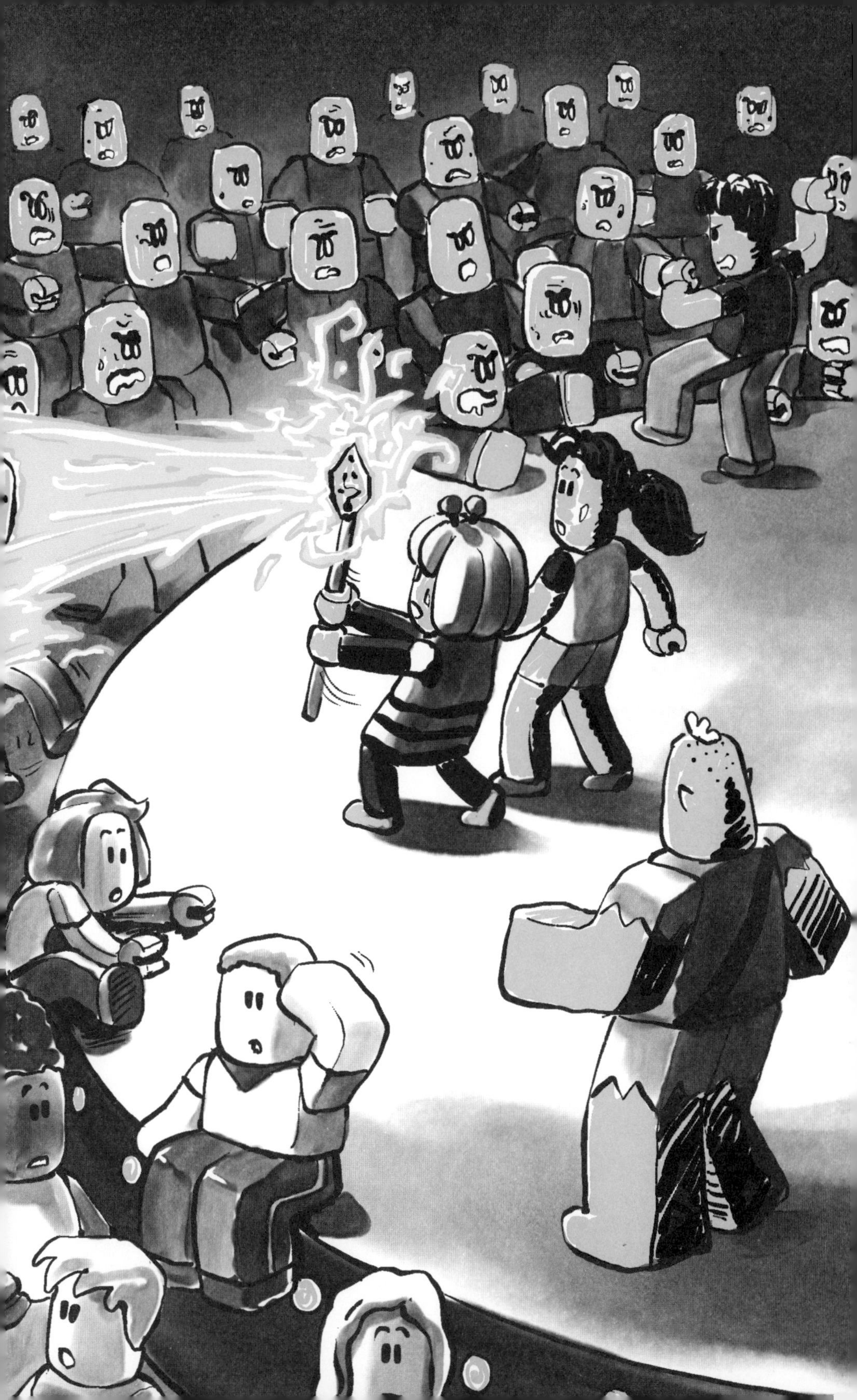

After a quick dip in the school pool to get rid of their zombie green coloring, the kids were then summoned by Principal Blox to an assembly.

"Each of you has shown extraordinary bravery and creativity today, and in doing so, you have saved our beloved academy," the principal said. "As a small token of my, and indeed all the school's appreciation, it gives me great pleasure to give you these." He handed each of them a small badge in the shape of a school crest. "These badges mean that you are now, officially, members of the Academy for Roblox Pros!" The school burst into applause and cheering.

"These badges will help you travel back to

your own world and, more importantly, return here so you can continue your learning at this academy."

Another loud round of applause drowned out the cheers and whoops of joy from Play, Bee, Dash, Ogre, Glitch, and Fritz at this news.

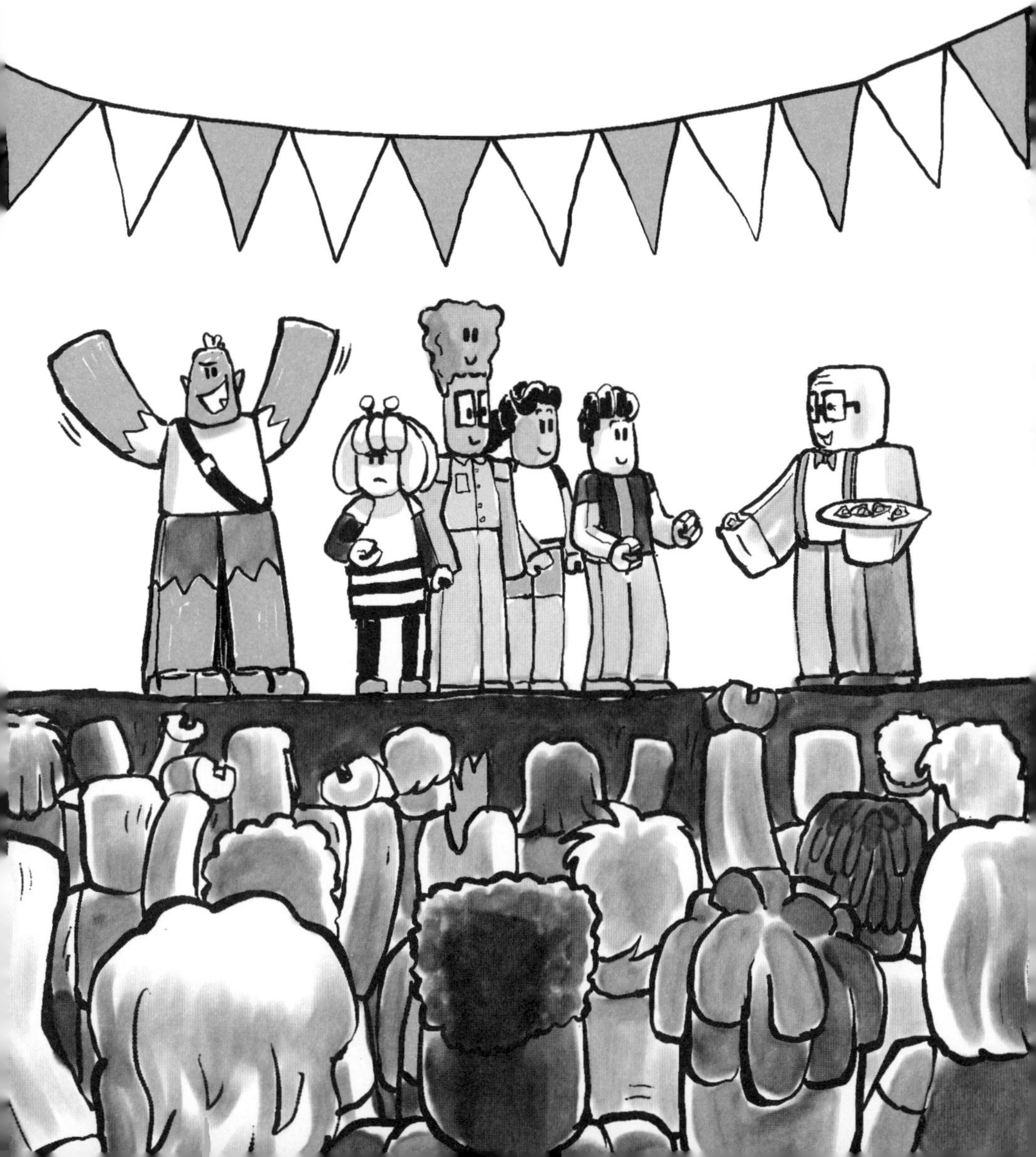

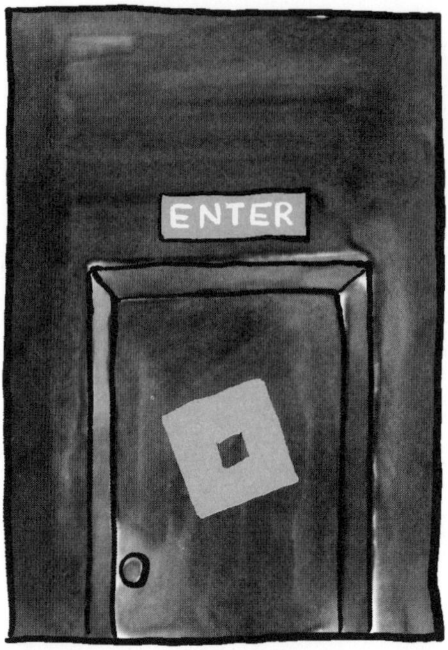
ENTER

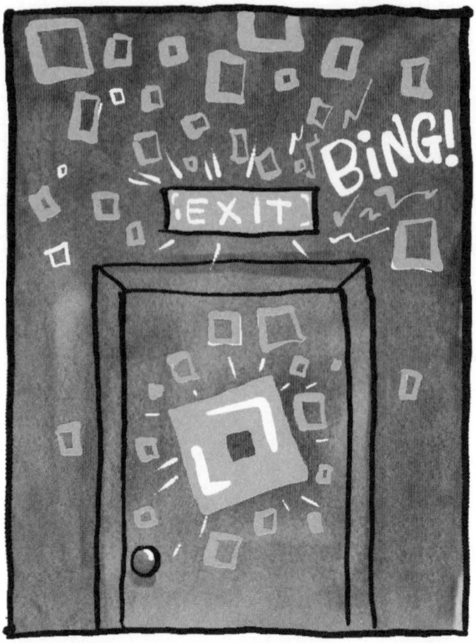
EXIT
BING!

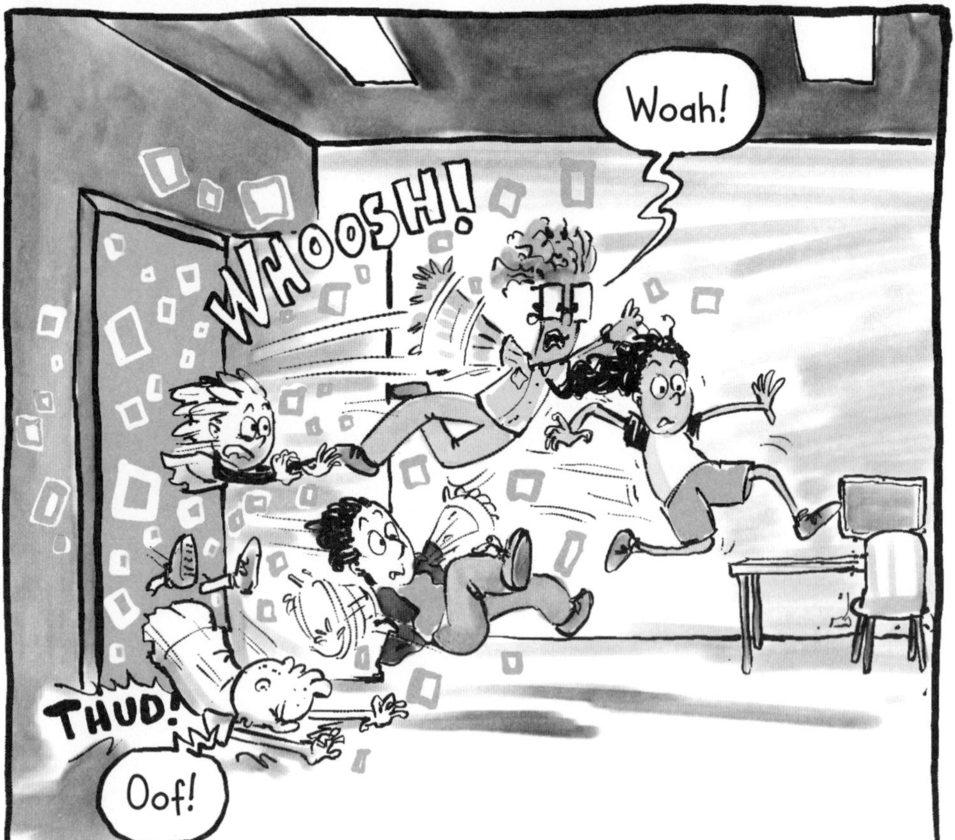
Woah!
WHOOSH!
THUD!
Oof!

Tash, Mitch, Jai, and (eventually) Bea headed back to class, and not even the thought of double math could dampen their spirits.

They knew that soon they would be returning to the Academy for Roblox Pros, where they'd have lots of exciting adventures, make new friends...and see what else there was to get in the cafeteria.

Having battled the Warlock and his zombie minions, they knew that together they could face anything, and overcome any obstacle... except maybe getting the bus on time.

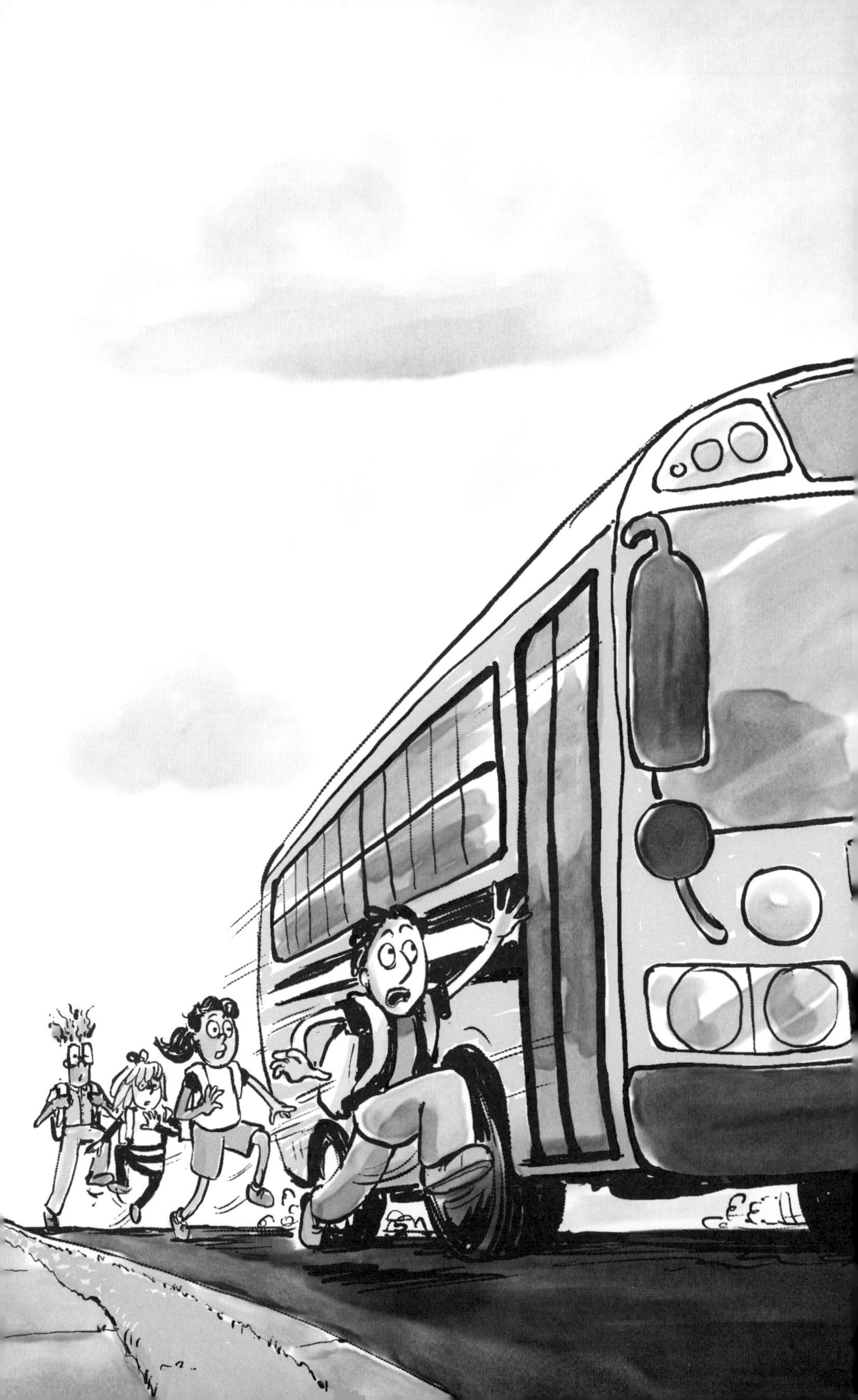

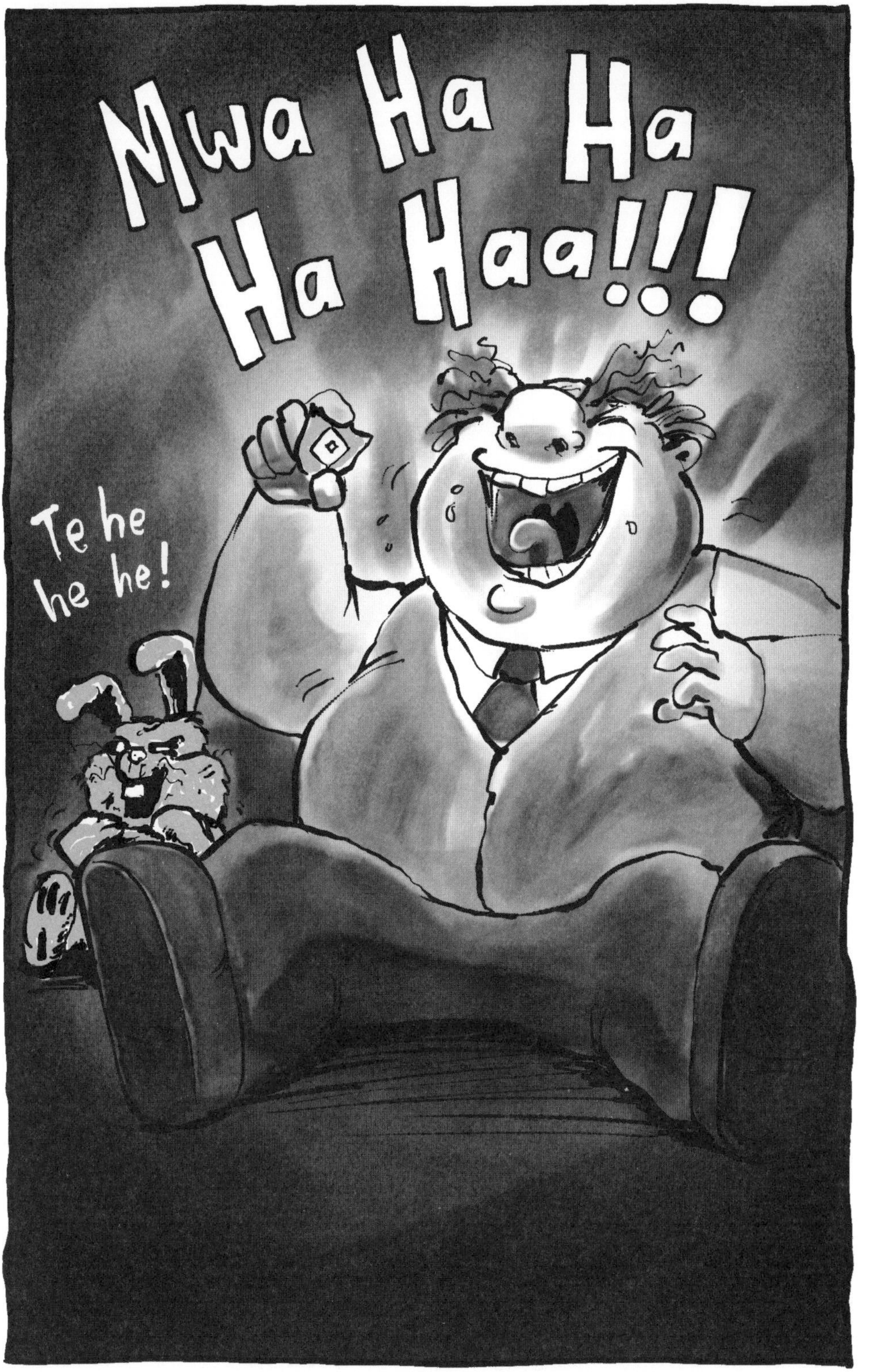
Mwa Ha Ha Ha Haa!!!
Te he he he!

ACADEMY FOR ROBLOX PROS

AN UNOFFICIAL ROBLOX GRAPHIC NOVEL

BOOK 2 COMING SOON!